Exit Wounds

Praise for VK Powell

"This story takes some unusual twists and at one point, I was convinced that I knew 'who did it' only to find out that I was wrong. VK Powell knows crime drama, she kept me guessing until the end, and I was not disappointed at the outcome. And that's not to slight VK Powell's knack for romance…Readers who appreciate mysteries with a touch of drama and intense erotic moments will enjoy *Justifiable Risk*." —*Queer Magazine*

"VK Powell has given her fans an exciting read. The plot of *Fever* is filled with twists, turns, and 'seat of your pants' danger…*Fever* gives readers both great characters and erotic scenes along with insight into life in the African bush."—*Just About Write*

"From the first chapter of *Suspect Passions* Powell builds erotic scenes which sear the page. She definitely takes her readers for a walk on the wild side! Her characters, however, are also women we care about. They are bright, witty, and strong. The combination of great sex and great characters make *Suspect Passions* a must read." —*Just About Write*

"If you like cop novels, or even television cop shows with women as full partners with male officers…[*To Protect and Serve*] is the book for you. It's got drama, excitement, conflict, and even some fairly hot lesbian sex. The writer is a retired cop, so she really writes from a place of authenticity. As a result, you have a realistic quality to the writing that puts me in mind of early Joseph Wambaugh, before his writing became formulaic."—*Lesbian News*

"*To Protect and Serve* drew me in from the very first page with characters that captivated in their complexity. Powell writes with authority using the lingo and capturing the thoughts of the law enforcers who make the ultimate sacrifice in the fight against crime. What's more impressive is the command this debut author has of portraying a full gamut of emotion, from angst to elation, through dialogue and narrative. The images are vivid, the action is believable, and the police procedurals are authentic…VK Powell had me invested in the story of these women, heart, mind, body and soul. Along with danger and tension, Powell's well-developed erotic scenes sizzle and sate." —*Story Circle Book Reviews*

By the Author

To Protect and Serve

Suspect Passions

Fever

Justifiable Risk

Haunting Whispers

Exit Wounds

Exit Wounds

by

VK Powell

2013

EXIT WOUNDS

ISBN 13: 978-1-60282-893-3

This Trade Paperback Original Is Published By
Bold Strokes Books, Inc.
P.O. Box 249
Valley Falls, NY 12185

First Edition: August 2013

Credits
Editor: Shelley Thrasher
Production Design: Stacia Seaman
Cover Design by Sheri (graphicartist2020@hotmail.com)

Acknowledgments

To Len Barot, publisher extraordinaire, and all the other wonderful folks at Bold Strokes Books—thank you for making this process so amazingly enjoyable and painless and for turning out a quality product every time.

My deepest gratitude to Dr. Shelley Thrasher for your guidance, suggestions, and kindness. You help me view my work through fresh eyes. Working with you is a learning experience and a pleasure.

For BSB sister author D. Jackson Leigh and friends Jenny Harmon and Joanie Bassler—thank you for taking time off of your busy lives to provide priceless feedback. This book is so much better for your efforts. I am truly grateful.

To all the readers who support and encourage my writing, thank you for buying my work, visiting my website (www.vkpowellauthor.com), sending e-mails, and showing up for signings. You make my "job" so much fun!

For my friends in Greensboro, NC

Chapter One

"Do you want to talk about tonight?" Loane Landry tugged on a tangle of wavy chestnut hair wrapped around the wireless receiver and tried to concentrate on the task instead of the sexy informant.

"Ouch. That *is* attached." Abby's husky voice reminded Loane of Melissa Etheridge's, reverberating deep in her soul and stirring yearnings.

"You're telling me. How the hell did you get hair this long twisted around something so small and tied in a knot?"

The corners of Abby Mancuso's pouty lips curled upward and her brown eyes sparkled with innocence. "I twiddle." She twirled the tip of her pale-pink fingernail around the shirt button between Loane's breasts. "Like this."

Loane's nipples tingled and her skin flushed. "I see how that could create a problem." She glanced around the dark, deserted shopping strip where they'd parked as if they were suddenly in a spotlight. "Is this thing," she waved toward the hair-entangled device, "still on?"

"Of course not."

"Good, because I doubt that Special Agent Dan Bowman of the Bureau of Alcohol, Tobacco, Firearms, and Explosives would approve of your twiddling demonstration." Abby laughed when Loane lowered her voice and produced an exaggerated imitation of the uptight agent.

"I'm sure my handler wouldn't approve of a lot of things we've done, but I'm not telling." Abby's mouth opened slightly as she moved toward her.

Loane wet her lips with the tip of her tongue. She felt hot and damp. "Abby—"

"I know what you're about to say. You're a Greensboro Police officer. I'm an informant. This is wrong."

"It is." Saying the words aloud didn't convince her any more than repeating them mentally for three months had. Logically, professionally she knew she'd gone too far. Sexually, hormonally—whatever drove her physical craving for this woman—she hadn't gone far enough. "I think—"

"Landry, do you copy?" Bowman's voice barked over the ATF radio hidden under the driver's seat of her Jeep. Loane jerked away from Abby, her fingers still coiled in hair. The hint of arousal dispersed like smoke in a stiff wind.

Abby pulled the knotted mass from Loane's hand and deftly unwrapped the tiny earpiece. "If you twiddle, you must learn to un-twiddle. Guess we better get to the office for the debriefing. Bowman's anal about procedure. Maybe we could stop at a drive-thru. You probably haven't eaten, have you?"

"I'm fine." Loane was anything but. The interruption had been like a sharp slap across the face, reminding her of the real reason she and Abby were together—to conduct surveillance and gather intelligence on an illegal weapons ring. The chief of police, her father's old partner, had given her the opportunity to work on the task force and possibly get a promotion out of it.

Looking straight ahead as she drove, Loane recalled the heavy sigh and quiet tone of her father's voice when he disagreed with something she'd done. She and her brother had followed in his footsteps, hoping to prove they were good enough to bear the family name. Her unprofessional behavior with Abby would appall her father and her brother. Guilt clung to the back of her throat like a bad taste.

"Loane, you wanted to talk about tonight. Did I do something wrong?"

"No. You covered well when Sylvia found you snooping in the basement. Taking the kid's toy down there with you was smart. You think fast under pressure and adapt quickly."

"Thanks. I detect a *but*."

"To find out about Simon Torre's illegal operations, you might have to branch out. You've checked his house and haven't found anything incriminating, not even records. Maybe he keeps home and business entirely separate, mistakenly thinking that if he's caught, his family assets will be safe."

Abby absently twirled a strand of her reddish-brown locks with her finger and a crease formed between her eyes. "You mean I need to get more involved in the business side of things?"

Loane nodded.

"Oh, joy. I danced in one of his *gentlemen's clubs* when I first went to work for Simon. The pay was great, but the humiliation of prancing around half-naked for strangers…"

Abby shivered and Loane placed her hand on top of hers. "It might not come to that. Besides, it's not my call. I'm just your cover officer."

"Why are you so good to me?"

When she looked at Abby's silky olive complexion, untamed hair, and cocoa eyes, warmth spread through her like hot coffee on a frosty morning, followed immediately by a twisting sensation in her gut. She was frolicking on a dangerous playground. She *should* have ignored her attraction to Abby when they met. She *should* have resisted the coaxing of her throaty voice and the temptation of that first searing kiss. But something about Abby Mancuso blasted the *shoulds* of proper conduct wide open.

"What do you mean? I like you, Abby."

"But you treat me more like an equal than a criminal informant. You offer advice about what to look for in the case and how to keep my sanity while I pretend to be somebody else. Bowman never does that."

"Bowman's a tool." She glanced at Abby as her smile turned to a grimace.

"You do know that being an informant isn't my life's goal, right? I mean, we've never talked about what happens after the case…or about…us."

"Probably best."

When they pulled into the ATF parking lot and stopped beside the only other car there, Abby turned to her. "I'd *like* to talk about us. Tonight after we debrief?"

Loane inched toward the car door and reached for the handle. "Okay, sure." Past lovers had always wanted more than she was prepared to give, accused her of withholding emotionally, and eventually left her. Abby was different. She'd never asked for anything but what they had. Was that about to change?

Loane had been doing fine until Abby Mancuso entered her life, and she assumed nothing would change after their fling. She'd continue remodeling her parents' home in the trendy Sunset Hills gayborhood, working as a beat cop and moving up the ladder in the police department. Having a tryst was nothing new. She always kept her feelings and casual sex separate, and if the affair proved problematic, she'd have to end it. She flinched at the unpleasant thought as she opened the door to the office and waited for Abby to enter.

Loane fidgeted in a leather swivel chair in the gray-walled conference room while Agent Bowman and Abby whispered in the corner. Her jaw tightened as Bowman invaded Abby's body space and excluded her from the conversation. *Note to self: never mix business with pleasure again.*

Abby made eye contact and nodded for her to join them. Bowman continued to ignore her. She wanted to rattle the muscle-enhanced agent, but antagonizing him would only make her job and Abby's more difficult. When the chief assigned her to the gunrunning case, he'd warned her to play nice with the feds. She was finding it more difficult than she'd imagined.

Bowman looped his arm around Abby's back just above her cuppable ass, and Loane couldn't contain her irritation. "Are we debriefing or what? I'd like to get out of here tonight."

He pulled a bottle of water from a cooler-sized refrigerator and straddled a chair at the table. "Keep your pants on, Landry." His green eyes twinkled and a blush crept toward his military-styled gray hair.

She mentally recited the chronological history of the Greensboro Police Department to halt a smart-ass response and focused on Abby. Her chestnut hair brushed the tops of her shoulders in waves as she stooped to grab another bottle of water. She offered one to Loane before joining them at the table. Always thoughtful, always taking care of others—that summed up Abby perfectly.

"What do you have for me, Abby?" Bowman asked.

Abby's gaze lingered on Loane a moment longer before she answered his question. "Nothing interesting. I did get a look in the basement but didn't find anything useful. Exciting night of family chitchat for Officer Landry." Abby bit her bottom lip to suppress a smile, and Loane's pulse quickened.

"Simon didn't get any calls, make any contact, with anyone?" He drummed his fingers on the tabletop. "I need actionable intelligence. We've been at this for three months. We need *something*."

Abby glanced down at the table and Loane said, "Back off. She can't fabricate evidence. I've heard every exchange too and there's nothing incriminating."

Straightening in her chair, Abby turned her full attention to Bowman. "I don't know what you expect, Dan. You told me to observe and report. If you want me to do something else, you'll have to be more specific. After all—"

"I know. You're just an informant working off drug charges."

Loane considered, not for the first time, if that was true. In field situations Abby performed like a fly-by-the-seat-of-her-pants informant, doing as she was told, improvising when necessary, and enjoying the perks of her situation. But as she spoke to Bowman, her tone and the certainty of her statements made Loane wonder. Abby was different from other informants, and it bothered her that she hadn't figured out how. She was usually a good judge of character and motivation, but their sexual liaison had clouded her ability in a rosy haze.

Opening herself emotionally, even a little, to a doomed situation also puzzled her. She was taking a giant gamble with this woman—exposing herself and risking her job.

Never show your hand. Her mother's playbook of how to conceal feelings could've been a *New York Times* bestseller. Until now, she'd never challenged those lessons, much less ignored them. At least she hadn't declared her love for Abby. They were having a fling. How could it be anything more? When playtime was over, it would end—Abby was a criminal and she was a cop.

"Sorry I can't give you what you want, Dan. I'll do whatever you think's best," Abby said. "I want this to be finished as much as you do."

Abby's sincerity tugged at her heart. How could she not be attracted to someone who wanted so desperately to please and didn't ask for anything in return? But Loane still held back and refused to surrender emotionally. She'd tried to show Abby that she was important, but that was it. Maybe it *was* time to end this liaison before someone discovered them or one of them got hurt.

Bowman slapped the table and stood, startling Loane out of her mental Ping-Pong game about Abby. "Guess we're done here," he said. "Another wasted day at the office. You two pick up in the morning and I'll see you back here for the debriefing."

Abby waited until Bowman slammed the outside door before she reached across the table and took Loane's hands. "Are you all right?"

Loane nodded.

Abby had seen how jealous, uncomfortable, and angry Loane had been when Bowman tried to provoke her. How had Loane restrained herself? Loane's calm façade provided the grounding Abby needed. She could manage the uncertainty of her life with Loane in it. How had this woman invaded her every thought and action in the past few months? "Thank you for sticking up for me, but you didn't have to. I've got to take care of myself."

"He shouldn't talk to you like that. Just because you're not an agent doesn't give him the right to be disrespectful."

"You softy, but I promise not to tell." Abby loved this part of Loane most—the tender, vulnerable side she never showed the rest of the world, and rarely to her. Abby felt privileged. "Can we go to your place?"

"Are you sure that's smart?" Loane tried to withdraw, but Abby held firm.

Her feelings for Loane were the only thing she was sure about right now. But she didn't have a right to them. Abby ignored her conscience, drinking in Loane's gaze like a balm to her soul. Her eyes relayed the truth more fully than her words or actions, and Abby took her cues from them. Right now, Loane was obviously as conflicted about their situation as she was.

Loane pulled away and combed her fingers through her thick hair. The platinum tresses feathered back around her oval face in a simple motion that made Abby's heart ache. Everything about Loane made Abby ache—the smoothness of her pale skin, the cool blue of her evocative eyes, the swollen fullness of her lips, her attempts to adhere to proper protocol, and even her pretense of emotional bravado. "Let's just talk. Okay?"

When she'd met Loane, she'd sensed an immediate connection, and Loane's aloofness fed into Abby's need to please like gin calls for tonic. She had always been the bridge builder in her expressive Italian family, the conduit between three brothers and her parents. But she was also the focus of her family's overprotectiveness, because she was small-framed and looked delicate. Even Agent Bowman often treated her as though she might break.

Loane had been different. Their first night on the job, she'd allowed Abby to decide when to contact their target and what listening devices would work best in the setting. She'd assumed Abby was competent and capable and hadn't judged her as only an informant. Their working relationship gelled naturally and a sexual attraction soon followed.

She'd never experienced the clichéd fire and ice of a stare until the first time her eyes met Loane's. Loane's crystal gaze had assessed and consumed her, her platinum hair and telling eyes a sharp contrast to her unassuming nature. Loane alerted every nerve in Abby's body on a visceral level. From the beginning she couldn't resist and had struggled to focus and to keep her secrets.

When she was away from Loane, she became more rational and could plan her life more clearly. She'd come to Greensboro, North Carolina, by way of Miami, to finish something she'd started eighteen months earlier. Here she had a chance to break out of the only-girl-youngest-child role in her family, and her dream didn't include love or lust or whatever she was feeling.

She wanted to tell Loane the truth, to ask her to wait, but she was still uncertain about too many things. Besides, she'd taken an oath of secrecy. Even Special Agent Dan Bowman wasn't special enough to know anything substantial about her.

Abby had accepted a once-in-a-lifetime opportunity full of deceit and danger, but so far she'd been nothing but an informant.

She moved around the table and knelt between Loane's legs. *Don't do it, Abby.* She pushed the nagging voice to the back of her mind and surrendered to her gnawing need. Sliding her hands up Loane's thighs, she felt the muscles tighten, and in that moment she wanted consummation instead of conversation. "So, your place?"

Loane nodded, her gaze fixed on Abby's lips.

Abby wanted to share herself completely with Loane. After she'd realized her feelings were more than casual, she hadn't had an orgasm during their lovemaking. She wanted to try again, but could she give everything while hiding so much? This might be her last chance.

❖

When Abby walked into Loane's bedroom, Loane was nude with a sheet pulled up to her waist. A dark ring on the pillow outlined the damp ends of her platinum hair, and the fresh scent of soap and toothpaste lingered in the adjoining bath. The arctic blue of her eyes deepened when Abby stared at her. She scanned Loane's exposed body and memorized each detail. "You look like a dessert." Loane held out her hand. "Not until I've showered."

"Need some help?"

"Relax. I won't be long." On the way to the shower, she undressed and looked around the bedroom. A set of new French doors opened to the private backyard, and a slight breeze barely circulated the late-summer heat that had settled in the room. As she took in the soothing wall color and cushioned furnishings, the tension in her shoulders drained. Her pulse slowed to the rhythmic *tick-tock* of the old mantel clock in the living room. As she kicked off her shoes, the plush pile of the Oriental rug squished up through her toes like sand on a Miami beach. This woman, this place called to her in a way she'd never experienced, and she wanted to understand why.

She stepped into the shower spray before the water heated, hoping a cold splash would help clarify her intentions toward Loane. Her body pulsed with the needs of a lover, and she wondered when her life had become so complicated. Love was supposed to make everything right, wasn't it? She washed away the day's residue and toweled off on the way to Loane's bed, still conflicted. *Think about what you're doing. Follow your instincts. Be honest.*

Diving in beside Loane, she wrapped an arm and a leg over her warm body.

"Jeez, did you shower in cold water? You're freezing."

"I wanted you to pucker up for me, hon." Abby closed her hand over Loane's breast. The soft flesh formed a tight knot against her palm. "I'll warm you up in a minute. Are you okay? Bowman was getting to you tonight."

"How could you tell?"

"Sorry, Officer, but you aren't as impenetrable as you think. I can usually tell how you feel about most things." *Except me.*

"How am I feeling right now?"

"Horny."

"You're good." Loane pulled her closer and Abby nestled her head into the groove of her shoulder.

"And don't you forget it." She motioned toward the French doors. "Every time I visit you've done something else to the house. Very nice."

"Thanks. It's been hard to make some of the changes, but I enjoy the process and the finished product." The sadness in Loane's voice was palpable.

"You're doing a great job."

"Sometimes I wonder if my folks would approve." Loane trailed her finger along the curve of Abby's waist and rested her hand on her hip. "I was never sure what they liked or disliked, beyond my father's love of history."

"Your parents would love that you're keeping the family home and updating it."

"I could probably be persuaded to live here forever." She shifted, and the heady scent of her desire fueled Abby's passion. Burying her face in Abby's hair, Loane blew lightly down the side of her neck and kissed her ear. "Are you feeling persuasive?"

"I could probably manage, Officer Landry, but we shouldn't even be having sex, much less thinking about a future." Greensboro was exactly the kind of culturally diverse community Abby could see herself settling into, but she wasn't here to settle down.

"Sometimes you can't argue with fate."

"Is that what we are, Loane, star-crossed lovers?" Abby heard the seriousness creep into her voice. She and Loane hadn't talked about anything beyond the present, probably because it wasn't possible. What kind of future could they hope to have? "Life is short but…"

"But what?"

"Circumstances get in the way. Things happen that you can't control." She stroked Loane's stomach and up to her breasts. "What would Bowman think about this?"

It was a rhetorical question. Dan Bowman would snatch her off the gunrunning case so fast she'd get whiplash. He followed the federal-agent handbook to the letter, and she made it up as she went. But some forces couldn't be contained. If she allowed this relationship to grow, Loane Landry could be that force for her. Looking at the woman lying next to her, Abby couldn't regret their meeting, no matter how untimely.

"Loane, you're a cop."

"And you're trying to stay out of jail, I know."

"That alone could get you seriously reprimanded, if not fired."

"Then we better make good use of our time, huh?"

Before she could answer, Loane circled Abby's lips with her tongue and poked gently. Her subtle request for entry always reduced Abby to a useless puddle. She sucked Loane's tongue in a rhythmic welcome, her pelvis pumping air and her vaginal walls gripping an imaginary finger. Her body always betrayed her.

"I need you, Abby."

She whispered, "You have me." The kiss was so light that she shivered. She blanked her mind and surrendered to the cascading emotions as Loane settled on top of her, their bodies undulating like choreographed dancers. Over and over they made love without thinking about duty, responsibility, or time. Only their overwhelming feelings and the physical expression of them mattered.

"Loane—please." Her voice hitched as Loane massaged her

abdomen above the pubic bone with her left hand, the slender fingers of her right buried inside her. Her skin slicked with perspiration as she rocked against Loane. This was their third round of lovemaking and she didn't want to stop. Watching Loane's hand piston in and out of her body stoked her passion.

Loane stared up at her and withdrew completely before reentering her with a slow, deliberate thrust. It was like watching an artist create a masterpiece. She gripped Loane's shoulders with just enough pressure to guide the pace. Slow, quick, quick, slow, like dance steps urging her to follow.

"Now, hon, harder, right there. Yes, like that." The orgasm built, coiling inside, just out of reach. Tension rippled up her legs and coalesced in her center. Her body quivered in anticipation, but she couldn't come. The relief she'd struggled for all night evaporated like steam off a hot kettle. "Loane, stop, please. I'm shattered."

"But you didn't come."

"It's all right. Guess I'm a little off tonight." Her body was raw, her emotions tender. If she didn't feel the emotional connection, she just couldn't let go, and she refused to fake an orgasm. "I need to breathe… and a drink of water would be nice."

"Don't stop yet. We don't have much time." Loane hovered over her, pale skin glistening in the filtered moonlight. Hunger burned in her eyes. "I'm not finished with you."

"You are if I die of dehydration." She grabbed the water bottle from the bedside table and drank deeply.

The hunger in Loane's eyes softened to a plea and Abby was lost. She dropped the water bottle and opened her arms again, letting Loane take over.

Loane slid her body against Abby's and the ache inside her eased. "Please, Abby." She'd never felt this needy, not sexually and certainly not emotionally. When she was with Abby, it was enough. *She* was enough. She wedged her leg between Abby's and groaned as their juices mingled, their dips and curves aligning perfectly, their movements in exquisite sync.

Abby sucked the soft flesh of her breast and teased her nipples. Her tongue was fire on Loane's skin, erasing thought and replacing it with a flood between her legs.

"How can you make me feel so—?"

"Don't talk."

Abby licked a moist trail toward her center and Loane shivered.

Her sex twitched and she tightened, readying for orgasm. "I'm about to pop. Please don't make me wait." Abby's brown eyes sparkled as they met hers and she lowered her head.

Loane couldn't speak as Abby captured her clit. She fisted a handful of chestnut hair as Abby worked up and down between her legs. The visual created an insistent pounding throb. Abby knew her body so well, too well. How was it possible?

1810 first Commissioners of Police established in Greensboro. Loane mentally recited historical facts, her distraction of choice, to prolong the impending orgasm. She wanted it, but she also wanted it to last. Her body stilled slightly.

"Stop that," Abby said.

"What?" *1819 first route of the Underground Railroad started in a cave near Guilford College.*

"Forget about history…stay with me. I want to make you come hard and fast."

At that moment she trusted Abby completely. Abby held her gaze and clamped onto her clit with her hot mouth. History became just that, history. She gave in, welcoming the orgasm but pushing on Abby's shoulders to slow it down.

"Make up your mind, hon. Do you want me to stop or keep going?"

"Don't stop." Clinging to Abby's hair, she rode her until the tingles of release started in her toes and exploded in her crotch. Abby stroked her with her tongue and she emptied over and over. She couldn't remember the last time having sex had seemed so effortless and enjoyable. Abby was gifted at pleasuring, maybe too gifted, and she couldn't get enough of her.

She pulled Abby up her body, needing to hold her, to feel their hearts beating in unison. Every inch of her craved the feel, the taste, and the smell of their joining. No one had ever bewitched her so totally. She'd found a shortcut to happiness, even if it was only temporary.

"I love you, Abby." As orgasm oozed from one end of her body, betrayal spewed from the other—betrayal of a time-honored family philosophy: never show your hand. Loane had never questioned it, until now. But had she actually spoken the words or just thought them in a moment of weakness?

Abby released her grip around Loane's shoulders and looked at her. Loane saw confusion in Abby's eyes as she said, "What is it, hon?"

Fingering strands of her long brown hair, Loane stalled for a clue. “Nothing.” Even if she *thought* she loved Abby, it was too soon for declarations. They were having fun, enjoying each other sexually. Perhaps the professional taboo had brought them together. She wouldn’t be the first cop to sleep with an informant, or even a crook, for that matter.

“Loane, are you okay? You look weird. Did I hurt you?”

“Not at all.” Obviously she hadn’t spoken those three words aloud, definitely a good thing. “Sorry, guess I’m getting a little tired.” She tried to sound convincing. “You should get some rest. You’re in play again in less than three hours. I’m going to get some water. Want anything?”

“Only you again.”

She felt Abby’s stare follow her out of the room. If she looked into her eyes right now, she’d say something she’d regret.

Never show your hand. Her relaxed defenses re-engaged with a thud as she gulped a glass of cold water. She was just experiencing a little postcoital dizziness. She and Abby were just sharing a period of mutual fleeting lust or infatuation, nothing more.

❖

Abby spooned against Loane’s back, enjoying the steady cadence of her breathing. The first night they’d spent together, Loane had tossed uncomfortably, unable to relax after their lovemaking. Now she slept the sleep of the sexually sated, nestled in her arms. The realization elicited guilt so powerful she flinched and eased away. If Loane woke up, they’d have to discuss the look in her eyes earlier. That single expression had said all the things she wanted to hear but had no right to expect or hope for.

As she eased her legs off the side of the bed, her cell phone vibrated across the bedside table and toppled onto the floor. She scooped it up, tiptoed to the bathroom, and closed the door behind her. “Hello?”

“Abby, you’ve got to help me.”

The woman’s voice was so strained and full of panic she almost didn’t recognize her. “Sylvia, is that you?” Sylvia was the wife of Simon Torre, one of the subjects of the gunrunning task-force investigation.

“Yes. Simon’s gone crazy. Says we have to leave tonight. He’s woken up Alma and Blake and is packing the car, talking nonsense.”

She considered how to refuse Sylvia’s request without raising suspicion. As Simon Torre's Girl Friday she'd done everything from babysitting his grandchild to dancing in his gentlemen's clubs. She'd even relocated with them from Miami to maintain her place in the family. As a confidential informant she was supposed to observe and report, take no action and no chances. But when the family called, she was expected to be accommodating.

"Sylvia, calm down. Has something happened?"

"He's been acting strange, drinking and smoking those smelly cigars his nephew sends him like it's his last day on earth. About an hour ago he announced that *they* were coming and we had to leave for Miami tonight. Please talk to him. He listens to you."

Abby thought Simon Torre was a good man and had difficulty seeing him as a gunrunner who used his dancers to transport weapons. But like with Loane, she'd violated another rule of the informant/undercover game and become emotionally attached to the family. After over a year together, she'd spent more time with the Torres than she had her own friends and relatives. She'd begun to think ATF was watching the wrong people. But that wasn't her call. This was.

"I'll be right there." She opened the bathroom door and nearly bumped into Loane, leaning against the door frame.

"I was about to knock, need to pee. Where you rushing off to?"

"Sorry, I have to go. See you shortly." Her instructions from Bowman were clear—never make contact with a suspect without approval and without cover. At least she could tell Loane where she was going. But this would be a quick handholding session and she'd be back. No need to involve her. Besides, if she was ever to stand on her own, she had to start somewhere. The petty side of her wanted to add, and if Loane can keep secrets, so can I.

"Anything I can do?"

She shook her head.

"Is it work?"

"I have to go, Loane. It's personal." She might as well have said *none of your fucking business*. The pained look in Loane's eyes couldn't have been any more heart-wrenching. So much for love and trust.

"Fine. Don't let me keep you." Loane closed the bathroom door with a firm slam.

Abby raised her hand to knock but changed her mind. She'd explain to Loane when she had more time, and if she learned anything significant about the case, she'd share it at the briefing. As she dressed,

Abby berated herself for accepting a job she couldn't tell anyone about, lying to everyone she knew, and mostly for hurting Loane. If she could tell the truth, life would be much less complicated. But honesty wasn't an option.

When Loane heard the front door close behind Abby, she pulled on the wrinkled T-shirt and jeans she'd discarded at the foot of the bed and ran to her car. Abby's inability to look her in the eye and the tone of her voice told Loane this early morning visit was anything but personal. She shifted into cop mode. If Abby was pursuing a lead in the gunrunner case, she wouldn't let her do it alone, no matter how unsettled their relationship.

The taillights of the undercover vehicle Abby was driving disappeared around the corner and she followed, hanging back enough to blend into the shadows in her residential neighborhood. The irritation she'd felt at Abby's dismissal quieted as the thrill of the chase took over. She darted in and out between parked cars and paralleled Abby's path until they merged onto Battleground Avenue from Benjamin Parkway. She slowed and turned on the headlights of her Jeep, thankful for night owls and early risers on the busier thoroughfare.

She trailed as Abby continued on 220 North, excitement deepening into anxiety. She rolled down the window and let the surge of fresh night air wash over her, hoping to purge Abby's scent and taste enough to think clearly. Before the Greensboro city limits, Abby turned on Strawberry Road. *Damn it, Abby.* She was heading to Simon Torre's. Why would she go to a suspect's home in the middle of the night without telling her handler and, more important, without backup? Maybe she was involved in this case beyond being an informant. And maybe Loane's hormones had blinded her to that fact.

Loane turned off her lights and waited until Abby made the first curve before turning onto Strawberry Road herself. The area was sparsely residential, and at this time of night, Abby could easily spot her vehicle. She drove slowly, allowing Abby plenty of time to arrive. Should she let Abby go in alone? Her informant role required unmonitored contact, but this felt wrong.

As she approached the residence, Loane passed two vehicles—a nondescript dark sedan and a Harley-Davidson motorcycle. She was glad they weren't highway patrol or she would've been stopped for operating without lights. When she cruised past the Torre home, the expansive ranch-style residence was lit up like Times Square. Loane pulled behind a stand of trees across the road to observe activity at the house and on the street. The only blind spot was the garage at the back.

She took her binoculars from between the seats and focused on the house. Through the sheer curtains in the front room she saw Simon Torre pacing back and forth, flailing his arms like a madman. Abby stood out in the lime-green blouse she'd been wearing when she left the house. She seemed to be trying to calm Simon as he paced. Why had Abby come here, especially if she knew he was upset?

The longer Loane watched the scene, the more uncomfortable she became. She couldn't go in or she would blow Abby's cover and jeopardize the case. But she had to do something. She pulled out her cell phone and dialed ATF Agent Bowman.

"This is Officer Landry. Abby Mancuso is at Simon Torre's house."

"How do you know that, Landry?" His question was more like an accusation.

"Because she called me. It's protocol." She lied, but she didn't want to get Abby in trouble. If Bowman thought she was acting outside the rules, he'd pull her from the case. "She's inside with this guy and he looks pissed."

"Don't do anything stupid. I'm already on the way."

"How—"

"I got a call, of course. It's protocol." He mimicked Loane's comment in his annoyingly superior tone.

His revelation sent a stab of disappointment and hurt through her. Why hadn't Abby told her? She thought they'd developed a strong partnership. Obviously what they'd shared didn't mean anything to her—professionally, and maybe not personally either. Maybe Abby had seen Loane's feelings reflected in her eyes tonight and was simply backing off.

"Did you hear me, Landry? Don't do anything."

Disconnecting the call, she threw the phone into the seat and slammed her fists against the steering wheel. When she looked back, Abby and Torre were gone. "Damn it, Abby. Damn it to hell."

As she thought about her next move, the house suddenly exploded in a ground-shaking blast. Debris spewed into the air. Pellets of scorched wood and fragments of brick rained down on the car as the building disintegrated. Cinders ignited the dry grass around the house, creating patches of flames between her and Abby.

She jumped out of her Jeep and ran across the road, dodging brush fires, and stared at the last spot Abby had stood. That spot no longer existed, nor did the house supporting it. "Abby!" She tried to get closer but the heat was too intense. "This can't be happening."

She ran toward the back of the house. The metal garage doors were twisted awkwardly off the hinges, revealing two vehicles. Inside a flaming SUV she saw the charred silhouettes of human bodies. *Abby. I have to get to her.* She fell to her hands and knees and crawled closer. Flames licked her skin and the smell of singed hair burned her nostrils. She took a deep breath, stood, and grabbed the garage door and pulled. The pain seared through her as quickly as the hot metal melted her skin. She started to lose consciousness. No way to reach her in time. She prayed that Abby had died quickly and that she would never wake up.

Chapter Two

Abby awoke to a quietness she could only associate with death—no rustling of trees, bird or animal sounds, traffic noise—not even her own heartbeat. She opened her mouth and screamed. The sound died like being underwater. Gasping for air, she panicked and grappled for anything solid within reach.

Lying facedown in a bathtub full of rubble, she swept her hands wildly above her head. A heavy weight pressed against her back. She couldn't get up. *At least I'm not dead yet.* Her head ached worse than a tequila hangover and her right leg throbbed. The air stank of scorched wood and burned her throat as she breathed. Her eyes stung as bits of dust and cinder made seeing difficult. *What the hell happened?* She remembered being in the Torre house and then… *Oh, God.*

Something moved under her and she pushed harder to rise. The weight shifted off her back and a slab of Sheetrock fell away. As she came to her knees, she looked down on Simon Torre's two-year-old grandson. Blake's mouth was open, his eyes tightly closed, and his face bright red. He appeared to be crying but she couldn't hear him.

She checked the boy for obvious wounds and watched for the rise and fall of his chest. He didn't appear to be injured, but she had no idea how long she'd been partially covering him or if he'd been hurt before the fall. She knelt in the small space, picked Blake up, and rocked, trying to reassure him as she scanned the area for a way out.

What am I supposed to do? Sweat trickled into her eyes and stung. She shivered while everything around her burned. It was like a scene from a postapocalyptic movie. The explosion had temporarily disrupted her thought process as efficiently as it destroyed the house. Her degrees in dramatic and performing arts were of no use. *Focus, concentrate—* one rule of acting: if you don't know what you're doing, act like you do. She looked at the child in her arms and knew she had to do more than act. *Move, get out.*

She recognized the basement bonus room of Simon Torre's home by its orientation away from and beneath the charred remains of the main house. Blake had needed to go to the bathroom and she'd volunteered to take him. She'd chosen his play area at the opposite end of the home, where he'd feel more comfortable practicing his new potty training. That little side trip had saved their lives.

But her relief was short-lived as she took in their surroundings. The main part of the building was still burning. Debris was falling and the structure continued to deteriorate under the wrath of the fire. She and Blake weren't in danger from the flames, but she didn't trust the stability of the remaining walls. They'd have to get out soon. *What about Simon, Sylvia, and Alma?* No one could've survived the blast she'd heard before she passed out. Perhaps the tub she'd been blown into had shielded her and Blake from further injury.

But the three people she'd spent so much time with recently would certainly be dead. She could see the garage at the back of the house and almost nothing remained. Had she missed something that led to such a tragic end? Could she have prevented it? The tears threatened but she forced them back. She had to save Blake. She owed the family that much.

Abby settled on the side of the tub and cuddled Blake in her arms, humming his favorite lullaby. Her hearing was returning but her head ached from the concussive blast. The air was thick with floating fragments, and the heavy scent of burning wood filled her nose and throat. She took a deep breath to clear her head but coughed instead. She flexed her shoulders and prickles of tenderness ran down her back. *Don't think about that now.*

She rocked Blake as she hummed, and his steady wailing slowly changed to broken sobs. His terrified eyes finally seemed to recognize her. "We'll be okay, baby boy. I promise. Now I've got to get us out of here." When he stopped crying, she gently laid him back down and tried to stand.

A splinter of pain shot up her right leg and she doubled over. She grabbed the side of the tub to keep from screaming. After a few deep breaths, she pulled her pants leg up, relieved to see only an area of red swollen skin and no protruding bone. She poked the angry flesh around the swelling and winced. The sensation was unpleasant but not as agonizing as when she'd broken her arm as a teenager. She needed something to stabilize her leg but didn't have time. Blake's safety was her first priority.

She searched the rubble within reach, finger-tested a few pieces of piping for heat, and chose a curved one as a crutch. Bending over the tub, she coaxed Blake into her left arm and gradually rose. Walking wouldn't be easy if her leg was broken, but if she waited for emergency personnel, it might be too late.

She settled Blake against her chest and took her first uneasy step. The makeshift crutch gouged her underarm and her leg throbbed, but she moved forward. She dodged shards of glass and jagged wood protruding from the walls and bare earth. A windowpane hung like a guillotine from what was left of the ceiling, and she circled wide to avoid passing under it. Before taking each step, she balanced on her left leg, pushed wreckage aside, and checked the stability of the ground. Her back already ached from the additional weight and awkward gait, and she wasn't even out of the house yet. To block out her discomfort, she focused on each movement as if it was a major project.

As she made her way through the ruins, the wind shifted and the fire seemed to follow, consuming the remaining building materials. Powered by adrenaline and fear, she moved faster until she lost track of time and the heat subsided. Then she turned and looked back. Only two walls of the main structure still stood, the ones above the basement bathroom where she and Blake had been. The realization made her weak. She pulled Blake tighter in her arm. She hadn't thought about looking for Simon, Sylvia, and Alma, knowing instinctively that they were dead. The recovery team would make it official.

Why wasn't the fire department here? Where were the first responders? Emergency personnel equals police equals questions. How would she explain her presence at an explosion of a suspect's home in the middle of the night? Loane or Agent Bowman could run interference. One of them would take her statement and leave her out of this investigation in order to keep her cover intact. First she'd have to contact them, but her cell had been destroyed, along with her purse and probably the car she'd been driving as well. She needed a phone.

A short distance away from the Torre home, surrounded by a dense grove of trees, was a neighbors' house. Though it wasn't visible from the street or the Torre home, Abby had seen it while walking around the property several weeks ago. Tonight she could barely make out the dim light from the windows.

With each painful step, Blake fretted more and seemed to grow heavier. Her left arm ached from his weight and her right from taking the pressure off her leg. The initial adrenaline rush was gone and she wanted to collapse in the field and wait for help. What had happened was unimaginable, the reason for it inconceivable.

Why would anyone want to kill the Torre family…and her? Maybe someone in the weapons case had become suspicious and wanted to eliminate her. But she wasn't supposed to be there at all. She'd made that decision—obviously a bad one. And why kill Simon if he was involved in the illegal operation? None of it made sense.

Hours seemed to pass as Abby picked her way through the woods. Still no emergency personnel at the Torre home. Strange, since they weren't that far out of the city. She wanted an EMT to check Blake and her leg but wasn't ready to answer questions. Before she made any decisions, she'd call Loane. She'd get a lecture about proper informant procedures, but it would be worth it to hear her voice right now.

As she approached the neighbors' house, the front door opened before she reached the steps. An elderly couple hurried toward them. The woman took Blake, and the man put his arm around her waist and helped her inside.

"Put her on the sofa, John," the woman said, pointing to a worn three-seater. The house was warm and cozy, with years of family memorabilia on the bookshelf and mantle.

"I'm sorry to intrude," Abby said.

"Don't be silly. You're hurt. I'm Susan Cooper and this is my grumpy husband, John. I'm an RN." She nodded toward a faded diploma on the wall as if to verify her qualifications. "Mind if I check you and the boy over?"

"That would be great. Him first, please." While Susan examined Blake and cleaned him up, Abby watched John pace back and forth in front of the window like a sentry.

"I've been trying to get through on nine-one-one, but the system is on the fritz. Happens occasionally. Technology." He spoke the last word like a curse.

"Keep trying, John," his wife said before turning her attention to Abby's leg. "We need to get you and the child to the hospital for a thorough examination. Either of you could have a concussion or internal injuries."

"You're right, but can we wait a little longer for the ambulance? I'm sure they'll be here soon." Abby had to stall long enough to figure out what to do. Blake should be cleared by a doctor, but how would she explain having custody of a child that wasn't hers without involving the authorities? She had to fly under the radar, at least until she got further instructions. "I hate to impose on you again, but could I use your phone?" Abby started to get up, but Susan patted her knee.

"Why don't I bring it to you? You've probably got at least a hairline fracture of the tibia. We'll need X-rays to know for sure. I'll stabilize it with a makeshift splint, but you need to stay off your leg as much as possible." When Abby didn't answer immediately, Susan said, "John and I'll get the little one settled upstairs."

Nodding her appreciation for the privacy, Abby took the cordless phone and started to dial Loane's cell. Halfway through the number, she stopped. Her instincts told her to make another call first. She needed answers before she'd know what to tell Loane.

But what would this call say about her ability to handle herself in difficult situations? Her instructions had been explicit—call Hector Barrio only in case of emergency. Dan Bowman was her contact in day-to-day activities, but if this didn't qualify as an emergency, she wasn't sure what did. The case had literally gone up in smoke, but only one man could officially end it. She dialed, waited for the prompt, and entered the Coopers' phone number.

At the first chirp of the phone, she answered. "This is Abby."

"Bad news?" Hector Barrio, ATF Special Agent in Charge of the Miami Field Division, was not happy. His tone implied that Abby better have a true emergency.

She succinctly relayed what had happened and waited for the words that would return her life to normal. The tightness in her chest eased and she realized how much she wanted that. Maybe this horrific event had a silver lining.

"Right. Stay where you are. Call Stefan Torre in Miami and tell him everything. Then do exactly as he says."

"But…isn't it over?"

"It damn well isn't. You've moved up a rung on the ladder. Congratulations."

"I don't understand." She couldn't continue as if nothing had happened. How could she tell Stefan Torre that his brother, sister-in-law, and niece had been killed in an explosion? But she was the only person who could. This wasn't a task she'd pass off to a stranger.

"You're still an informant and I still need information."

"Who'll be my Miami contact?"

"I will. In the meantime, get acquainted with the new family boss, whoever he is. It'll be good for you to lie low for a while until your leg heals. You don't need to contact me unless something significant happens."

"Are you going to tell Bowman about—"

"He doesn't know the daughter-in-law was visiting, does he?"

"No."

"Perfect. He'll believe what everybody else does, that you're dead and the case is closed, at least until we know who we can trust. Remember your assignment. Get information on the weapons dealer and identify the leak in the Greensboro ATF office. Bowman might be the mole. Think about it, Abby. Somebody wants this investigation shut down. What if the Torres weren't the only targets tonight?"

"You mean me?"

"And anybody else connected to the family."

Her heart fluttered and she stifled a gasp. Loane. "What will you tell the local authorities—the officers working on the task force?"

"Nothing. This will close the case as far as they're concerned. You and I are the only ones who'll know it's still ongoing."

She wanted to demand that Loane be told the truth about the case and her involvement in it. She owed her that much, but Hector Barrio was not a man who gave in or gave up. "Sir, what if these officers are in danger? Don't you think they have a right to know?"

"They'll be safe if the gunrunners think the case is closed."

Leaving Loane's safety to chance didn't set well with her. She wanted to get a message to her somehow. At least tell her to be cautious. "Are you sure it shouldn't be? We haven't found a connection between the Torres and illegal weapons in over a year. Are you certain we're watching the right people?"

"Absolutely. The big fish are always the hardest to catch. Stick with it."

"I'm not sure I can—"

"Of course you can. You're an actress. That's why I hired you. Shake it off."

Abby heard the click and stared at the phone in disbelief. What if she couldn't shake it off? The emotions of the past two hours churned inside. Simon, Sylvia, and Alma Torre hadn't been just suspects to her. They were people with feelings and dreams for the future. They'd treated her like family. Could she repay their kindness and disrespect their memory by betraying them further?

She thought about Blake asleep upstairs. At least he wasn't

seriously injured. She'd done one thing right. Now she had to get him back to his father, where he belonged. Nick would be grief stricken and frantic. She dialed Information and the operator provided the number for Stefan Torre and connected the call. It took all her strength not to break down as she told him about the explosion and his only relative who'd survived.

"You and Blake come home now." Stefan's thick Italian accent reminded her of her father and she stifled a wave of nostalgia. Mr. Torre was on the verge of tears so she needed to stay strong. "There is airport near you, no?"

"Yes, Air Harbor." It was the one she and the Torres used when they came to Greensboro in their private jet.

Stefan asked. "Where are you now?" She flipped over a magazine on the coffee table and read the Coopers' address. "I send a car and doctor for you and the boy. The jet will be there soon—two hours most. Tell no one where you're going. Understand?"

"Yes sir, I understand." His cough sounded like a strangled cry. Abby wanted desperately to say something helpful but words failed.

"And thank you, Abby. You have done the Torre family a great service today."

Helping Blake was the *only* thing that made sense about this day. She'd left Loane without sharing her feelings, lied to her about where she was going, and agreed to continue on a case she didn't believe in—a case that might still jeopardize Loane's safety. She'd never felt so lost and in need of guidance.

She started to dial Loane's cell again. Hearing her voice would be comforting, but she thought about Hector Barrio's question. *What if the Torres weren't the only targets tonight?* What if contacting Loane put her at risk? She had too many unanswered questions that might get Loane hurt or worse.

Her feelings were raw and the memory of their lovemaking made her ache. Why hadn't she told Loane where she was going tonight when she left her house? It wasn't that she didn't trust Loane. She trusted her with her life, and the next time she saw her, she'd tell her so, along with the fact that she was in love with her.

Life was too short to risk things like this happening without those she loved knowing how much they meant to her. Tonight she'd simply wanted to help Sylvia, then get back to Loane as quickly as possible. It seemed like such a small thing, but she'd managed to screw it up. As usual, her need to please everyone resulted in helping no one.

When she looked up again, Susan Cooper was coming down the stairs. Abby said, "The boy's family is sending a car and their personal doctor."

The woman nodded. "That's good."

Abby wiped her cheeks as tears dropped onto the phone she held in her trembling hands. She could've been killed tonight. A two-year-old could've been killed. It seemed surreal that they were safe in a neighbor's home while only a few hundred yards away his mother and grandparents lay dead. What law of nature or God decided who lived and who died? She understood protecting the life of a child, but why was she worthy of deliverance?

She had to protect Loane. If further contact would even remotely jeopardize her safety, Abby would close that door until the case was finished, the suspects arrested, and she was free to tell the whole truth. She'd have to let Loane believe she'd died in the explosion tonight. The thought ripped at her insides like a sharp razor.

As she considered the injustice of it all, Susan Cooper cradled her and told her everything would be okay. She doubted it ever would. Three people she cared about were dead, she was returning to Miami in a role she no longer wanted to play, and she'd made a conscious decision to mislead Loane.

❖

"Let me..." The words hung on the parched sides of Loane's throat and refused to come out. She tried again. "Let me the fuck up." Her voice was raspy and she wheezed like a heavy smoker.

"You've been injured." A paramedic moved into her field of vision. "You need to be still. We've got to get you on oxygen and transport you ASAP."

She struggled and then fell back, unable to catch a deep breath as paramedics strapped her to a stretcher. "She's still in there." She pointed toward the building and gauze bandages fell from her hand. The pain hit her with blinding force and she remembered. Abby. She'd tried to save Abby—and failed. The emotional pain momentarily masked the physical.

"Why don't you relax and let the paramedics help you, Landry." Dan Bowman stood over her. "You've got some nasty burns on your hands, smoke inhalation, and who knows what else. They need to get you to the hospital."

She tried to get up again. "No. She's still in there."

"It's too late for anybody in there." He inclined his head toward the burning building behind them.

Loane wanted to argue with him, to hit him, to lash out at anything, but he was right. She'd seen the explosion and the bodies up close, too close. Abby was gone. She surrendered and collapsed on the stretcher, tears burning her cheeks.

The medics cupped an oxygen mask over her face as another man joined Bowman. She had never been officially introduced to the resident agent in charge of the Greensboro ATF office, but she recognized Gary Fowler from television and newspaper coverage.

"Bowman, I want this scene locked down, and I do mean *now.* This is an ATF investigation and I don't want the local cops or sheriffs fucking it up. Understand?"

"Yes, sir."

"I've got some other agents on the way to relieve the locals. They'll be here before the firefighters release the scene. Nobody talks to the press. Nobody releases names. Nobody breathes a word about this case except me."

Why wouldn't ATF want assistance from local police? They'd worked together for three months. She tried to say *she* would still be on the case, whether Fowler wanted her or not, but she started coughing and the paramedics rolled her away. She automatically clenched her hands into fists and the pain made her light-headed. Her last thought before she passed out again was that she'd been too late, too slow, and too weak. She'd failed, and this time it cost Abby her life.

When Loane woke up again, her brother, Tyler, was standing beside her bed, along with Eve Winters, an old friend of her mother, and her partner, Thomasina. "How long have I been out?" Her throat hurt when she spoke and her voice was still rough.

Tyler moved closer. "Couple of days off and on, mostly because of the pain meds. How do you feel?"

"Like road kill." The mention of death prompted visions of bodies inside an SUV. "Have to get out of here." She tried to get up, but Tyler put his hand in the middle of her chest and eased her back onto the bed.

"You can't leave yet. Another day or two."

"But I have to get to…"

Tyler shook his head. "No, you don't." It took her a few seconds to realize he was tactfully reminding her that what she'd seen had really happened. He motioned toward Eve and Thom. "These two have been here almost as much as I have."

"Hi, guys," she said. "Thanks."

"Where else would we be?" Eve asked. Her wavy gray hair fell across her forehead and she brushed an impatient hand through it. Eyes the color of blue sky stared at Loane, and she could almost read the questions behind them. Thom stood next to her, the epitome of grace and controlled worry. She was a shapely package of all things soothing and nurturing rolled into one. Her dark-brown eyes and thick auburn hair reminded Loane of two things she loved, chocolate and coffee, and the comfort she got from both.

"I'm so glad you're awake," Thom said. "Maybe I can get some decent food into you now. That stuff they've been peddling as healthy would make anybody sick." Hospital food obviously offended Thom's gourmet sensibilities.

Loane's head felt fuzzy, but she was aware that Eve and Thom probably had questions about how she'd ended up in the hospital. She looked at Tyler and he shook his head slightly.

"Anybody want coffee?" Nobody took him up on his offer. "I've got a cop's stomach, so I'm used to the hospital cafeteria. See you guys in a bit."

When Tyler left, Eve and Thom stepped closer. "Could I have a sip of water, please?" Loane asked, and raised her bandaged hands. "I can't do much of anything, including feed and water myself." Thom held the plastic cup and straw so she could drink, then placed it back on the bedside table. "I know you're wondering what happened."

"You think?" Eve wasn't one to hold back. She was notorious for saying the wrong thing at the wrong time and not caring who liked or disliked it.

"Eve, you promised." Thom's reminder did little to slow Eve, the emotional steamroller.

"I want to know what the hell is going on."

Loane took a deep breath and, between coughing spells and breaks for water, told them as much as she could about the gunrunner investigation without breaching confidentiality. "And because I didn't do what I should've, three people are probably dead."

Eve rolled her eyes. "Did a tree fall on your head? You can't take responsibility for a bomb some nut job set. Contrary to what you might believe, you're not the savior of the world."

“I should’ve followed her, been there sooner, something.” She felt as helpless as she had that night.

Thom combed her fingers gently through Loane’s hair. “You couldn’t have prevented this, even if you’d been there with her. It wasn’t your fault.”

The words echoed inside her hollow chest but didn’t ring true. “I have to find out what happened. Where’s my cell? Maybe she’s tried to call.”

Eve pulled a cell phone out of the table drawer. “It’s been right here since the night you checked in, and I’ve left several messages on her voice mail. She hasn’t called.”

Loane stared at the offending device and hope seeped out of her body. If Abby were alive, she’d contact her. They cared about each other, and she wouldn’t let her suffer unnecessarily by thinking she was dead. Abby wouldn’t be that cruel.

CHAPTER THREE

Four weeks after the explosion

Loane looked out on Eve and Thom's 1920s granite Greek-revival-style house from the window of their garage apartment. The sandy rock shone in the morning sun against a backdrop of greenery that looked more like an English-castle setting than a neighborhood in Greensboro. A bright-red apron hung over the back of a chair in the sunroom—her signal that their morning quality time was over and she could join them for breakfast. She pulled on a pair of elastic-waist pants, careful to use the tips of her fingers, and slid into a T-shirt. This had become her uniform when the bandages on her hands prevented full maneuverability. As she descended the stairs, she wondered what she would've done if these amazing women hadn't taken her in after the explosion.

"Good morning." Thom gave her a hug and held her in that motherly protective way she had of making everything seem all right, then pointed to her place at the table. "Blueberries or strawberries with your cereal?"

"Blue, please."

"Have a seat, sport. We need to talk," Eve said.

"Eve." Thom's emphatic warning clued Loane that whatever was coming had been the reason breakfast was slightly delayed this morning.

"Oh, Thom, she can handle it." Eve directed her steely blue gaze on Loane and she knew she was in trouble. "So, I've been patient, for me anyway. What *in the hell* were you thinking, grabbing hold of hot metal?"

Loane sipped the lukewarm coffee Thom had prepared through a straw and wondered when she'd be able to have hot coffee again in a real cup she could hold instead of a kid's sippy cup. "I wasn't thinking, Eve. I just acted."

"That proved to be a costly mistake, didn't it?"

"Eve!"

"No, she's right, Thom. It was an impulsive decision, not one of my finest moments." She took another sip and met Eve's stare. "Imagine if you thought Thom was trapped in a burning building and you might be able to save her. What would you do?"

Eve looked back and forth between her and Thom, grunted, and dug into her bowl of cereal and blueberries. That was as close to concession as she'd get. "I wasn't aware that your relationship had progressed that far. We only saw her once and it seemed…casual."

Loane wasn't sure how to answer. She'd told herself the same thing that night. But the explosion had magnified her feelings for Abby, and she was trying to understand them. She still wasn't sure what to call their relationship. "I've been thinking it's time for me to move back home. I can manage on my own now."

Thom stood behind her chair and rested her hands on her shoulders.

"That's not why Eve brought this up, is it?"

With her mouth full, Eve shook her head emphatically.

"But I've been a burden too long, unable to bathe myself, wash my hair, or change my bandages. Hell, I couldn't even lift a cup of coffee. You've already been way too generous with your time and your home."

"Nonsense." Thom squeezed her shoulders, then took a seat across from her. "We love you, Loane. You can stay here as long as you want."

"She's right," Eve said.

"I know, guys, but I'm ready to go home. The hard part is over. The doctor says I can return to most activities but should probably wear light gloves for a while to protect the new baby skin."

"What about scars?" Eve took another mouthful of cereal as nonchalantly as that famous bull that crashed things in a china factory.

Loane stared at the raw pink flesh of her palms and flinched. Gloves would be a must. She didn't want people asking about the injury, and she didn't want to be reminded every time she looked down. "Shouldn't have much scarring, but my palms will be sensitive for months, maybe even years, especially to heat and sunlight."

"That's good. So…you heard anything from Abby?" The china continued to crash.

"Eve, really!" Thom gave her a look that would stop any creature great or small, but Eve didn't even acknowledge her.

Loane had heard this question from her brother, Eve, and herself so many times that it shouldn't be a shock, but it still felt like a brain freeze from eating ice cream too quickly. She stared at her cereal. She'd tried to get confirmation from ATF that Abby was one of the victims of the explosion. Even though she'd been there, she needed to hear the official verification. They'd refused comment. It gave her hope that Abby might still be alive.

"We called her from the hospital that night and several times since, just in case." Eve was relentless. She probably wanted Loane to face facts and move on with her life. "Why do you think she hasn't called?"

Loane mustered the courage to say the words aloud for the first time. "Because she's dead."

Thom's soft gasp seemed to echo around them in the small sunroom. "Oh, Loane, there might be another explanation."

"Yeah, like she doesn't care enough to let me know she's still alive and where she is?" Either option was unacceptable.

"Have you checked your messages lately?" Eve asked.

"Several times a day. I've called her, but nothing."

Thom scooped a wedge of grapefruit and looked up at Loane. Her smiling eyes and soft expression always instilled comfort and hope. She was the Mother Teresa type who made everyone around her feel special. "Don't give up. Maybe something else is going on that we don't know about. Give her the benefit of the doubt, and take care of yourself. The answers will come." She pointed to Loane's bowl. "Eat. You've lost too much weight. You could give a girl a complex about her cooking skills."

Thom had started a gourmet baked-goods company that had gone nationwide out of this kitchen, so Loane doubted anything could challenge her culinary confidence. "I haven't been hungry. Sorry."

"Thom thinks anybody who doesn't eat isn't well. Right, sweetie?" Eve stroked Thom's hand in a rare display of affection, and the look that passed between them was pure love. "Can we watch the news before I go?"

Thom clicked on the small television beside the table as the local anchor pitched a segment outside the police department's main entrance. “This morning Councilwoman Brenda Jeffries and ATF Resident Agent in Charge Gary Fowler announced the wrap-up of an extensive investigation into illegal weapons in the Triad.”

The camera focused on the two as the councilwoman spoke first. “This case confirms once again that Greensboro will not tolerate criminal activity, organized or otherwise. I have run on a law-and-order platform for years and will continue to do so in the next election. I’m honored to have supported ATF in this effort.”

Jeffries looked at Fowler, obviously the cue that it was his turn to speak. “We’re happy to have successfully closed this case, and we couldn’t have done it without the endorsement of Councilwoman Jeffries.” They stepped away from the microphone.

“Were any arrests made?”

“Have the victims of the explosion been identified?”

“Why is the press being denied access to public documents about this case?”

Jeffries and Fowler waved off the reporters’ questions and walked away.

“Well, that told us absolutely nothing,” Eve said.

“Exactly,” Loane replied. “That’s what I’ve been saying. Everything is smoke and mirrors. There’s been no connection to the Torres and gunrunning. They own gentlemen’s clubs, but that doesn’t mean they’re dealing weapons through them. At least three people are dead, a whitewashed murder investigation, no arrests, and yet these *politicians* are taking credit for a win against crime. Did you notice she didn’t even mention the Greensboro Police Department? How can Jeffries claim to be pro-law enforcement when she blocks us at every turn?”

“The truth will come out. Give it time,” Thom said.

“I don’t have time. I need to know the truth…now.”

Eve kissed Thom, patted Pretty Kitty, the big gray-and-white cat by her chair, and started toward the door. “While you two figure out the inner workings of our local political system, I’ve got to meet with my Realtor on the way to the museum.”

“Why do you still go there?” Loane asked. “Didn’t you finish the renovation months ago?” Eve was a self-made millionaire from prime real-estate investments, but she still worked from a small office in the historical museum.

“Because, like your father, I love history…an interest that you picked up. If we remember our history, maybe we won’t have to repeat it. Remember that, grasshopper." Eve waved good-bye and she and Pretty Kitty left.

"I don't get it," Loane said.

Thom shook her head. "She likes being surrounded by the things she loves, old buildings and history, while she works. I think that place got to her. I'm sorry about her questions. You've known her since you were a child. She says what's on her mind and there's no stopping her. If you tell her not to mention something, it's like waving a red flag in front of a bull."

"I still can't believe she and my mother were friends. They're so different. Eve is out there, and Mom was always guarded. I don't think my dad knew what she was thinking, ever."

"That's why they were good friends. It's that old opposites-attract thing. So, are you going to work?"

"If you can call it that. Answering phones all day is not my idea of work, but it's all I can manage at the moment. I can barely hold a pen to write notes." She raised her hands in frustration.

"Let me put some more vitamin E on your palms before you go." Thom rose and looped her arm through Loane's. "The better care we take of your injuries, the sooner you can get back to real work."

Forty-five minutes later Loane sat behind a desk in the watch commander's office off the main lobby of the police department. This was the dumping station for non-emergency calls from the Communications Center and walk-ins from the street. All day she listened to whining citizens complain about everything from bad cops to smelly garbage and cheating lovers. No cop wanted this assignment because it had nothing to do with real police work and everything to do with public relations. The only saving grace of the duty was that the office had views to the lobby and outside that made daydreaming easier during lulls.

She was doodling on a notepad and doing hand exercises when a squad mate, Terry Cox, walked through the lobby. He glanced toward the office and quickly averted his gaze. Pushing back from the desk, Loane hurried to catch up.

"Hey, what's up, Cox?"

"Nothing, late for lineup." Terry was a lanky lateral transfer from a small county department who thought he'd died and gone to heaven when Greensboro hired him. He was becoming an okay officer, but he sucked as a liar. Lineup wasn't for another thirty minutes.

"Any news on that thing I asked you to check on?" All she'd requested was a copy of the report about the explosion—simple.

"*That thing* is closed, or didn't you catch the morning news?" Cox tugged at his utility belt as if bolstering his courage. "I can't get it. Everybody has been warned off. The other guys—"

"The other guys what?"

Cox flicked at a sprig of red hair that brushed the top of his collar and glanced away. "Nothing."

"Come on, Terry. What are the guys saying?"

"Look, you've been good to me, helping me adjust to city policing, but you're jamming us up. Word is that you messed up an assignment and now you're trying to cover your tracks." He raked at his collar again. "I don't believe it, but I don't have enough seniority to stick my neck out too far. Sorry. I gotta go."

He walked away as Loane struggled for something meaningful to say and failed. "Get a damn haircut…and thanks for nothing."

She'd gotten pretty much the same response from everyone she'd approached about the gunrunner case, which only made her more certain that something was terribly wrong. Cases like these didn't magically disappear, and cops didn't stop asking questions because they were told to—exactly the opposite.

CHAPTER FOUR

Three months after the explosion

Loane stared at the nondescript door to the police conference room that stood between her and the rest of her life. A typewritten sign taped to the worn frame announced CLOSED MEETING. She wished that included her. Her supervisors strongly encouraged her to cooperate with the unofficial fact-finding inquiry. Translation: play nice to preserve interagency relations and limit political fallout. What happened once she entered this room would determine her manner of play.

Nerves churned in her stomach like sour milk. *1829 John McClintock Logan appointed Greensboro's first public officer.* Would this be her last day in a similar role? She paused before grabbing the door handle and looked at the gloves that had become a normal accessory. The black leather served as camouflage for beige compression gloves that kept her scars from contracting and becoming too thick. Since that night she never touched anything metal without a second thought. Fighting a flashback, she took several deep breaths and opened the door. "Officer Loane Landry, reporting as requested."

A single straight-back chair faced a table with seven individuals that she recognized as Greensboro Police detectives and ATF agents she'd worked with in the past, along with the resident agent in charge of the Greensboro ATF field office, Gary Fowler. The setting felt less like an informal meeting and more like a firing squad. As far as she was concerned the exercise was just that, and she couldn't have cared less. She'd shown up only to ask her own questions. If she didn't get the answers she needed, she was prepared to walk, from the proceedings and the job.

RAC Fowler occupied the center seat and spoke first. "Officer

Landry, just so we're clear. This isn't a formal hearing or an official interview. It's more like a debriefing."

"Then, with all due respect, sir, why aren't we sitting around the squad room sipping coffee and eating doughnuts?"

Agent Bowman, seated beside Fowler, tugged at his perfectly Windsor-knotted tie and glared at her. Over the past three months of badgering Bowman for answers about the case and Abby's death, Loane recognized the gesture as his only nervous tell.

He didn't wait for his boss to answer. "Because I—we—thought it would be more productive to let you tell your side of the story—"

"*My* side of the story? And exactly who is telling another side? I was the only one there at the time of the explosion."

"Exactly. And you call yourself a cover officer." Bowman sat back with a self-satisfied smirk.

He was right. She'd thought Abby was working the case and she should've been Velcroed to her that night. Hearing Bowman say it aloud didn't hurt any less than hearing it over and over in her mind. The guilt didn't vanish because she admitted it.

"We've allowed you time to heal from your injuries…and to grieve," Bowman said.

Loane's anger flashed and the room turned red around her. *Grieve?* How could she grieve something she wasn't sure had happened? And what could these people possibly know about her personal involvement with Abby? She tamped down her anger before responding.

"And why would I need to grieve the death of an ATF informant?" Asking the question made her chest tighten. Months of searching for clues through official channels and paying for useless information had left her too exhausted to grieve.

Bowman glanced at his row of co-conspirators as if relishing his starring role. "I just meant the two of you worked very closely on the case."

"Or maybe there was more going on," Fowler added without looking up from the folder in front of him. Both of the GPD detectives and Agent Bowman looked genuinely shocked.

"If you're implying something, Agent Fowler, please be more specific." She didn't plan to deny her relationship with Abby, but she wouldn't confirm it either. That information had no bearing on the events that led to her death, and Fowler damn well knew it. He obviously intended to discredit her, but why?

"I'm wondering how an ATF confidential informant ended up…"

the word hung in Loane's throat, "dead on your watch, Bowman. I think there's a cover-up. What happened and why can't I get any answers? Your office wouldn't even give me her address or family contact information so I could send condolences." She'd promised herself she wouldn't cry, and she struggled to keep that promise.

"We don't release CI details to anyone."

"What difference could it possibly make now?" Bile churned in her stomach as she recalled the charred bodies in the SUV.

"It's policy. Surely you understand policy, though in this case it looks like you and Mancuso may have violated a few."

Fowler attempted to regain control of the situation. "Bowman, the more important issue is why an informant made personal contact with a suspect and didn't take her cover officer. And what happened once she was inside the residence?"

Loane had to say something. "At least you admit Abby was actually there and I didn't imagine the whole thing. She wasn't even mentioned in the newspapers. Not even reporters can get an accurate head count of how many people died that night." The whole situation seemed surreal—back talk, double talk, no talk, and for no apparent reason that she could see.

Bowman wouldn't relent. "ATF doesn't release confidential information to the press or to *nonessential* parties. By your own admission, Mancuso didn't mean anything to you."

She gripped the chair arms to keep from vaulting over the table at him. He was baiting her but the callous words still stung. She'd told herself that what she and Abby shared was simply a situation-induced fling, nothing more, but the feelings wouldn't die.

"Bowman." Fowler warned him.

"Well, maybe you can tell us how you knew Mancuso was at the Torre residence. You told me on the phone that she called you. I checked your cell and there was no call from her."

She'd been taken to the hospital by ambulance, her vehicle and cell left at the scene. Why would Bowman feel the need to check her cell calls? "We're going around in circles. You have my written statement."

When Bowman started to respond, Fowler shook his head and said, "Which appears to be misleading at best and absent a few details. Maybe you were already at the residence. Maybe you had something to do with the explosion. Why didn't you call Agent Bowman sooner? You knew Mancuso's late-night contact was a violation of protocol."

"Why are we having this conversation?" Loane asked. "You've already decided how the story ended and closed the case to prove it." Why was she being questioned about an inactive case? Were they trying to find out if she'd uncovered anything new?

"We're wrapping up loose ends. You need to answer our questions," Fowler said.

She felt like she'd been dropped in a foreign country and everybody was speaking a different language. Nothing was getting through on either side of the conversation. Was he actually suggesting that she was involved in Abby's death, or was he taunting her? "And maybe you were already there yourself, Fowler. Maybe you and Bowman are orchestrating a cover-up. Bowman left pretty quickly that night after you shut out the other agencies on the scene."

"I don't owe you an explanation of my activities," Bowman said.

"Maybe you should give *somebody* an explanation. Or maybe you and your boss only answer to politicians." Loane turned the tables on Bowman. She'd heard the rumors that someone in ATF was Councilwoman Jeffries's puppet in her law-and-order agenda.

"I'm not the one under review." His response was too calm, too predictable.

"Which brings up a good point. If this isn't a criminal investigation or an administrative hearing, I'm pretty much done here."

Why wasn't Fowler keeping this fiasco in check? The answer became obvious as the senior agent unnecessarily shuffled papers. He was the politician and Bowman was the soldier. He'd given Bowman his marching orders and offered only token interference. The other officers avoided eye contact, adding to her feeling of isolation.

"Are you going to answer our questions?" Bowman asked.

She dug her fingernails into her gloved palms and they tingled with the sensory memory of hot metal slicing through flesh. The pain helped control her outrage at the unresponsive and unproductive course of events. "Until you're willing to answer some of my questions, you can take your informal hearing and go straight to hell." She stood and stared Bowman down before turning to leave.

"If you don't answer our questions, your job could be in jeopardy."

"What job?" She'd made her decision. Anything Dan Bowman could do to her now was inconsequential.

As Loane walked out of the room, the past three months seemed like a bad dream. She'd initially been in such a drug-induced state of recovery, depression, and pain that she didn't remember much of anything except Thom's gentle touch and words of encouragement.

The shroud of secrecy surrounding Abby's death convinced her that she was on the right track, but the harder she looked for clues, the fewer she found. Her feelings for Abby had been branded into her psyche as clearly as the scars on her hands. Without answers those feelings were eating her alive. It was a vicious cycle.

Bowman was right about one thing. She was supposed to be Abby's backup. Her failure to protect Abby was one of the blades that twisted inside her; another was her undefined feelings for Abby.

She walked into the chief's complex and placed the envelope from her back pocket on his secretary's desk. "What's this?" the woman asked.

"Notice of my indefinite leave of absence."

"Chief Hastings wants to see you before you go."

She didn't want to explain herself, not that she could. There had been enough talk and not enough action. She started to leave.

"Officer Landry." Chief Brad Hastings stood at his office door and motioned her inside. "I can't believe you weren't going to talk with me about this."

"Nothing to say, sir." She couldn't look at her father's best friend without remembering the backyard cookouts and basketball games their families had shared.

"What's this about a leave of absence?"

"I need to get away for a while, clear my head." His gray eyes bored into her like a sharpshooter pinpointing a target.

"What's gotten into you, Loane? It's not like you to go off the rails like this. You've always been a straight arrow and followed the rules. Now I hear that you're digging around in a closed case, challenging your peers, and questioning their loyalty. What's this all about?"

"Something's wrong, Chief. Something about this case is off, and if I have to leave to find it, that's what I'll do."

Chief Hastings removed his glasses and pinched the bridge of his nose. "I'm not exactly crazy about the way the feds handled this case either, but sometimes we have to compromise to keep the peace."

"I can't. Not this time. Don't ask me to."

"Can I at least ask you not to get into trouble? You can't investigate anything while you're on leave. You'll have no authority and no liability coverage. I don't want to see you get jammed up or worse."

She turned back toward the door. He'd cautioned her about rogue behavior and liability. He and the department were covered. "I won't do anything stupid." For her that allowed a lot of leeway, but it probably did little to reassure him.

"I'll approve your leave of absence, but I expect you back as soon as possible. How will we get in touch with you?" the chief asked as she opened the door.

"You won't."

❖

"What the fuck, sis?"

Loane held the phone away from her ear. Tyler sounded so much like their father when he was angry. She didn't need to listen closely to hear the same frustration.

"Guess you heard." On an impulsive behavior scale this was off the charts.

"What were you thinking?"

"That you'd have a better chance of promotion if your older sister wasn't around?" It seemed she and Tyler had always been in competition for everything, from toys as kids to martial-arts training in their teens. Only two years apart in age, they'd become cops like their father, and their rivalry intensified in the breeding ground of machismo and testosterone.

"I'm not worried about rank, especially after your stunt today. If this is a hair-trigger decision, Brad can fix it."

"He had months to *fix* this. Like everybody else, he hasn't done shit."

"Really, sis, maybe his hands were tied? He wasn't happy about the feds taking over an investigation in his city. If you'd been to the Police Club the last few months, you might've picked up on that. What *are* you thinking?"

"Let me see, maybe that I'm sick of being left out, stonewalled, and lied to by people I considered my family and friends? If they can't trust me with the truth, I can't trust them, any of them." She tried to contain her anger. *March 1830, first Citizen's Patrol was formed in Greensboro to augment their only public officer.* Loane felt like the only sane officer left in the city as she recalled even Tyler's reluctance to help her since Abby's death.

"Is this still about that woman?"

"*That woman* had a name. It was Abby, Abby Mancuso."

"Yeah, well, she's dead and you're still alive. Get on with your life."

If she'd been standing next to him, she would've kicked him in the balls. He might've felt that. Her emotions were frayed and she wanted to lash out at someone, to make them pay. "Has anyone ever told you that you suck at empathy and compassion?"

"My wife, every day. Can I help it if I have a simple mind that works best with facts? Feelings are like old oil, they clog up everything."

Tyler was a true devotee of the never-show-your-hand philosophy. How had his wife put up with him for ten years? The same way their father put up with their mother until he couldn't take it any longer.

"Why won't you help me, Ty?" She wanted to believe in her brother. She needed that last thread of connection to her family. Though theirs had always been a contentious relationship, it had always been solid.

Tyler let out a long, exasperated sigh. "Because there's nothing to do. The wom—Abby—is dead, and ATF has shut the lid on the case. Nobody has access."

"And doesn't that sound the least bit suspicious to you?"

"No. Simon Torre, the suspect, is dead and the case is closed. They don't want to air the fact that they lost a civilian informant too. It's the government covering its ass."

Why couldn't she accept his explanation and move on? She'd experienced a special connection to Abby, and in an instant it had evaporated. The tether that had bound them was still too tender to retract and simply put away. So it fluttered on every breeze of hope, reaching for some piece of her still out there. "And what if she's not dead?"

"Jesus. How can you even think that? Nobody could've survived. She's gone." As if a lightbulb suddenly went off over his head, Tyler was momentarily quiet. "Wait…did you, were you two…"

"She mattered to me."

The line was silent for several minutes. "Jesus H. Christ. I'm sorry."

I'm sorry was her family's all-encompassing expression of compassion, followed by an awkward pause before moving to another topic. It was now her responsibility, as the injured party, to decide the length of the pause and signal the shift. Then life resumed as if nothing had happened. "Yeah. I know."

"If she isn't dead, sis, why hasn't she contacted you?"

That was the same question Eve had asked and Loane still didn't want to hear. She hadn't come up with an answer she could live with. If she were alive, Abby had consciously chosen to disappear and forget her. The thought was almost as painful as losing her.

"I'm taking some more time off, Ty."

"What about your job?"

"I don't know, and I don't care. I want to rent out the house, if that's all right." She wanted Tyler to have a say about the home place even though she'd inherited it after caretaking her mother in her final years.

"Do whatever you want with the house. It's yours." He cleared his throat in the nervous manner she associated with a rare surfacing of emotions. "I know it was hard for you to be there with Mama those last two years. You thought she hated you, but she didn't."

The memory of that awful day when she was fifteen flooded back. Her mother's adamant statements still haunted her. *"I will not tolerate a child of mine being that way. It's not normal."* Her father had tried to reason with her for years until the stress became too great and he left. "If she didn't hate me, she did a great job of acting. And after Daddy left, she turned against me even more."

"Dad didn't leave because of you, Loane."

"And he didn't stay because of me…or you. Look, I didn't call to talk about this crap. Will you handle the house rental or not?" A year after her mother's death, the house still felt like a connection to people she'd failed, and though the renovation was helping, she couldn't face it right now. The ghosts of her mother and Abby were too strong.

"Sure. Let me know where to send the checks."

"Deposit them into my account. I can access whatever I need electronically."

"I don't like this. It sounds like I'll never see you again. What's wrong with hanging out at Eve and Thom's again for a break?"

"It's complicated."

"Always is with you. I know better than to argue when you get in this mood. Who will I practice my moves with? You're the only decent sparring partner I've got. Speaking of sparring, how are your hands healing?"

"Fine." She appreciated his concern but didn't want to rehash the healing process. "And thanks for being there for me after the accident." Not that it was an accident, but thinking of it in those terms occasionally allowed her to mentally gloss over the details. "I'll keep in touch. It's not like I'm leaving town. I need to be a little less visible for a while. If anybody asks, say I disappeared or whatever."

"You'll keep your cell phone, right? I just got used to the number."

"Yeah, I'll keep it...for you. If you'd save numbers in your phone, you wouldn't have to remember them. You need to step into the technology age, little brother."

"Now you sound like my wife. Nag, nag, nag."

"Give my nephews a big squeeze for me."

"Will do. Take care, okay? You looked like a walking skeleton the last time I saw you. Eat occasionally."

"Bite me, Ty." She wanted to say *help me*, but things had gone too far. She'd lost trust in everyone, even her brother. Her heart ached for the easy banter of their childhood and the competition over things that didn't really matter. This mattered too much.

Loane disconnected and made a to-do list. It was easier to tell Tyler she was taking a break than try to explain her real intentions. Maybe she simply needed a respite from the pressure and disappointment of not knowing. Maybe she wanted revenge. If so, the more she distanced herself from her home and the people she cared about, the better.

The life she'd known didn't exist anymore, and no amount of going through the motions would change that. She loved Greensboro—its rich history, mild climate, and diverse population. But the city was still small enough that blending in would challenge her skills and her determination.

Chapter Five

Loane sat in Center City Park, sipping coffee and petting Parker, the city-center kitty. She glanced in the direction of the Greensboro Historical Museum. Eve deserved a chance to organize her day and have several shots of caffeine before Loane complicated her life. She'd spent three days mulling over how to present her unusual request and had tried out several versions on Parker. He was more interested in having his ears scratched.

She listened to the gentle splash of the fountains as she looked down at her gloved hands, remembering the hurt of that day. She still experienced tenderness when she touched something without thinking, but the sharp pain had lessened. Would she have scars? If so, would she ever be able to touch a woman without feeling self-conscious? Scars would be constant reminders of her failure and of the internal anguish that never subsided.

She tried to shake her morose mood as she walked toward the historic red-brick Romanesque building with round arches and large towers that began its life as a Presbyterian church. Could Eve help flesh out her plan? *What plan?* She'd been talking to herself a lot more since moving back to her place. Not surprisingly the conversations often resulted in the same questions and answers. She needed a different perspective.

Eve Winters embodied her mother's practicality and her father's love of history. She had always listened when Loane needed a sympathetic ear. Loane had even tested her coming-out story on her before springing it on her parents. She had thought it would be easier for her mom to accept her sexuality because she'd known Eve. That assumption had proved grossly inaccurate. But Eve had stood by her during that difficult time and had offered her continued assistance through the years in any way possible. Loane was about to test her sincerity.

When she walked into Eve's office, Eve greeted her with a big smile that then faded slightly. Eve pushed a button on her phone and without preamble said, "Hold my calls and cancel my appointments until further notice." No one responded. You didn't question an edict from Eve Winters, who stood and opened her arms.

Loane hugged her and rested her head on Eve's shoulder. At seventy, and in better shape than most forty-year-olds, Eve wasn't the grandmother type, but at that moment she felt like home—warm and accepting. Loane couldn't remember the last time she'd held someone and known without a doubt that she was loved. She fought the urge to cry. If she did, she was afraid she'd never recover. They hugged until Loane reluctantly pulled away.

Eve motioned to a cozy sofa nestled among artifacts in the corner of her office. "You look like a scarecrow. You obviously needed to stay at our place longer. What the hell is going on and what can I do?"

Eve wasn't exactly sensitive and tactful, but Loane had always admired her ability to suss out the problem, get to the point, and solve it. She'd become wealthy in real estate using that approach. If you needed help, there was no better person to have on your side. And you got the added bonus of Thom, who was tremendously sensitive, loving, and diplomatic.

"I have a big favor to ask, Eve."

"Name it."

"Please listen to everything before you try to talk me out of it. I've thought about this a lot." She'd thought through some of it, not other parts, like leaving her job. Eve would know that. She'd guided her through her impulsive years as a young, horny lesbian testing her sneakers and butch card.

"This should be refreshing." Eve smiled, clearly teasing.

"I need to get to the bottom of this weapons case, and I can't do it living my life like normal." The slight darkening of Eve's blue irises indicated her surprise. Talk about vague. She had to do better if she expected Eve's help. This woman dealt with concrete facts, not philosophies and ambiguous notions. "It's Abby, the explosion, and not knowing whether she's dead." Loane still found it difficult to talk without a choking sensation in her throat. "I want to sort of blend into the background for a while."

"I hate to state the obvious, Loane, but you're not exactly a high-profile citizen with immediate facial recognition."

"I know, but a little distance from family and friends might be a good thing right now."

"Maybe you better tell me the whole story."

She relayed the details about the gunrunning case and explosion that she hadn't already shared. The hardest part was explaining that her fellow officers refused to help her. "So I took a leave of absence."

"From your job? With the police department?"

Loane nodded.

"Did a tree fall on your head?" Eve's blunt sayings were legendary in the community, and Loane had grown to accept them as part of her eccentric personality. "That seems a bit rash, though I understand your frustration."

"It's more than frustration, Eve. I don't trust anyone. I have to find some answers. If she's dead, I'll know for sure. If she's not—"

"You need to think about that one. If she's not dead, can you forgive her for letting you believe she was all this time? It's almost killed you."

She shrugged. She didn't have that answer yet.

"I don't think I'll like this, but what do you need?" Eve swiped an unruly lock of gray hair from her forehead as Loane pulled a crumpled note from her pocket, handed it to her, and waited for the fallout. "I'm not sure I can do this."

"Please, you're the only one I trust."

Eve placed the list beside her and took Loane's hand. As she traced the stitching on the leather glove, her eyes filled with tears. "What if something happens to you? I can't be part of that directly or indirectly."

"I'll be fine." The words sounded mechanical. Was she only lying to Eve or had she started to believe it herself?

"I know you. You're going after these people—the gunrunners, maybe a killer, and possible corrupt police. All of it sounds pretty dangerous to me."

Loane wasn't sure what she'd expected. Everybody else had let her down too. No problem. She'd manage. "Then you won't help me?"

"Don't take that tone with me, young lady."

"What tone?"

"That Little Red Hen I'll-do-it-all-myself attitude. This isn't a game. I'd highly advise against trying to play it alone. At least with the police department, you had backup."

"I work best on my own."

Eve stared with those penetrating blue eyes, as if drawing the facts from her. Loane finally looked away.

"Is this about revenge?" Eve asked.

Loane considered her answer. Would Abby contact her if she were still alive? She wanted to believe she would. They'd shared long nights wrapped in each other's arms, told stories of their lives, and reveled in the joy of sex. And if she weren't dead, someone had to know. Maybe Bowman was hiding the truth. Perhaps he'd heard from Abby and wasn't passing along messages, lying to Abby at the same time.

"It's about the truth." At least it was right now, but her answer could change. If Abby was dead or someone had intentionally kept them apart, revenge would definitely be an option. Eve didn't need to hear that.

"All right. Remember that we all need help sometime. We might not always recognize it, but we do."

"Does that mean I can count on you?"

"Under one condition."

With Eve there were always safeguards or conditions, probably a result of her successful career in business. Loane tried to imagine what she'd require. "Okay."

She placed her hands on either side of Loane's face and forced her to look her in the eye. "You give me a contact number for emergencies, and I promise not to call unless there is one. Sorry, but that's my condition and it's non-negotiable."

Loane considered the pros and cons of what Eve was offering. "I can live with that."

"You want me to find you a temporary place to live under my corporate name, pay the bills, and not tell anyone where you are. That's it?"

"Pretty much. I'll arrange to pay you in cash for the bills. It's not a foolproof plan, but at least if anybody is looking for me, they'll have to work for it."

As Loane detailed her plan aloud it sounded lame. It was almost impossible to disappear off the grid entirely. But the more invisible she became, the better her chance of sliding unnoticed into the underground of gunrunners. She had to appear to have crossed over to the criminal element. With her current non grata status with fellow officers and the unfavorable publicity the case had received, it shouldn't be difficult. Criminals always seemed willing to accept another convert into the fold. If Eve agreed, this would be the first step.

"I assume everything else will remain intact—bank accounts, retirement—and Tyler will get forwarded mail? And your house?"

She nodded. "He's renting it for me, for now." Once Eve made a decision, she was full steam ahead and God help anyone who got in her way.

"And what about Abby? Were you in love with her?"

It's not like the question hadn't crossed her mind a million times, but she still couldn't answer it. "I'm not sure. I can't walk away until I know the truth."

"What if she isn't dead and tries to find you?"

The possibility should've filled Loane with hope, but it settled into her consciousness with a dull thud. Maybe deep inside she already knew the answer she was seeking. Abby wasn't going to call because she couldn't. She shrugged, unwilling to voice the morbid thought.

"Grief is like an infection, Loane. It can be fatal if you ignore it. At some point you'll have to let all this out. Don't wait too long."

She couldn't look at Eve. What Eve said was true, but she couldn't deal with it right now. What was the point of grieving something that might not be true? And if it were, time could make it easier, though that hadn't worked so far.

Eve squeezed her arm. "Any particular requirements for your new place? Single-family ranch, condo, townhouse, yurt, or hovel under a bridge?"

"You know what I'm trying to do, so something easy and anonymous."

Eve handed the slip of paper back as she got up from the sofa. "Take care of yourself. You look like you've lost twenty-five pounds. That's not healthy."

It had been easy not to eat. No appetite, no food. She'd lost track of how much she weighed before and after the explosion. It didn't seem important.

"You're sure about this, Loane?"

She nodded, but she wasn't sure at all. The thought of being alone in the middle of a dangerous case without the legal authority of the police department or fellow officers for backup worried her.

She preferred order and at least a small degree of certainty. She found comfort in structure and procedure, but the system had let her down. She had no other choice.

"I still advise against this," Eve said.

Loane pulled her into a hug. "I know. Give Thom my love, and don't worry."

"Those aren't very reassuring words. Be careful, and don't be too damn proud or stubborn to ask for help."

"I'll check back in a few days, and I'll be careful. Promise." Even she wasn't convinced. At least Eve didn't know what she planned to do next.

❖

Loane backed into the doorway across the street from the Sky Bar, blending with the shadows. Neon glowed over the club's opaque glass windows and door, giving it an eerie, otherworldly sheen. When patrons entered they disappeared, swallowed by a huge sightless monster. The bar was popular because it allowed folks to check their morals and values at the door. She'd answered calls here and seen young and old engaged in behaviors from pot smoking to full-on sex, unusual for a quiet Southern town in the middle of the Bible Belt.

She watched a couple of bouncers set up orange cones down the center of the sidewalk in front of the bar and string rope between them to form a cueing line for the patrons who would arrive later. Raising her night-vision camera, she focused on the two employees she hadn't seen before. Fuck the Greensboro Police Department. By the time her surveillance was over, she'd know every employee of this dive and how they were connected to the Torre family.

In the months she'd worked with Abby on the case, they'd never made a definite link between the club, the Torres, and illegal weapons, but it was the only place she had to start. There was bound to be more going on here than a little pot smoking and sex play. Experience had taught her to dig deeper than the initial layer of grime.

As she snapped pictures of the bouncers, a brisk wind whipped around the corner and kicked a plume of dust into her face. She stepped back too quickly and slammed into the door behind her. The thud echoed across the street as she tried to balance the camera with one wounded hand and keep from falling with the other. She lost both battles. The camera skidded across the sidewalk toward the street and she landed flat on her ass in the doorway, unwilling to slap the concrete with her palms. The bouncers' heads swiveled in her direction like lions stalking a gazelle.

"Hey, you, what the fuck?"

By the time Loane got up, they were on top of her. The camera dangled from the taller one's fist like a prize. "Lose something, cop?"

She tried to be professional in spite of her clumsiness. "Who said I was a cop?"

The short one with a ponytail sniffed around her like a bloodhound. "Smell like pork. Not too subtle. Taking pictures where you don't belong. Spells cop to me."

She automatically reached toward her belt for her walkie-talkie. Maybe it was best to let them believe she was a cop for the time being. "Then I guess you better give me that department-issued equipment, or I'll have to charge you with theft." Invoking authority she didn't have made her uncomfortable. Bluffing wasn't her forte.

"Looks like it got broken in the fall. Even the card is missing. Too bad." The tall guy handed the camera over with a shrug. The card slot was empty.

Damn it. This wasn't a fight she could win with her hands still tender. She grabbed the strap and yanked, immediately regretting it. The rough cord dug into her palm through the leather glove, and she bit her lip to stifle a groan. "You two better get back to work before I make up a reason to arrest you."

They simultaneously stepped closer, pushing her farther into the darkened doorway. "Think you could pull it off?" One of them reeked of cheap cologne and the other of cigarettes, not smells she'd want to be her last.

"Hey, I know you," Ponytail said. "You're the cop that's been stirring up shit—the department dumped you. I'm right. So, photography your new profession?"

How the hell did he know about her leave? Personnel issues were supposed to be confidential. But his information might play nicely into her plan to switch sides as a disgruntled cop. "So what? Screw the police department…and you too."

"If you're not a cop, whipping your ass won't be quite as much fun, but I'll still enjoy it."

Getting a street beating to prove she wasn't a cop wasn't her idea of fun. She glanced around for an escape route, but they had her pinned. Ten officers had been killed in the line of duty in Greensboro since the department was formed. She didn't want to be number eleven. Loane calculated how much elbow room she needed for an effective martial-arts move and was about to try it.

"Hey, dudes, there's a cop coming this way." A young girl, late teens or early twenties, stood behind the two hulking thugs. She had red hair cropped so close Loane could almost see scalp and a backpack over her shoulder that looked like it weighed more than she did.

The two guys parted like the Red Sea and Loane walked through. She and the kid knew there wasn't another cop within miles, but the bluff worked. She hoped it hadn't blown her rogue persona. As they walked away, Loane said, "Thanks, kid."

"Next time," one of the men murmured as they crossed the street toward the club.

She couldn't resist. "Any time, assholes."

The girl looked at her like she was an alien. "Yo, really?"

Attitude wafted from her as heavily as the goon's cologne. Loane wasn't in the mood to deal with an annoying adolescent. The fruits of her surveillance were gone. She'd been challenged by a couple of losers she could've taken blindfolded before her injury. And now some street urchin wanted to give her attitude. "Yo, what? I said thanks." She kept walking.

"You're like a total mimbo." She fell in step beside Loane, her black, unlaced Vans slapping noisily against the pavement.

"I have no idea what you said, and I don't care. Get lost, kid."

"Stupid. Know what that means?"

Loane spun toward her so fast that she stepped back, probably afraid Loane might hit her. Then she really saw the girl for the first time. She looked younger, maybe mid-teens, with a cherubic face. Her eyes were wide and inquisitive, hard to tell the color in the shadows, but something light. She looked like a tomboy with tattered jeans hanging low around her slight ass and a tight red T-shirt revealing two small nipples as breasts. Earrings lined the rim of both ears like jewelry displays. The overweight backpack completed the picture of a lost or runaway kid looking for a handout. Not interested. "Whatever," she said, and walked away.

"Look, cop, I did you a solid."

"What? You want money?" Loane dug into her coat pocket.

"Forget you." She pivoted and headed away from Loane. "Flash, Einstein, you've been made."

It took a second for her statement to sink in. "Wait." She thought her surveillance had been pretty well camouflaged in the shadows and from rooftops, until her swan dive tonight. She didn't want to broadcast what she was up to, but it could already be a moot point. "What do you mean?"

Urchin girl stomped back around the corner, her flat chest puffed a bit. She had something Loane wanted and she knew it. "Could you be any noisier?" Loane asked.

"Could you be any more clueless?"

"All right. What do you mean by made?"

"Not here, Dude. Lower level, LF deck in five."

"What the hell do you think this is, a freaking spy movie? And why the Lincoln Financial parking tower?"

"That or nothing." The girl was already heading in the opposite direction.

Kids. Thank God she wasn't one, didn't have one, and didn't work with them. They didn't even speak in complete sentences any more. What a pain.

All the way to the parking deck Loane argued with herself about showing up. Trust had never been her strong suit, and she was less inclined since the explosion. Not even cops she'd once worked with deserved her confidence anymore. Why would she trust a street kid? She couldn't possibly have anything Loane needed.

As she reached the bottom step on the lower level, the girl stepped out of the shadows. "Jeez. Are you trying to give me a heart attack?"

"Jumpy for a cop."

She didn't have the time or inclination to exchange barbs with this kid any longer. "If you have something to tell me, get on with it. If not, I'm out of here. And speak English, none of that street crap."

"Whatever. Everybody at the Sky Bar knows you've been staking it out."

"How?"

"You suck at it. And you're like a freaky billboard."

"What does that even mean?"

"You're starving-baby thin, and that weird white hair stands out like an elephant on a power line."

"It's platinum blond, not white," Loane said.

"Whatever. The point is you're too obvious. Students pimp you out. Even the winos are taking bets on how long before the bouncers give you a righteous thumping."

"I'm trained in surveillance. I know what I'm doing." She couldn't believe she was listening to a street kid critique her abilities and defending herself.

"That's the problem, you're too trained. You don't fit in."

"Look, kid, I—"

"And cut the kid crap. Call me Vi."

"Vi? What's that?"

"A nickname, but it beats the hell out of *kid*."

"You look like a kid. How old are you anyway, twelve?"

"Why is it always twelve when old people want to insult you? Why not thirteen or fifteen? And I'm twenty-two."

"Fine." Loane had enough back-and-forth going nowhere with her. She'd have to be more careful or get the information she needed another way. "Look, ki—Vi, I appreciate the heads-up, but I have to go." She turned back to the steps. Her hands ached and she couldn't wait to slather them in vitamin E.

"I could help…if you want." Her voice was more confident and Loane detected a note of cockiness.

"With what exactly?"

"The fitting-in part, or be your eyes and ears."

"Why would you help me?" Not that she would trust her for any reason.

"I'm a law-abiding citizen?"

"Right, not buying that one, Vi."

"Have my reasons."

Loane had learned that hidden motivation usually equaled dangerous motivation. She didn't need any more complications. And even if Vi was right and she'd gotten sloppy, she could adjust. Citizens had far fewer restrictions than cops when it came to surveillance and intelligence gathering. "No thanks. I'll manage."

"Great job so far."

"I'll work it out."

"Brill, your funeral."

"If only." She took a few more steps and called back to the girl. "And thanks again for the save tonight. I owe you."

"Right. So what's your name, cop?"

"Loane."

"As in a-lone…explains a lot."

Loane felt like she'd stepped out of a bad reality-TV show where a cop encounters a throwaway kid and their roles are reversed. In this version, the kid saved her from an ass-whipping by a couple of thugs. She was out of her trained-and-organized element. She needed to pay better attention.

CHAPTER SIX

Abby whacked the side of the walking cast with her cane, and a dull ache traveled up her shin. *Damn it. I have to get out of here before I go crazy or kill myself.* The Torre family had doted on her since she and Blake returned to Miami. His father, Nick, had showered her with praise and gifts so often that she dodged him in the compound. She was a hero, and no amount of protesting slowed the accolades. The affirmation felt good, but her guilt fluctuated in direct proportion to their attention.

She'd saved a child's life—that was something to be proud of. But after so long in the Torre home, she felt more connected to them and more disconnected from her own life. Her contact with Hector Barrio had been sporadic, limited by her ability to move about easily and make discreet phone calls.

The worst part of this whole scenario was that she hadn't talked to Loane. What if the person who'd set the bomb was waiting for her to make contact? She couldn't take even the slightest risk of placing Loane in danger. She'd called from a pay phone only once to hear Loane's voice but hung up when her message came on. Every day she argued with herself that she was doing the right thing, and every night she cried herself to sleep wondering if she had. She raised the cane to tap her cast again but thought better of it.

"Not good for a broken leg." Maria Torre, Stefan's wife, stood in the doorway of their South Beach sunroom and smiled. With a plump figure, rosy skin, and gray hair, she was the perfect matriarch, full of nurturing and advice. "How about a trip downtown? You look like you could use some fresh air."

"You have no idea." In her enthusiasm, Abby stood too quickly and forgot to compensate for the cast, almost toppling over. She grabbed the chair arm and brought the cane alongside her injured leg. "That would be fantastic, Maria."

"I remember when my boys were born, I felt trapped after only three weeks in the house. You've been here much longer and you're younger. We could take a slow stroll along Ocean Boulevard. There are lots of shops."

"Sounds perfect." Maria loved the Art Deco district, and it would be easy for Abby to sneak away and make some calls. The Torres had given her a cell phone with a new number after hers was destroyed, but she'd been reluctant to use it. They paid the bill and she knew Carl, the elder son, would check any calls she made.

He was stepping up as the new business head of the family, with his father Stefan's endorsement. But she got the feeling he didn't trust her. Surely she'd proved her loyalty at the risk of her own life. Was he suspicious of her for some other reason? Had she slipped up during three months of recuperation, given herself away with an offhanded remark? Maybe he held her responsible for the explosion that killed Simon, Sylvia, and Alma. Or maybe he was just being cautious, afraid for the safety of his family and her by extension.

"Are you going out, Mother?" Carl asked from the hallway as Maria walked with her to the front door.

"Yes, we're going window-shopping. Would you call for the car, please?"

Carl's tanned face tightened as he swiped at a shock of bleached-blond hair. The surfer look might have been attractive on a younger man, but on Carl it looked like he was trying too hard. "Abby is bored with our company?"

"Not at all," Abby answered. "You've been too generous, nursing me back to health when I couldn't walk. It's time to get out a bit, even look for my own place. I've inconvenienced you enough."

"Nonsense. We owe you a great debt. You should be with us. Right, Mother?" His tone was more of a command than a genuine invitation.

"Of course…unless you have family elsewhere." Maria's concern and the gentle weight of her hand on Abby's arm were distressing. Maria truly cared for her, and her thoughtfulness during her convalescence had been sincere.

Abby shook her head. The lie poked at her conscience. Her family didn't even know if she was still alive, much less that she was in the same city. She meant to remedy that today.

"Good, then it's settled," Carl said. "Mind if I come along? I have some business on the strip. It would save taking two cars."

"Of course not, dear."

Abby's enthusiasm dissolved. If Carl came it meant more security. It had been weeks since she'd contacted her family. They would be worried to distraction. And Loane—God, how she missed her. Abby had no idea what she must think of her after all this time without so much as a phone call or text message.

Today she was determined to sneak away from Carl and his bodyguards long enough to reach out again. A person could only live a lie for so long before it became reality. She wasn't about to become a Stockholm victim, no matter how self-imposed her isolation. The line between the Torres as gunrunners and the Torres as family had already blurred too much. Hector Barrio paid her well as an informant, and the Torres kept her on their payroll as a personal assistant, but no amount of money was worth her sanity. She reached into her purse, fingered the small pouch of coins she'd squirreled away, and prayed that somewhere in downtown SoBe there was one pay phone that still worked.

"It's such a beautiful day," Maria said. "A walk will do us good."

"I don't have time to walk." Carl spoke with the arrogance of a man accustomed to a life of privilege. As the long white limousine pulled in front of the house, he dialed a number on his cell phone and unnecessarily shushed them before launching into a conversation about one of the gentlemen's clubs.

The ride was quiet except for Carl's self-important chatter. Maria, a woman of elegance and impeccable manners, shook her head apologetically when the car stopped and he was still on the phone. "Men and business." They stepped onto the sidewalk. "Which way shall we go, darling?"

Maria looked right toward her favorite clothing establishment. Abby pointed left to a row of shops and an electronics store and said, "I'll be fine. I need the practice. Go treat yourself."

Carl, still on the phone, stood outside the car, snapped his fingers and pointed toward Abby with his index and forefinger, then repeated the motion toward Maria. Four bodyguards got out of the vehicle behind them, two of them following Maria and two heading after her.

"I don't need protection, Carl," Abby said. "Let them take care of Maria."

Carl shook his head and motioned for the men to follow her. So much for sneaking away. She slowly walked along the storefronts, stopping occasionally to peer inside and simultaneously scan the surrounding area for a pay phone. The guards hung back, but not far enough for her to slip out of sight. The constant supervision was getting on her nerves. If she hadn't wanted possible criminals to know about her family, she could've made her calls in the open like a normal person.

Abby considered her options. Brute force wouldn't work. She'd have to play to her strengths…being female and acting. She whirled around on the two men and they stepped back off the sidewalk. "Look, guys, I don't want to be a bother, but I need a little space."

"Boss told us to protect you." Obviously the articulate one. The other guy shrugged.

"And I appreciate that, but could you at least wait *outside* the stores so it doesn't look like I'm under arrest? I'm feeling premenstrual and your hovering is starting to annoy me."

That registered. They backed up farther, looked at their shoes, and nodded in mute agreement.

"I'll be in the electronics store. Unless I yell for help, don't bother me. I could go off at any minute. Okay?" They nodded again. She loved the power and mystique the female body held over men.

They watched her go in, then positioned themselves on either side of the door. She stared at them and circled in the air with her finger. They obediently turned to face the street. *Finally, somewhat alone at last.*

She wasn't sure how long her luck would hold, so she went directly to the cell-phone counter. "Could I have your least expensive prepaid model?"

The young woman behind the counter launched into a rehearsed sales pitch. "We have some nice models on sale this week that come with only a ten-dollar monthly fee. Or I could offer you—"

"I don't mean to be rude," she glanced at her crooked name tag, "Ellen, but could you offer me what I asked for? And can you activate it *now*? I'm in a bit of a rush." She nodded toward her escorts, and the young woman's eyes widened as she saw the two men standing guard at the door.

"Are you in trouble, ma'am? Do I need to call the police?"

Abby motioned for her to come closer and whispered. "You're very kind, but I just need a phone, quickly."

A little added drama seemed just the ticket for speedy service. "Got ya." Ellen pulled a phone from under the counter, ripped it out of the box, and slid the battery into place. "You only have about fifteen minutes' talk time before you have to charge it." She whispered now, the role of co-conspirator obviously appealing. "Let me give you a quick one, two, three on how it works."

She reached for her lifeline to the outside world. "I've got this."

"Actually, that won't be necessary." Carl's voice behind her sent chills up her spine. How the hell had he slipped in without her knowing? "Is there something wrong with the phone I gave you?"

Ellen's eyes widened like a scared kitten's. Abby smiled to reassure her and put on her most innocent face before turning from the counter. "Not at all. It's time for me to start paying my own way."

"I thought we covered this back at the house. You're family now, and we take care of each other. Use the phone. I write it off the business anyway." Further discussion would only raise suspicion. "Now, are you ready to go? Mother is getting hungry." He motioned toward the door.

"I need to use the restroom before we leave." She looked back toward Ellen, who had inched closer to the desk phone as if expecting trouble. "Could you show me the way, please?"

"Of course." Ellen led her to a back room behind the storefront. Before Abby closed the door, she shoved a phone into her hand. "Use mine. I'll stand guard."

Abby didn't argue. Her first instinct was to call Loane, the same instinct she'd had every time she'd been near a secure phone for the past three months. But what would she say? How could she explain her long absence? She looked back at the restroom door. She was running out of time. She *had* to make one call and she needed to hold it together. Her mother answered on the first ring.

"Mom."

"Thank God! Child, are you all right? Where are you? How have you been? Can you come home?"

Her mother's voice quivered with emotion and Abby stifled a wave of tears. "I'm okay, Mom, but I can't tell you where I am or when I'll be home. I'm so sorry. I wanted you to know that I'm fine and that I love you all."

"Your father and I don't like this new job, whatever it is. Nothing is worth abandoning your family. It's not good. Listen to what I say. Your brothers have looked everywhere for you. We thought you must be…dead."

Abby was grateful her mother didn't know how close she'd come to being just that. Her mother's concern carried through the phone as clearly as if they were in the same room. She wanted to surrender, to return to normalcy and safety, to be protected again, but it was too late. She was too far in and too much had happened to too many people she cared about. She had to redeem herself and prove she could stand on her own. Her mother wouldn't understand how important that was to her…as important as family and love.

"Are you okay in there?" Ellen whispered through the door. "You better hurry. The natives are getting restless."

"I'm sorry, Mom, but I can't come home yet. I have to go now. I'll be in touch."

"Abigail, please…" She disconnected, unable to bear the sadness in her mother's voice. She wanted to make a difference in the world, but it seemed all she did was cause more pain. Now she understood the necessity of intelligence agents and spies without personal attachments. She had to find a way to see her family, if only briefly. She owed them that peace of mind.

"Here he comes," Ellen whispered through the restroom door.

She closed the phone, pretended to wash her hands, and opened the door, slipping Ellen's cell into her pocket as she passed.

"Are you ready?" Carl's voice relayed his characteristic impatience.

"Ready." She gave Ellen an appreciative smile and followed Carl out.

"We need to talk when we get home." He guided her to the car and held the door as she got in. His tone wasn't friendly, and the thought of being alone with him made her cringe.

"About what?"

"Business. We need to discuss business." Carl Torre had never consulted her about business. He seemed content to have her perform miscellaneous domestic tasks. Why the sudden change? Perhaps she'd judged him too harshly. Maybe underneath his façade of bravado was a gentler, more caring man, like his uncle Simon. She wanted to believe in the good.

On the way back to the Torre compound, she stared out the window and thought about the phone call she'd made and the one she hadn't. Each broke her heart for similar and very different reasons. She loved her family and Loane, but she could return to her family at any time and be welcomed. She doubted Loane would be so forgiving. Did she think Abby had simply abandoned her? Would she even allow her to explain if their paths crossed again? How would she feel if their roles were reversed? She hoped Loane would at least understand her commitment to follow through on an assignment.

The only thing she knew for sure was that Hector Barrio wanted her to stay with the Torre family and pursue any leads that developed. He hadn't given her an informant's handbook when he hired her, and she wasn't sure exactly how to proceed. She was playing it by ear, but he seemed to trust her judgment. She'd have to make another decision soon because her cast was coming off in a few days. Right now her more immediate problem was the talk with Carl.

After lunch, he asked Abby to join him in the study located at the back of the residential complex. The place reminded her of a panic room made of solid walnut paneling and bulletproof windows. He could hole up in here for days with the food and drinks in the stocked refrigerators. It wasn't a comforting thought.

He closed the door behind her and motioned to one of the tufted-leather wingback chairs. "Do you know what I want to talk to you about, Abby?"

"No." She was more certain of her answer than anything else at the moment.

"You were very resourceful and dedicated the night of the explosion. I saw a different side of the young, petite woman who'd been only a family assistant. You have potential. I've been watching you since you came back to Miami."

A flutter of panic rippled through her as she waited for Carl to tell her that he knew she was working with ATF and to what…have her snuffed out, kidnapped and dropped in a third-world country? If he'd seen potential, what else had she inadvertently revealed? Her imagination was getting the best of her. She remained silent, afraid that if she said anything her nerves would give her away.

"You risked your life for Blake and you've been loyal to my family. I'd like to offer you more responsibility with the business, if you're interested."

It took a minute for her to realize that Carl wasn't upset but asking for help, and that was very uncharacteristic. He'd never indicated that he liked her, much less considered her particularly capable. She had to be careful not to appear too eager. "It depends on the offer."

"Would you go back to Greensboro and manage the Sky Bar for me?"

It took a moment for the question to register before the internal struggle began. A lot had happened there, most of it still unresolved. She flashed back to Loane—naked, incredibly sexy, head thrown back as she climaxed. Her heart leapt at the thought of seeing her again, then plummeted. How would Loane react to her now? She had every right to be angry. Hell, she didn't even know if Loane was still there. Could she handle it if Loane rejected her?

"I'm asking a lot. I know it'll be hard for you to return." Carl's voice had taken on a gentleness she'd never heard.

Her grief tipped over the edge and she let her tears fall. "I'm sorry, Carl."

"You were very close to Simon, Sylvia, and Alma."

"Yes, I was." Her tears were for Loane, but she was relieved he had misread them. "I miss them. I wish I could've done something."

He patted her on the shoulder. "It's not your fault, Abby. No one blames you." He handed her a tissue and waited until she stopped crying. "Do you have any idea who would want to hurt them?"

They'd discussed this almost every week but found no answers or resolution. The questions always filled her with sadness and guilt. She wanted to find out who was behind their deaths. What if she failed? The weight of unwanted responsibility settled on her again and she struggled to breathe. "I…I…"

"My sources tell me a local female police officer was investigating my uncle. She's been dismissed and has disappeared—perhaps she was involved. Do you know anything about that?"

The air seemed to have been sucked out of the room. Her mouth went dry as she tried to keep her expression neutral. "Simon was under suspicion? For what?" Her first impulse had been to ask about Loane. She hoped she'd covered well enough to fool him. If Carl believed Loane had something to do with the explosion, she was in danger, and Abby couldn't vouch for her without revealing their relationship and blowing her cover.

"I'm not sure. Did he ever say anything to you about being investigated?" Carl asked. "Anything to indicate he suspected something illegal was going on?"

Abby shook her head. The question struck her as odd, but she was more concerned about the implications for Loane in this mess. If Carl was right, why had Loane been dismissed? Was she blamed for letting Abby go to the Torre house unprotected or for the explosion? Possibilities bled into facts, coloring them with uncertainty, and a prickle of fear shot up her spine.

Carl had never mentioned specifics of the investigation before. What other information did he have and where had it come from? Abby had to find Loane and warn her—but what if this was a trick? What if Carl knew they had been lovers? They hadn't told anyone except Eve Winters, and Loane trusted her with her life. Strange that it could come down to exactly that. If she returned to Greensboro and contacted Loane, she would lead Carl to her, and he might not take time to find out if she was guilty.

A band tightened around Abby's heart as she struggled to cover her emotions. She fought the urge to escape and take the first plane back to North Carolina. Her earlier thoughts of a reunion with Loane and the fear of possible rejection now seemed selfish. She wanted to find and protect her. She could handle a lifetime of rejection as long as Loane was safe. Suddenly her decision not to call Loane seemed justified, but it gave her little consolation.

"I'm not sure what the police thought Simon had done, but they were wrong."

Carl's statement returned her to the task at hand—keep herself in Carl's favor long enough to somehow warn Loane and close this case. "I can't imagine. Simon was one of the kindest, most honest men I've ever met."

"Yes, he was, and that's why I have to find out what happened to him. Can I count on your help?"

"And my working in Greensboro will help?"

"I've asked Father to let me take over the Greensboro club, and he's agreed. It's very profitable, and it would be a shame to let all my uncle's work go to waste. With you in charge, I can focus on this other matter. If you need time to think about it, I understand, but I want you there as soon as possible."

In Greensboro she'd be positioned to locate Loane, work the case, and keep tabs on Carl. Maybe his offer was exactly what she needed. "I don't have any experience managing nightclubs."

"Yes, but you know people, and that's all management is—understanding people. The rest is bookkeeping, and you can hire whoever you want to handle that part of it."

"Pardon me for saying this, but I have to know where we stand. You've never seemed particularly fond of me, so—"

"I'm a businessman and I want what's best for the company and the family. We don't have to be best friends to work together, do we?"

"No, but you do have to trust me and give me more flexibility."

"You mean the bodyguards?"

"That's part of it, yes. But I'd also expect to have a life outside work, to pay my own way, and live where I choose…without being under surveillance twenty-four seven. Personal privacy is important to me and I haven't had much of that recently. It makes a woman surly. I want to date again…date women." The dating part was a lie, but it would give her more freedom. "Will that be a problem?"

Carl's lip curled into something resembling a smile. "My wife tells me I can be overbearing at times. And your *preference* has never been a problem for the family."

She inclined her head in agreement. This was a dangerous negotiation, but she needed to establish boundaries that would not only ensure her sanity but also help with what lay ahead.

"I'll give you whatever you need, but in return I expect your complete loyalty." Carl's voice assumed the hard edge that Abby was used to, and there was no doubt about his implication—*cross me at your own risk.*

"Then we have a deal. When do I go?" She felt guilty about leaving Stefan, Maria, Blake, and the rest of the family, but it was best. They'd grown closer during her convalescence, and that wasn't good for someone in her position.

"As soon as you're out of the cast and I've made a few arrangements. I'd like you to drive a small van back for me. We're taking some furniture from here and I don't want to wait for a moving company. It takes too long to schedule one this time of year."

"I should be one hundred percent once this thing is gone." She tapped the cast and smiled to cover her confusion. If her presence in Greensboro was so necessary, why was Carl wasting time by having her drive a van? Maybe this was all a ruse and she was being used as a mule to transport weapons. At least she'd be back in Greensboro before he arrived and would have time to find out and to warn Loane. "I'm ready to be doing something productive." That meant locating Loane, reconnecting with her family, and eventually returning to a life without role-playing.

CHAPTER SEVEN

Loane wiped sweat from her forehead as she stood on Elm Street in front of the sleek granite-and-glass Center Pointe high-rise building. Glowing with accent and up lighting, it looked regal and imposing against the night sky. Like many other structures in the downtown area, it had been something else—a seventeen-story Wachovia Bank. Like her, it had been repurposed. But her new function wasn't yet clear. A shiver of excitement and anticipation dimpled her skin as she followed the clean lines of the building skyward. She'd often wondered what this place was like, but Eve wouldn't—would she? She double-checked the address.

"You're at the right place. This is your new home." Eve hooked her arm through Loane's and guided her around the corner into the Lincoln Financial parking deck.

"Are you serious? This place is mega expensive."

"I figured the city center would be a bonus, and you asked for discretion."

"And this qualifies how exactly? A concierge works the front desk, the doors are locked every evening, and there's only one entrance from the street. Sounds like more security than my parents' home when I was a teenager. Do they make you sign in too?"

"Ever the cop. Be patient. Not your strong suit, I know." They took an elevator up one floor to a covered walkway between the parking deck and the condo building. "You can park your car in the garage here, in the underground facility, or behind the museum." She pointed toward the high-rise. "Here's the second entrance. You have an entry fob, and once you're inside, there's a private elevator to your penthouse suite."

Loane stopped at the door and turned to Eve. "Penthouse? How did you pull this off in three days?"

"It was the only way I could ensure your privacy. It's rented under one of my company names, Winterland, LLC."

As they rode the elevator to the sixteenth floor, Loane's chest swelled with gratitude. Eve had stepped up when others let her down, even though she didn't agree with Loane's methods. She had gone above and beyond anything Loane expected. It had been months since she'd felt this supported by anyone.

"I don't know how to—"

Eve patted her on the back. "You can thank me by reconsidering this madness."

"To move on, I have to find some answers." More than that, she had to know if Abby was alive or dead. Her thoughts bounced like a Ping-Pong ball, back and forth with no evidence to support either theory. Without that knowledge, the aching void in her body that neither food nor drink nor activity could fill would remain.

"I knew you'd say that. So, let's look at your place."

When the elevator opened, Loane stepped into surroundings she could've only imagined. Rooftops three or four stories high had been her greatest vantage point until now. The eastern landscape flickered with thousands of tiny campfires of light. Stars dotted the night sky like pinpoints poked in black paper. The view extended as far as she could see—an unobstructed vista of earth and sky. Floor-to-ceiling windows stretched the length of the east and west sides of the unit, and Loane felt like she was floating. "Oh, Eve. This is…"

"Beautiful isn't adequate, is it? I hoped you'd like it."

"Like it? I love it, but it's too much." How would she ever repay Eve and Thom for their kindness? They'd provided years of support when Loane was coming out, encouragement and backup as she cared for her ailing mother, a sanctuary after the accident, and now this.

"Let me know how you like living here. Thom and I are considering it when we're older. There's been a big hoopla about music from the clubs. Personally, I could give a fat rat's ass. You expect a little noise when you live in the city center." She waved her hand in an encompassing gesture. "How do you like the décor? I hadn't seen this myself."

Loane took in the dark, rich cherry flooring and cabinets, slid her hand across the cool, black granite countertop, and marveled at the straight lines of the contemporary furnishings and accents. "Thom nailed my taste."

"She had a great time setting it up."

"Please thank her for me. It's perfect."

"You can stay as long as you like, but I hope it's a short visit. I want you back in the real world, living your life, not fighting battles on your own."

Loane heard the hint of disapproval in Eve's tone and was grateful she didn't say more. "I appreciate this. I hope I can wrap it up soon."

"Well, I'll let you settle in." She handed Loane the key fob and walked toward the elevator. "You have a phone number for me?"

"It's the same, but remember—"

"I know. Nobody gets this number." She gave Loane a quick hug and stepped onto the elevator. "Thom stocked the refrigerator for a few days. Enjoy."

When Eve left, Loane looked around the unit and couldn't believe how spacious it was. Three sizeable bedrooms, one outfitted as an office, with expansive windows and ten-foot ceilings that made them seem even larger. The living space was divided into two separate seating areas, both with wall-mounted flat-screen televisions. A dining area off the kitchen could easily accommodate a dozen people. She would've been happy with a small one-bedroom unit, but Eve believed in value for money, and this one had it all.

Loane slid open the door to the balcony, stepped outside, and looked down Elm Street toward the Sky Bar, a direct view to the front door. Eve had no idea how perfect her selection was. Loane could use her binoculars to watch the activity without ever leaving home.

She was anxious to start but needed to set up her base of operations. A trip to the storage facility she'd rented and she'd be set. She grabbed one of Thom's signature Irish meat pies and a bottle of Guinness, and headed for the elevator. As she took a long pull of the rich stout, she remembered the last time she'd drunk one.

Five months ago she and Tyler had finished an exhausting round of martial-arts training and stopped by M'Coul's at Hamburger Square. Since their father died, they'd met at least once a month to practice and remember him. He'd introduced them to his own modified version of hand-to-hand and close-quarters combat techniques when they were teenagers. They practiced unarmed fighting, edged weapons, and weapons of opportunity. As they became more proficient through the years, almost every encounter ended in a draw, and they always celebrated with a beer on the way home.

After the explosion, she'd lost not only the ability to participate in sparring but also the interest in doing so. As she downed the last sip of Guinness, she realized how much she'd missed those sessions, physically and emotionally. Granted, Tyler wasn't an affectionate guy, but he was her brother and all she had left of a family. And it wasn't his fault ATF had shut everyone out of the information loop on Abby's case.

In the elevator, she dialed Tyler's cell and waited for him to answer. "Hey, bro. What's happening?"

"Damn, I thought you fell off the face of the earth." His voice cracked and he cleared his throat. "It's good to hear from you, sis. I know it's only been a little while, but it seems longer."

His uncharacteristic emotions surprised her. "Uh, thanks. Thought I better let you know I was still alive and still in Greensboro. I've got the same cell number, so save it to your phone…but don't use it unless you have to, for a while."

"Are you okay?"

"Yeah, got some things to take care of."

"Anything I can do to help?"

His offer sounded genuine. Had she been too hard on him? "Not right now, but I'll keep in touch."

"Good. The boys are asking about you already, and I don't like not hearing from you—plus, my body's going to hell without our workouts. I bet you're getting pretty flabby too. Admit it." He laughed, returning to their old repartee.

"Look, Ty, if you hear anything…about me or the gunrunner case, let me know."

"I'll keep my ears open. Whatever you're doing, just be careful."

"I will. Tell the boys I'll see them soon." She missed Tyler's three rambunctious children. They always kept things real, saying whatever was on their mind without editing. She envied kids that freedom before socialization took over. "Check you later." She didn't wait for his good-bye. Tyler had been much more supportive and understanding. Maybe after this was over, they'd have a chance to really connect. But that would have to wait.

As she walked toward her Jeep, she thought about leaving her family home and living in the downtown high-rise. She'd always wanted to try it, but now the experience seemed hollow. The thought of walks along the greenway or attending cultural events made her ache with the loneliness of doing those things alone. Life should be shared, but she'd lost the desire to do so. Instead of enjoying the vitality of downtown with family, friends, and a lover, she planned to isolate, blend into the crowd, maybe even go underground a bit, and observe. Nothing seemed to carry the same promise or significance without Abby.

❖

Two hours later Loane parked her old Jeep behind the historical museum to walk back to Center Pointe. Everything she needed was in her backpack and a small gym bag. Funny how compact and portable life became when necessary. She zigzagged between the buildings, enjoying the slightly cooler temperature and the more tranquil pace of the city at night.

As she stepped onto the sidewalk, she heard fast-approaching footsteps behind her. Adrenaline kicked in—her heart pounded and breathing quickened. Her cop senses tingled as she prepared to fight. When she turned, a figure in dark clothing and a hoodie darted out of the shadows, snatched her gym bag, and ran toward the Bellemeade Street parking deck.

"Hey, what the—come back with that." Damn it. She'd been distracted by her leisurely stroll, not paying attention. She ran after him, but her backpack slapped against her hips, slowing her down. The thief was getting away. If she didn't chase him, maybe he wouldn't run. She stopped and listened. His footsteps echoed through the garage, running and then slowing to a walk. She followed the sound, careful not to make any noise. Rounding the corner of the garage, she heard heavy breathing behind a half wall separating two levels.

She inhaled deeply to steady her heart rate and crept closer. Pulling her Walther PPK .380 from her waistband, she stepped from behind the wall and pointed her weapon at the culprit. "Freeze. Police."

Huge green eyes against a blanched face stared up at her from underneath the hoodie. "Really? You guys still say that crap?"

"Vi, is that you?"

"'Course it's me. Took you long enough." She nodded toward the gun still pointed at her chest. "Put that thing away before you hurt somebody, like me."

Loane wanted to snatch her by the collar and shake her until her row of silver earrings fell like coins to the pavement. She could've gotten herself killed. Instead, Loane reholstered and grabbed her gym bag from between Vi's outstretched legs. "What the hell are you doing snatching my stuff?"

"Taking you to school."

"What?" Loane was irritated that she'd allowed a street urchin to sneak up on her. She hadn't been expecting anything to happen, and that's when things always did. Like the night of the explosion. When would she learn not to let her guard down?

"That cop training doesn't mean crap in the real world. I proved you need me."

"Like hell I do." She wasn't about to admit she needed anyone, especially a kid whose only degree was in street life. Vi was wearing the same clothes she'd had on the first time they met, and her attitude definitely hadn't improved. She scolded herself for not checking Vi out sooner. She might have a criminal record already. "I ought to take your ass in for theft."

"Can't. You're not a cop at the mo, are you?"

"Where *do* you get your information?" She recalled her last run-in with Vi. She definitely hadn't volunteered anything about her leave of absence. Either she was a plant or she had some pretty good sources.

"Be surprised what cops talk about while having a smoke, taking a piss, or eating donuts and drinking coffee."

"And how do you get these pearls of wisdom?"

"I listen. Street grapevine, hundred times more reliable than cops." Vi got up from the garage floor and hiked a seat on top of the half wall. "Impressive, huh?"

"Depends. What else did you hear?" For the first time since they'd met, Vi seemed reluctant to speak. "Go on. I have to know if your sources are reliable."

"You were working a case and some people ended up dead in an explosion."

Loane wasn't ready for that one. The statement registered like blows to the chest over and over again…*ended up dead, ended up dead.* She grabbed the concrete wall to steady herself. It shouldn't be so hard to hear the words out loud again, but they always took her off guard. The two things didn't belong together—Abby and death.

"Sorry, dude." Vi looked at the ground as if allowing Loane time to regroup. "It's not like you went all Lizzie Borden on your parents."

She had Vi's sweatshirt clutched in her fists and was inches from her face before she realized it. Vi showed no fear; instead her innocent grin stopped Loane cold as she realized the girl was trying to make a joke. "You're crazy."

"You needed to lighten up," Vi said.

"You're lucky I didn't snap your head off." She'd taken quite a chance on Loane's reaction. Maybe this kid was smarter than she looked. She released Vi's shirt and stepped back, the emotional ebb leaving her weak. It wasn't like her to lose control so easily, but her nerves had been on edge for months, lapses were bound to occur. "Sorry…I overreacted."

"You think?" Vi was still smiling. "It's a tough break. You're allowed to get pissed, hit shit, and take it out on people. Teenagers don't have the market on that."

"Actually, it's not allowed. I'm a cop. I'm supposed to take everything in stride." Loane gave her the once-over and settled against the wall beside her. "You're not just another pretty face, are you, ki—Vi?"

"Nope, and I never lie."

Shaking her head in disbelief, Loane said with all the certainty of her life's experience, "Everybody lies."

"Not me. If you take me on, I'll be your intel source, not to mention gossipmonger."

She couldn't figure out why Vi wanted to hook up with an out-of-work cop hell-bent on starting trouble with criminals and the police. "You don't even know my plan."

"Duh—that's a no-brainer. You want to find out who caused the big boom and why."

"Not exactly." Uncanny, this kid's ability to read her. It was disturbingly reminiscent of how easily Abby had become a part of her life. "But close enough. What do you want from me? I don't have any money, so I can't pay you. I'm too screwed up and too old to be your friend."

"I want to help."

"Nobody does something for nothing."

"Is that even proper English?" Vi grinned again, her teeth only slightly whiter than her colorless complexion.

"Look who's talking about proper English. If you want to hang out with me, you have to tell me why."

"I can't spill my guts. Trust has to be earned, dude."

"And I should trust you because you say so? Not likely."

"Let me count the reasons." Vi held up her closed fist and raised fingers as she talked. "Saved your ass from two goons the other night. Snatched your bag and didn't rip you off. Told you where I get my info. I can help you fit in on the street. *And* I'm getting a gig at the Sky Bar as soon as the new manager arrives. 'Nuff said?"

The last comment caught Loane's attention. "What new manager?"

"Am I in? If not, no more free info."

No way she would trust Vi with this case, but she could use her for information. It would be helpful to have someone on the inside in case she didn't make it. Vi couldn't get hurt just watching and reporting. *Abby did.* The thought was sobering. "Tell me about the manager."

Vi shoulder-bumped her. "Word is that Carl Torre is taking over Simon's businesses and bringing in a new manager. When that person is in place, I'm getting a job. Need the cash."

The offer was almost too good to be true, if it wasn't for the fact that three people associated with the Torre businesses had already been killed. Maybe it was too risky no matter what the circumstances. She couldn't be responsible for placing anyone else in danger. "I can't let you do that."

"Hey, you can't stop me. I'm of age. If they'll hire me, I can work anywhere I want. If you don't want my help, that's on you."

Vi was almost as stubborn and independent as she was, but she admired her determination. "Do whatever you want. I'm not asking for help."

"I get that, hard-ass. You can do it all yourself. Right?"

"Stay out of trouble. I don't exactly have access to backup or unlimited police resources anymore. Do your job, watch, and listen. What is your job, by the way?"

"I can do anything—a Vi of all trades."

"If you say so." The nonstop chitchat had exhausted her. If it went this way every time they talked, she'd never have the need for internal dialogue again. "Do you have a place to go? A home?"

"Don't use it much, but I have one. Too much shit happening all the time to sleep."

Loane hefted her backpack and gym bag and turned to leave.

"Hey, what about the fitting-in part? You need some serious help," Vi said.

"Later. I'm older and I need rest. How will I get in touch with you?"

"Don't worry, dude. I'll find you soon for your makeover."

"What makeover?" When she turned around, Vi was already gone. Weird. The girl was plain weird. What had she gotten herself into? She hated to admit it, but having a street-savvy kid on her side wasn't an entirely unpleasant thought. As long as Vi didn't get hurt and Loane didn't let her guard down, she'd be fine.

CHAPTER EIGHT

Abby slowed the old U-Haul truck and coasted into the service plaza off I-95 North. Saying good-bye to Stefan, Maria, Blake, and Nick had been more difficult than she imagined. It was hard to leave behind the flesh-and-blood reminder of the most significant thing she'd ever done. She'd been on the road almost six hours since leaving Miami. Between traffic, pit stops, outbursts of emotion, and a temperamental vehicle, she was lucky to have gotten this far.

In less than half an hour, her parents would be here. They'd been visiting relatives in Daytona Beach when she called, which made a meet-up on the interstate easy for everyone. Her conscience wouldn't let her leave Florida without reassuring them she was okay. And she needed to reconnect, if only for a few minutes, with the touchstone of her life—her family's unconditional love.

She parked the truck on the back row between two tractor-trailers, unwilling to explain to her family why she was driving such a cumbersome vehicle. It would only lead to more questions she couldn't answer. She hurried into the fast-food restaurant, picked up a variety of items, and settled at a picnic area under the trees just in time. Her parents' silver Cadillac pulled up, and before it came to a complete stop, her three brothers—Bobby Junior, Carter, and Will—bailed out of the backseat.

They ran toward her like the children they used to be. She thought about holding back, uncertain if they'd notice how she favored her right leg, still stiff from the recently removed cast. She also wanted to show them that she wasn't the same little girl who once needed their protection, but her heart was so full she ran and hurled herself into the midst of them, knowing they would catch her. They fell to the ground, poking and jabbing at each other like kids on a playground.

"Stop this." Her father teased them as he exited the vehicle. "You're grownups."

"In body only," her mother said.

The boys pulled her from the ground and presented her like a gift to their parents. They looked as if they'd aged years since she'd seen them. Her father's thick black hair was peppered with gray, his forehead more deeply wrinkled. Her mother's face appeared unchanged, but her eyes had lost some of their characteristic sparkle. Abby feared she'd caused the subtle changes.

She hugged her mother and inhaled the familiar scent of her lilac perfume mingled with the smell of baking. The fragrance reminded her of childhood when life was simple and parents could solve any problem with love and a loaf of fresh-baked bread.

Her father waited patiently, and when he delicately turned her into his arms, she almost broke down. His hulking six-foot frame belied the gentleness of a sensitive man. She smiled when he nuzzled her neck and his beard stubble scratched her skin. He always complained that the electric razor his wife insisted he use never did the job as well as a *real* razor. She was so caught up in the reunion that she forgot why they were meeting halfway between Miami and Daytona Beach at a rest stop.

She stepped back, pointed at her brothers and the food she'd bought, and shrugged. "You're on your own. I didn't know you were coming."

"How could we not come?" Bobby said. "Go get us some burgers, Will, and don't forget the fries. I'm starving." He gave Will a handful of money. The youngest always got fetching duty but never complained because he kept the change for carrying charges.

Carter draped his arm across her shoulder and added, "You're lucky Mama and Papa didn't invite the whole neighborhood."

"Thank you" was all she could say.

They gathered around the picnic table and ate, telling stories about relatives and friends but avoiding the real subject for almost two hours. Her parents were too respectful of her privacy to intrude.

That had never been an issue for the boys. When the conversation lulled, Bobby went for the hot topic. "So, where have you been, what are you doing, and, most important, when are you coming home?" Everybody stared and she could feel the answers being urged from her. "At our last family gathering, you said you'd gotten a job and would be away a lot—understatement. We've hardly seen you in eighteen months. What gives?"

"It's complicated."

Will said, "Try us. We'll keep up."

"We don't mean to pry." Her mother was always afraid of offending. "We're worried."

Abby recognized the look on their faces. She'd seen it growing up—concern mixed with an overdose of protectiveness. That expression and the well-meaning, but suffocating, attentiveness had driven Abby to move almost completely out of her family's sphere of influence. She'd chosen a difficult course, but now she had to see it through.

She worded her statements carefully enough to convey reassurance without offending and without saying anything. "I can't give you details because I've signed a confidentiality agreement. I work for a company with interests around the world, so I travel a lot. I'm sorry I can't tell you more right now, maybe in the future. But I'm fine, as you can see."

"We miss you, baby," her father said.

And that was part of the problem. Her parents still thought of her as their baby, and her brothers still felt like her protectors. "I know, Papa. We'll get together properly very soon. I promise. But I have to go now."

"What are you doing on I-95?" Bobby asked.

"I'm driving back up north on business."

"Are you dating anyone?" Will elbowed her and winked. "We can't wait to meet whoever she is."

Abby stifled the urge to surrender emotionally and throw herself into the comfort of her family's love. She cherished how they accepted her sexuality and encouraged her to settle down with a "nice" girl. But right now she couldn't find an answer that covered all the emotions Will's question evoked.

"I'm sorry. Did I say something wrong?" he asked.

"No, it's this job..." She let them fill in the blank. If she didn't have time for family, certainly she wouldn't have time to date. They'd understand that. She stood, hoping they'd follow her lead, but no one did. She'd told them everything she could. "I have to leave. Let me give you my new cell number."

As she reached for her jacket, the phone in her pants pocket vibrated—the Torre work phone. "Hello?"

"Abby, what's wrong? Did you run into trouble?"

"Who is this?" She knew it was Carl, but she needed a few extra seconds to decide how she'd answer his questions with her family standing around her.

"It's Carl. You've been stationary for over two hours."

"How do you know that?"

"GPS tracking. I have it on all my vehicles as a safety precaution."

Sometimes she hated technology. "I'd driven for six hours and wanted to rest a bit. No problems. I'll be back on the road shortly."

"Wait where you are. I have a couple of guys on another job in the area with the chopper. They can be there in about thirty minutes. I want to be sure you're okay."

"That's not necessary. Everything is fine." She couldn't afford to sound too insistent or her family would get suspicious, but she had to deter Carl. "Remember our talk about this job?"

"Yeah, more flexibility."

"And…"

"Trust," he added.

"Exactly. I don't need an escort."

The long breath he exhaled signaled that he wasn't happy with the outcome. "Fine. I'll call the guys back."

"And I'm leaving now. I'll let you know when I arrive." She closed the phone and turned back to her family, edging them toward their vehicle. "Sorry." She hugged everyone good-bye and gave them her new phone number. "You can call me anytime. Please don't worry." With teary eyes, she watched them drive away.

The brief visit had been worth the risk. She needed to see the caring in their eyes and feel their love again before facing whatever lay ahead. Carl couldn't possibly find out she'd met them. The chances were at least fifty-fifty that he wouldn't care, but she couldn't take even that much of a risk with her family.

As their car disappeared down I-95, Abby thought about Carl's phone call. Was he so worried about her safety that a two-hour stop caused concern? Her earlier suspicions that there was more to this furniture shipment than she'd been told seemed more likely. She walked to the back of the van to inspect the cargo. The door was secured with a tamper-resistant lock and a red warning label that an alarm would sound if disturbed. Strange precautions for a simple furniture shipment.

Perhaps Carl was taking extreme measures against theft, or maybe he was shipping guns. She'd check it out when she arrived in Greensboro; after all, she'd be the new club boss. That was second on her agenda. The first thing was to find Loane without alerting anyone else, warn her of the potential danger from Carl, explain everything that had happened over the past three months, and pray that she'd understand. She didn't know where she and Loane stood, emotionally or professionally, and that hurt more than she cared to admit. Abby climbed into the truck and drove north, pleased with the way she'd handled Carl and her family, hoping her luck extended to her search for Loane.

❖

"'Sup, A-lone."

Loane whirled around on the park bench as Vi dropped her backpack beside her. "Why do you always sneak up on me?"

"Wasn't sneaking."

"How'd you find me?"

"You like this park and that dusty old dump over there." Vi inclined her head toward the historical museum.

"I don't like being followed."

"All I did was wait." Vi flashed a cocky grin that made Loane want to prove her wrong, but here she was, as predicted.

She was planning to stake out the Sky Bar again tonight to identify the rest of the employees, and she didn't need Vi messing things up. "I've got work to do."

"After your makeover." Vi reached into her bag and pulled out an electric razor, shears, and a plastic bag of miscellaneous jewelry. "Where to start?"

"I didn't agree to any makeover." She wasn't inclined to let Vi anywhere near her with sharp instruments. She didn't trust close friends that much. And she certainly didn't need a makeover to work stakeouts and surveillance.

"Look, dude. You can hang around on the fringe or you can get into the action. What's it gonna be? I can get you *inside*, if you'll think outside your stuffy cop box."

"I had no idea you could speak in complete sentences."

"No need for insults. Wanna hear my idea?"

Whatever this kid had in mind was probably illegal, immoral, or unethical—things she was sworn to fight in her profession. But since she wasn't technically a cop at the moment, it couldn't hurt to listen.

Brainstorming with a street kid might spark a different approach. She was tired of standing outside taking pictures. "I'll listen. No guarantees."

Vi's young face glowed as she scrubbed her knuckles across her chin and scooted closer. "First, we gotta do something about that hair—can you say *obvious*?"

"I like my hair." She raked her fingers through the collar-length strands and let them fall around her face. "What's wrong with it?"

"It's too long and it *glows*." Vi scrunched her face like the word held a particularly distasteful connotation. "It's like white. Can't be natural."

"It most certainly is natural—platinum blond, and I'm not changing it. I might consider a cut, but no color."

"I'm sensing resistance to the plan."

Loane was weary of the back-and-forth, but something about it felt familiar. "I'm not hearing any plan."

"Okay, okay. I can live with the color, I guess. Let's cut the hair, funk it up a little, and add a few baubles, maybe a tat."

"No freaking way am I getting a tattoo."

"We gotta sell you as the clean-cut cop gone rogue. Feel me? You gotta look different, act different, *be* different. If you're the same as them, you're no threat."

Maybe the kid had a point. It was her goal to be taken into the Torre organization, or at least considered harmless as she floated around the edges. Could she hide her feelings well enough to pull it off? She'd have to be a damned good salesman, but maybe… "What else?"

Looking at Loane's lap, Vi said, "Nice gloves. Trim the tips."

She rubbed her gloved hands together and a painful memory sliced through her. *Abby died and all I got was scarred palms.* She wanted to scream, to rant at the injustice of life. She'd tamped down her rage until she could almost taste the bitter edge of it with the slightest irritation. Her control would fracture if she didn't find some answers soon. *Focus. Keep it together.* She splayed her fingers dramatically and tried for humor. "But they're real kidskin."

Vi shrugged.

"As in, they're expensive."

"Buy a cheap pair. They look cool. Do you wear them for a reason?"

Loane couldn't tell the story, especially not to a kid almost young enough to be her daughter. The extent of her injuries, her identity, the names of the dead, and other pertinent facts about the explosion had been excluded from the newspaper and television accounts. All anyone knew for sure was that the Torre home had gone up in flames and no one knew why or how. But like most airtight cases, this one leaked details like a sieve.

She shook her head and refocused on the different look and new role Vi was painting for her. The loyal-and-dedicated cop had failed to produce results. If she could pretend for a while, she wouldn't need anybody's help, and that was appealing. "Let's do this."

Vi jumped off the bench, her stash of transformative items flying in all directions. "For real? I'm in? You'll do it?"

The picture was so childlike that she stifled a laugh. Vi didn't need encouragement. She was a precocious pain in the ass, but she might have the answer to Loane's current situation. "If you can change my look without turning me into a freak. Can you do that?"

"Totes, dude."

"And whatever that was, don't ever say it again. Speak English."

"Well, let's rock and roll! Is that more your era?"

"Smart-ass. Where are we going to perform this grand renovation?"

"Your place?" Vi picked up her goodies and stuffed them into her backpack.

"Not happening."

"O-kay, how about the women's?" She pointed to the park's restroom. "Open until eleven. Should be enough time."

Surveying the smattering of people throughout the park, Loane assessed the likelihood they would be disturbed. Summer was waning, the leaves were beginning to change, but a final surge of Indian-summer heat kept most folks inside. "That'll work."

She felt a bit like a prisoner in the claustrophobic space, and when Vi plugged in the electric razor, she started to panic. *1890 first residences in Greensboro receive electric lines.* The vibrating noise and menacing teeth of the device did little to calm her anxiety. Why had she agreed to this? A makeover was not her style, and trusting a street urchin she'd just met with a razor and shears seemed like suicide. "Let's get it over with…and be careful with those things."

Her instincts about people had always been keen, and something about Vi felt harmless, even genuine. She wasn't sure why, but she'd go with that until she found out her real name and ran a check on her.

Thirty minutes later she sat on the toilet seat with her hair scattered around her like fallen leaves. She'd given Vi free rein and was beginning to regret it as her head cooled. "It's a bit drafty up there. Did you scalp me?"

"Crybaby." With an exaggerated flourish, Vi fingered the front of Loane's hair and pointed to the small wall mirror. "Take a look."

She stood and, out of habit, reached to flip her now-nonexistent hair.

"Don't touch it," Vi said. "Look…and no blood either."

The image in the mirror was so different that she turned to see if anyone else was there. Without hair feathered around her face, her cheeks appeared sunken and her eyes ringed with dark circles. Her blue eyes were iridescent against pale skin, and her full red lips looked like crayon drawings. She raised her hand and traced the neat cut-out around her ears. The rest of her hair was trimmed close to the scalp except for a twist at the front. In place of the bangs that had concealed her high forehead, a gelled spike stood about three inches tall. If she encountered this person on the street, she'd immediately think drugged-out rocker.

"Yeah?" Vi practically vibrated with enthusiasm, obviously pleased with herself.

"It's different. I had no idea I looked so…"

"Wasted? Spooky, right? Phase one complete."

"Isn't this enough of a change?" She now understood why her brother and Eve thought she looked unwell. She hadn't paid much attention to herself recently. Her clothes had gotten looser, but she cinched her belt tighter and kept going. The old image of the walking wounded certainly applied.

"You need more. Jewelry and a tattoo maybe…something temporary if you're afraid of needles or too chicken to scar that lily-white skin."

Loane shook her head. Vi taunted her like Tyler used to do when they were kids, and it stirred a wave of nostalgia. "Temporary, definitely."

Vi reached into her backpack and pulled out a plastic bag of jewelry. "I've got earrings, finger rings, toe rings, lip rings…" she sang the choices like a street vendor, "brow rings, nose rings, navel rings, and clit rings."

"No piercings, absolutely not."

"Temps, Chicken Little. They're fake, with spring hoops. See?" Vi clamped one of the silver rings on her bottom lip. "Doesn't hurt and looks hella cool." She offered the bag to Loane, then turned her head from side to side as if preparing to paint her portrait. "I suggest one lip, one brow, and several on each ear."

"I don't need to look like the poster child for piercings. You've got that covered."

"Ouch."

She chose several understated pieces of jewelry and handed them to Vi. "Where should they go?" She felt like she was having a dress-up day with a kid sister, though she'd never had either. Looking completely different was starting to appeal to her.

Vi took the clips she'd chosen and gave her several pages of tattoos. "Look at these while I hook you up."

Loane found the perfect tattoo on the first page, a heart with an exploding bomb in the center. Pieces of the mangled organ were blown away, and she envisioned them stretched down her arm toward her gloved hand. Pretty much said it all.

"Yeah, I can see that for you—damaged," Vi said as she gently placed a small silver hoop over the left side of Loane's bottom lip and one over her right eyebrow. "My work here is done. Now let's get you tatted up."

Loane had no idea why Vi's touch hadn't sent her running. Maybe lack of sleep and nutrition had compromised her resistance. Maybe she was too tired to care about herself anymore. Or perhaps on some gut level she trusted Vi. But that wasn't likely, not after almost everyone she knew had betrayed her. Her defenses were securely in place. She'd experienced a momentary weakness that wouldn't happen again. Kid or adult, everybody should come with warning labels.

"And where would I get a temporary tattoo?"

"Seven Sagas on Spring Garden Street. We can walk there in fifteen."

Two hours later Loane walked out of the tattoo shop with an impressive henna tattoo on her right forearm. She'd never admit it, but she sort of liked the reckless feel of having her body marked. Her mother would've approved of the design, a constant reminder to keep her guard up. "Not bad."

"Not bad? It rocks." Vi ran in front of her, turned, and walked back, her gaze roaming up and down her body. When they met, she slid a finger around Loane's ear, down her arm, and past the new tat. "You're looking mighty bootylicious."

Loane recoiled. "Get off me."

Vi stumbled backward and dropped her backpack. "Jeez. Chill. Can you say kidding?"

The shocked look on her face told Loane she'd seriously overreacted, again. Vi probably thought she was a basket case, and she wouldn't be far wrong. "I'm sorry. It's—"

"No sweat. You seriously need to get laid or something. Later." She retrieved her backpack and pointed in the opposite direction. "And get some clothes that fit. Jeans and T-shirts."

"Yeah, sure." Loane watched her shuffle away, Vans slapping the pavement in a rhythm uniquely Vi. What was wrong with her? She'd almost assaulted the kid for touching her arm. Earlier she'd hardly flinched as Vi cut and styled her hair, much more familiar, intimate contact. Her emotional and physical responses were all over the place, though they should be leveling off after this many months. If she didn't find a way to channel her pain and frustration, she could hurt someone else or herself.

CHAPTER NINE

Tap, tap, tap. Abby shifted and a dull pain throbbed in the lower half of her body. She tried to straighten her legs but they felt stiff and heavy. *Tap, tap, tap.* What was that annoying sound? Turning sideways, she rolled off the truck seat and onto the floorboard. *Damn it.* Then she remembered. She'd arrived in Greensboro after the club closed and parked in the rear lot, unwilling to pay a night's rent at a hotel for only a few hours.

From her landing spot on the floor, she saw a young woman peering in through the window, preparing to tap again. She put up her hand. "Don't. I'm awake." She pried her legs from under the steering wheel, and they tingled with sleep needles. "Give me a minute." Mornings were not her thing, especially after sixteen hours on the road in a rickety truck.

"Need some help?" The woman's green eyes sparkled with what Abby interpreted as amusement at her less-than-gracious position.

She climbed off the floorboard and sat on the edge of the seat, glancing at herself in the rearview mirror. "More than you know," she mumbled. Her hair was scattered like she'd been in a wind tunnel, runny mascara darkened her cheeks, and something akin to dried saliva clung to her chin. She rolled down the window just enough to not seem rude. "Can I help *you*?"

"I have a job interview at noon with the new manager of the Sky Bar."

"Early much?" Abby pulled her cell phone out of the glove compartment, along with a wet wipe, and checked the time—twelve thirty. She didn't know anything about an interview. As she wiped the remnants of yesterday from her face, she saw the envelope that had been taped to the club door when she arrived. After the drive, she'd been too exhausted to deal with anything else, even trying to find Loane.

She ripped the envelope open and emptied the contents into her hand. A barely legible handwritten note read,

M, here are keys to the club. Hope they're still here when you arrive. Interview with Kinsey Easton at noon for a job. We need more dancers. I'll be here at two.
Ray

She made a mental note to discuss security with Ray ASAP.

"You're Kinsey?" she asked the woman still staring at her like a rare specimen. She nodded. "Great, wait over there." Abby pointed in the direction of the club's back door. "I'll be with you shortly." What a great first impression she'd made as a boss.

She emptied the wet wipes, trying to make herself visually and aromatically acceptable. Her wrinkled blouse and jeans would have to suffice until she retrieved her suitcases from the back of the truck. She brushed her teeth with her finger and rinsed with bottled water from the trip. A shower would've been heaven.

When she stepped out of the truck, her right leg buckled. It was fully healed, but after periods of inactivity, she needed to move slowly. She'd forgotten. Kinsey Easton was at her side as she grabbed for support.

"Take it easy. Are you all right?"

She straightened and met the young woman's concerned gaze. "Quite, but thank you. My leg went to sleep. Sorry." She shifted her weight to her left leg, slowly redistributed to the right, and made her way across the uneven gravel lot. Would she always bear the physical and mental scars of that horrible night? If she could only find Loane, talk to her and have her understand, she'd gladly bear the rest.

"Sure you're okay?" Kinsey asked.

She nodded. "Shall we?" She made an effort to walk normally as she led the way to the club, unlocked the heavy metal door, and stepped inside with Kinsey close behind. "I wonder where the damn lights are." Feeling around the dark walls until she located a panel, she flipped several switches. The bar lit up. "Good enough."

"Are you M? I sure hope so or I'd feel like a complete ass."

"Guess so. Have a seat. Tell me about yourself and why you want to work," she motioned to the vast open area, "here." Why would an innocent-looking, freckle-faced woman be interested in a job in a topless club? She certainly didn't have the assets necessary to command big tips. Maybe it was as simple as needing a job, any job. She fought her caretaking urge to tell Kinsey to look elsewhere for work.

"I recently graduated. There's a glut of grads unable to find jobs. I need to repay some loans and heard you pay well."

"What position are you applying for?" Ray's note had been specific, but she could ask about other qualifications.

"I'll do anything. I learn fast."

Unfortunately the available job didn't require much skill—expose breasts and shake. "I'm afraid we only have openings for dancers at the moment."

"I could do that."

"You realize this is a topless bar, right?"

"*Topless*, as in show my tits?"

Abby nodded.

"Couldn't I wait tables? I mean, look at me." She pointed at her chest, small mounds barely evident beneath a tight T-shirt.

The desperation in the young woman's voice registered like a cry for help. If Kinsey were her younger sister, she'd advise her to run from this place and find a decent job that didn't require her to strip and act like a whore. But any such advice could come back to haunt her. She was in character and needed to maintain her cover. "Leave your contact details and be here tonight at eight."

"You're hiring me?" Kinsey jumped off the bar stool like she might break into a happy dance.

"We'll see how it goes. Maybe I can make you bartender's assistant or something. No promises, understand?"

Kinsey started to hug her but stopped when Abby held up her hands. "Understood and thanks, M. You're awesome."

Wait until a sleazy old man grabs your ass. She watched the young woman walk out of the bar and a man the size of a tree trunk walk in. Could this day get any worse? She wanted a shower, fresh clothes, Loane, and a chance to look in the back of the moving van, in that order. Instead she was faced with Paul Bunyan and whatever fresh hell he had in store.

"You M?" he asked, his breath and clothes reeking of stale cigarettes. His bald head shone even in the dull light. Cue ball came to mind.

"I'm Abby Mancuso, and you?"

"Ray." As if that should be obvious. "Left you the key and a note, duh."

"Of course." Now the dreadful penmanship made sense. "About that—"

"Never had a woman boss. Some of the guys won't like it."

She started to comment.

"But I can grease the rails for you. I was Simon's right hand. Not gonna change much, are you?" She tried to speak again. "Probably not a good idea right away. Guys don't like change."

"Ray, if you were Simon's right hand, I trust you can handle the day-to-day operations. I need to get into the back of the van, grab my luggage, and find a place to live at least temporarily. I'll leave everything else to you until I get settled. Agreed?"

By the stunned look on Ray's face it appeared all the sentences strung together might have been too much for him. "Uh-huh, I mean no, yeah, I can handle it."

"What's the *no* part?"

"Carl said nobody gets in the van except me and Tiny, the other guy coming to help me unload."

She was too tired to be tactful and Ray probably wouldn't notice if she was. "Do you *really* think he would've put my suitcases in the back if that included me? I'm the new boss. Carl trusts me. Open the damn lock and get my clothes out or you'll be unemployed."

Ray's massive chest seemed to shrink as he considered her words. "Yeah, okay, that makes sense." He scratched his head as if conjuring up another thought. "Nothing but furniture in there anyway." Abby doubted he was telling the truth.

"Exactly." She followed him to the truck and memorized the security combination as he plugged it in. Luckily her luggage was nowhere in sight. Whoever packed the truck had shoved boxes of furniture in last. "Damn it. Where's my stuff?" She stood aside as though uninterested in the rest of the shipment. "And where's your helper?"

"I'm right here." A shorter version of Ray but with a ponytail and a trail of cheap cologne stepped from around the side of the van. "Are you M?"

"What's this M stuff? My name is Abby." Maybe sleep deprivation fueled her irritability, but she felt like she was dealing with a couple of kindergartners.

Ray said, "We thought you were gonna be a guy, but…anyway. Kind of James Bond, huh? Get it, M?"

Kind of moronic but she didn't have the energy to debate with him. "Sure."

While Ray and Tiny searched the truck for her luggage, she scanned the contents. Each container was the same—long, rectangular, and nothing like a sofa, chair, or bar table. She had to look inside one of those boxes. "When do we unload the furniture?"

Ray and Tiny exchanged a look and the shorter man shook his head. Unlike Ray, he seemed to actually consider his response. "We'll take care of it later."

"But—"

"Here we go. Found them, M." Ray held up the two suitcases like prizes he'd won at a carnival. "Now you can get cleaned up and change clothes."

Further objection would raise suspicion. "I need a hotel…and a car."

"The Biltmore on Washington between Elm and Greene Street. Easy walking distance," Tiny said. "A little pricey, but Carl's picking up the tab until you find a place. And he rented that for you." He inclined his head toward a red sports car in the lot.

"Great." It wasn't, but she needed to get away from these guys and sleep. "I'll see you in a few hours." She had a feeling her life was about to get complicated, and she needed to find Loane before it did.

❖

Abby woke after five hours physically rested but mentally exhausted, as if her mind had been constantly working. Her first thought was of Loane, but before she could savor it or decide what to do next, her personal cell rang.

"Hello."

"What the hell is going on, Mancuso?" ATF Agent Dan Bowman was clearly not a happy man. They hadn't talked since before the explosion. Barrio hadn't mentioned anything about reconnecting with him during their call before she left Miami, yet he'd obviously given Bowman her new number. What was she supposed to say? Was this Barrio's way of testing Bowman, feeding him bits and pieces of intel to see if and when it floated to the surface? If so, which bits was she supposed to provide? Or had Barrio learned something that led him to trust Bowman?

"I'm shut out of the case, told you're dead, hear nothing to the contrary for three months, and now I'm back in again. I'm not a goddamned yo-yo. What's happening?"

"I'm sorry, Dan. I don't know." He'd obviously already gotten his marching orders from above and could not be softened. She let him vent.

"Don't give me fucking *sorry*. Why wasn't I read in on this operation? Why am I the only man standing—never a good position. I can't even report to my own supervisor."

She understood Bowman's frustration but Hector Barrio had made that call. He'd decided she should stay on assignment and Bowman should be left out of the loop until they found the leak in the Greensboro ATF office. Bowman was lashing out at her because he felt like a peon and couldn't rant at his superiors.

"I don't know what to tell you, Dan. I'm only an informant."

"Exactly! You're a freaking informant. Why is everything so damn top secret?" She couldn't tell him. Besides, if she said anything, truth or lie, it would only fuel his anger. "Now my orders are to serve as an information gatherer. Either you've got something big on somebody or you're sleeping with the director."

She couldn't win. Best to stick to the case facts. She could only assume that Barrio intended her to funnel information to Bowman. It was the only thing that made sense. "I drove a van back from Miami full of furniture, or so I was told. It's parked behind the club on Elm Street. I haven't been able to look inside the crates, but they don't look like furniture boxes to me. Want me to snoop around?"

"Sure, whatever. Do what you've been instructed to do and keep me in the freaking loop this time. Got it?" He hung up before she could answer or ask about Loane. Bowman would know what happened to her. Whether he would tell her was another story.

As she showered and dressed, Abby considered her next move. She needed to check out the boxes in the van, but she also needed to find Loane. No contest. She listed all the places they had been together, places she might look for her. She could call her cell phone and leave a message, but too much time had passed. A call wouldn't suffice. She needed to face Loane, to see the look in her eyes when they met again. Then she'd know if there was still hope. She'd start with the police department.

She dialed the central contact number she'd memorized and prayed.

"Guilford Metro Communications."

"Yes, I'm trying to get in touch with Officer Loane Landry."

"What is this regarding, ma'am?"

"It's a personal matter."

"I'm sorry, ma'am, but we don't release information about officers to the public."

"But I'm a friend. I need to get in touch with her. It's important." Her status as a confidential informant wouldn't win her any points, so she couldn't play that card.

The operator was insistent. "I'm sorry. If you'd like to leave a name and number, I'll try to get the information to the officer."

"Can you at least tell me if she's still with the department?"

"Ma'am, if you'd like to leave your name and number, I'll have a supervisor call you."

"This is important."

"If you have an emergency, I'll be glad to dispatch someone who can—"

"Never mind." Abby could barely see the End key on the touchpad through her tears. If Loane was still with the police department, she wouldn't find out this way. Loane had a brother who was also a cop, Tyler. Maybe he'd be more helpful.

She dialed directory assistance and asked for a listing for Tyler Landry, surprised when there actually was one. Most police officers she knew weren't in the phone book. Either Tyler was more grounded than most or more reckless. Either way, it put her one step closer to Loane. She dialed the number and held her breath.

A man with a deep, rumbling voice answered. "Yeah."

"Tyler Landry?"

"Who wants to know?" Smart-ass, like his sister. In spite of the gruff greeting, her heartbeat raced in anticipation of news, any news.

"I'm a friend of your sister and I'm trying to locate her." Abby didn't identify herself. She couldn't afford for Loane to hear she was in town from anyone but her. "Can you help?"

"Nope."

"It's important that I get in touch with her."

"Lady, I don't know who you are. Even if I did, I couldn't help you because I don't know where my sister is. She disappeared." He hung up without further explanation.

Abby's hope vanished and her imagination went into overdrive. *Disappeared?* Maybe she went on vacation and hadn't returned yet. Did she leave of her own accord or was she taken? He didn't say kidnapped. He said disappeared, which she hoped implied a level of choice. Anything else was unacceptable.

She dropped into the chair beside her hotel window and stared out. Why would Loane leave Greensboro, her job, her family and friends? What if she'd gone to look for her? She wouldn't have known where to start. Dan Bowman didn't know where she was. She wouldn't know to call Hector Barrio. For all Loane knew, she'd died in the explosion on Strawberry Road that night.

Someone should've told Loane that she was still on the case and would resurface when possible. Abby's head pounded. Only she and Hector Barrio knew the whole story. Who *could've* told Loane everything? Who *should've* trusted her enough to tell her the truth? Her chest tightened as guilt and remorse filled her. She should've. How could she ever explain why she hadn't?

Her need to find Loane grew more urgent. She'd go back to the place where they'd connected. A few minutes later she rapped on the solid wood door of Loane's home until her knuckles ached. No answer. If she'd known that she wouldn't see Loane for almost four months when she left, would she have made the same decision? The empty feeling in her chest as she looked around the house made her wonder. Loane had ignited something in her that she hadn't felt before. Maybe she would've made the same decision, but she would've been honest with Loane about why. She would've been honest about everything.

Abby walked around the side of the house and opened the privacy gate into the backyard. The last time she'd seen this view she'd been in Loane's bed, exhausted after a marathon lovemaking session. Her body warmed with the memory and ached for a repeat. How could she have let something so special slip away? She could hear her parents now. *"We taught you better."* The heavy sadness settled over her as she checked the area for any sign of Loane.

The grounds were well groomed and the patio spotless, like someone still lived here, but nothing looked familiar. She knocked on the back door, but still no answer. *Where are you, hon?*

"Can I help you?"

Abby turned toward the voice and saw an elderly woman in a baseball cap standing outside the gate. "Sorry?"

"Can I help? You don't seem like a burglar or you're a bad one, too noisy."

"I'm looking for Loane Landry."

"Moved out." The woman delivered the news like a boring headline in the paper.

Abby couldn't believe Loane would've left this place. She had some pleasant memories here and had enjoyed making the home come alive again through her renovations. "Moved…do you know where she went?"

"Nope. She didn't offer and I didn't ask. I'm not one to pry."

What happened to nosey neighbors are good neighbors? Abby would've been grateful for a curious, meddlesome old lady. "Somebody obviously still lives here. Do you know who?"

The woman shook her head. "Young girl, not around much. You know how kids are these days, in and out at all hours."

So she did notice some things, just nothing that would help locate Loane. "Did Loane have any friends who might know where she went?"

"Lady, does it look like we'd run in the same circles?" The woman turned and started back across the yard toward the house next door.

"Thank you." Why didn't she know that? They'd talked at length about Loane's family, their dysfunctional dynamics, and the sibling competition, but she'd never mentioned her friends, other than Eve Winters and her partner, Thom. Abby felt a degree of separation from the woman she loved. She'd held Loane so closely in her heart these past months, savoring every moment they'd shared, remembering every detail of their short time together. Now it seemed there were things she didn't know about her.

What did Loane think and whom did she turn to when Abby disappeared? Eve was the perfect person for Loane to confide in. Loane considered her not only a friend but also a surrogate mother. She'd tried to protect Loane when her mother railed against her lesbianism. Why hadn't Abby gone to Eve first? She glanced at her watch. It was almost nine at night and the museum where Eve's office was would be closed. She had been so preoccupied with finding Loane that she hadn't noticed when day turned to night. She looked at her watch again, nine o'clock. Work.

As she drove back downtown, she tried to stay positive about the prospects of finding Loane. It had been a long time since she had to consider a work schedule, and now she was late for her first day on the job. But since she was the boss, who would question her? She hoped that the moving van was still there and she'd have a chance to look inside it. Something good had to come of this day. Her spirits sagged, as did her enthusiasm for her roles as informant and now manager of an *upscale* titty bar—had to be an oxymoron.

She dashed back to the hotel and changed into something that looked more bar-bossy—a pair of black leather slacks and a red silk blouse. Fingering her hair, she let it fall loosely around her shoulders. Good enough. She wasn't working for tips.

Abby heard the heavy bass thump of music from the bar outside her hotel. A younger clientele strolled between restaurants and clubs, replacing business-attired people who hours earlier had dashed between work and lunch. The line of patrons from the Sky Bar stretched two blocks down Elm Street as she approached. Tiny saw her coming and cleared a path to the door, giving her only a cursory nod.

She stepped inside and stood against the wall while her eyes adjusted to the dim lighting. The room seemed huge, even crammed with people. It was a daunting thought that everything that went on inside this large piece of real estate was now her responsibility. Was it even possible to control so many alcohol-fueled individuals in a room with half-naked women? One thing in her favor was that only three people knew she was the boss. She could observe with anonymity and get a feel for how things worked.

Abby inched her way around the perimeter of the room to one of the bars and ordered a vodka tonic. A blond bartender with particularly nice breasts handed her the drink and a napkin with a phone number scratched on it. If Abby's heart hadn't been so full of Loane, she might've been tempted, but no one else stirred her interest in the least. She took the drink that was only intended for camouflage and downed a gulp so fast her head throbbed in protest. Leaning against a support pillar, she reminded herself that she had to stay focused to pull off her double duty. Any slip could prove costly.

As she looked around the room again, Abby saw the young woman she'd hired earlier, Kinsey. In a pair of low-slung jeans and a rib-hugging T-shirt, she was trying to balance a serving tray in one hand and fight off a groping patron with the other. The tray wobbled precariously before tumbling to the floor as she gave up in favor of self-preservation. She was obviously not waitress or dancer material. Abby thought again that she should fire her for her own protection. But she liked her and wanted to help her.

As she was about to intervene, Ray rushed to the table. From her vantage point he appeared to be chastising Kinsey for her clumsiness and apologizing to the man who'd been groping her ass. She couldn't hear the exchange, but Kinsey was not happy. With hands on her hips, she faced off with Ray.

Unfazed, the beefy bouncer reached out and grabbed Kinsey's breasts in his huge hands, turned back to the patron, and grinned. Abby moved closer and heard him say, "*This* is what you're getting paid for. Got it?" Kinsey shoved his hands away, slapped his face, and bolted toward the back door.

Abby left her drink on the bar and started toward Ray, her feet stomping the floor like a raging stallion's. She didn't care if this was a topless bar; nobody disrespected her employees. Halfway across the floor her anger cooled. If she allowed her caretaking gene to emerge, she'd certainly blow her cover. She forced herself to back away and instead went after Kinsey.

She found her sitting on the back steps and joined her. "You okay?"

"Sure."

"I tried to warn you."

"I can handle it. Set boundaries at the start."

Abby admired her strength. She'd put Ray in his place but was still willing to work somewhere she didn't like. "The point is that you shouldn't have to, especially not with fellow employees." She didn't want to say what came next. "Kinsey, I think maybe this job isn't—"

The young woman turned to her, reaching for her hands. "Please, M, don't fire me. I need this job. I'll be all right."

"It doesn't seem to suit you. Can you do anything else?"

"What do you need?" Her eyes burned with desperation and Abby felt compelled.

"Do you know anything about bookkeeping, records, stuff like that?"

"Isn't it all a bunch of numbers?"

"More or less." Oh, the innocence of youth. How simple they made things sound. "Come back tomorrow around noon and we'll look at the accounting software. If you can help with that, we might be able to work something out. But please, no more waiting tables." She smiled and gently squeezed Kinsey's arm.

"What about Ray?"

"He's about to feel the wrath of the new boss."

Kinsey started to get up but put her hand over Abby's where it rested on her arm. "You got a boyfriend? I know that's a personal question, but I like you."

Abby didn't usually get into personal discussions with anyone, especially not employees, but Kinsey was different—innocent and unthreatening in a way that reminded her of a teenager before know-it-all-itis set in. Maybe it was her large inquisitive eyes that begged for trust. "I'm not into men."

"A girlfriend, then?"

The question was a painful reminder that she had no idea where she and Loane stood. Should she answer based on her desires, Loane's perspective, or current circumstances? "Yes, no, I'm not sure."

"Well…I don't know much about you, but you seem like an awesome woman. When you figure out where you are, give me a shout. I know people—"

"Thanks, Kinsey, but I'm not in the market. I appreciate it."

"Okay, see you tomorrow." Kinsey smiled and strolled toward the front of the building.

When she was gone, Abby walked through the parking lot toward where she'd left the moving van. With everybody busy inside, this was a good time to check out the cargo. She'd be in and out in minutes. As she rounded the corner of the building, she stared at the vacant space in the lot. The truck was gone and with it her chance to inspect its contents. For the second time today she felt totally unproductive—no closer to Loane and no closer to finishing this seemingly endless case.

Chapter Ten

Standing in line at the Sky Bar, Loane felt like she was trapped in a glass bubble, able to see and hear, but not truly connect—totally out of context. She was shoved along with the crowd pushing its way toward the door. People talked but their voices didn't register, like wind through trees, saying nothing of significance.

As a cop she would've observed from a distance, listened for information, and been unaffected. After Vi's makeover, she wanted to test her new look, not be a cop, and see if she could fit in. But the whispered words around her—words of want, need, desire—only made her feel more separate and isolated. As young, hard bodies rubbed against her and pushed closer to the door, she ached to be touched, but her heart and mind railed against it.

She hadn't thought about love or sex for months. Gorgeous, dark-haired women were easy enough to find, but she couldn't delete one, insert another, and carry on like she had in the past. Abby had triggered something in her that defied logic and transcended sex. But those once-tender feelings had started to harden and corrupt everything she encountered. The sweetness now tasted bitter. Passion morphed into anger. And hope too closely resembled revenge. That was, after all, why she stood at this moment at the enemy's door.

"What the fuck do we have here?"

She recognized the ponytail-wearing bouncer as one of the employees who had accosted her across the street. Time to test her new role. "A paying customer."

"We don't let pigs into our establishment. It's a respectable place."

The crowd moved back, probably anticipating an altercation or perhaps an opportunity to slip past the preoccupied bouncer. "I'm not a cop anymore. Just looking for a good time."

Ponytail gave her a sideways evaluation. "You might look different but you still smell like pork."

"Fuck you, man. I don't need this shit. I can spend my money somewhere else." She bluffed and turned to leave but got help from an unexpected source.

A guy in the crowd said, "Come on, Tiny. What's the holdup? Move along."

Another yelled, "Yeah, what the fuck?" The crowd joined in, chanting, "Let us in."

Tiny buckled under the pressure. "What the hell. Give me your damn money…and you better not cause any trouble. Got it?"

She handed him the cover charge and waltzed inside. Tonight wasn't about being on alert or reconnaissance. It was about inserting herself into this scene. She'd never been in the club out of uniform and felt a bit naked. At the same time, her body hummed with excitement. Being in a target-rich environment of recklessness and temptation was quite an aphrodisiac. The emotions she'd suppressed for months surged to the surface, seeking a means of escape.

A curvy brunette brushed up against her. "Buy you a drink, lover? I'm Rachel." She was definitely Loane's type—long, dark hair, nice breasts, and a sexy voice.

"Why don't I buy you one? Find us a quiet spot." Loane took her order and came back to the table with four shots of tequila and two beer chasers. If she wanted to fit in, she had to play the part. Nothing like alcoholic lubrication to loosen up her behavioral monitor.

Loane wasn't a big drinker, so the first shot of tequila flooded her system with heat. She welcomed the immediate buzz, happy to relinquish any portion of the sadness that clung to her like black to a widow. Refusing to think about the past, she downed a second shot and rested her head against the cushioned booth.

Rachel scooted closer and Loane felt the heat of her body. She remembered a time that would've been enough of an invitation, but she wasn't into subtlety these days. Rachel pressed her lips to Loane's neck, kissed her lightly, and licked a trail to her ear. No doubt what Rachel wanted now, if her body would cooperate.

She took in Rachel's tight skirt and low-cut blouse. They cradled her shapely ass and generous breasts to perfect advantage. Normally she would've been wet already from looking at Rachel's assets, but she felt nothing. She closed her eyes and imagined Abby instead—long, wavy hair sifting through her fingers, full lips sucking on hers, curvy body sliding hot and wet against her. Instantly aroused, she opened her eyes, trying to hold the image, and ordered another shot of tequila. It would take more than two to pull this off.

"Would you like a lap dance?" Rachel asked.

"From you or one of the dancers?" At this point she didn't care, as long as someone touched her before the inspiration passed. She didn't want to want it, but she had denied herself any emotional outlet for so long that her body seemed constantly on edge. She'd even lashed out at Vi a couple of times. Sex was a safer and less complicated outlet than the depression and volatility she'd been experiencing. She chugged the third shot, praying for mental numbness and sexual abandon.

"Whatever you want, lover. But the dancers aren't allowed to do much and you can't touch them." Rachel inched closer and rubbed her breasts against Loane's arm. "I don't have those limitations."

"Why not both?" The alcohol had definitely sunk in. Loane hardly recognized her own voice. "Her." She pointed to a topless dancer with long chestnut hair that fell in curls past her shoulders.

Rachel approached the young woman, slipped several bills into her bikini bottom, and pointed toward Loane. The two women walked toward her and she thought how alike they looked, both short, brunette, and curvy—how similar to Abby.

Rachel nodded toward the dancer. "This is Erin. Erin, meet… oops, I don't even know your name, lover."

"Loane."

"I like that," Rachel said as she slid a chair away from the table and indicated that Loane should relocate. "It'll be easier."

Loane sat down and stretched her legs, the new skinny jeans feeling a bit too snug in the crotch. Erin's body was lean and rhythmic, swaying back and forth in a cadence that would've kept a hula hoop spinning for hours. She drank her beer chaser as Erin danced a slow, seductive number. "Nice." Her breasts were perfectly palm-sized, nothing to waste. "Very nice." She reached out but Erin spun away.

"Not allowed, but I can touch you." Erin straddled her lap and rubbed her breasts against Loane's chest. "You like that?"

Her breath caught in her throat as bare flesh teased too-sensitive skin. "Yes." Everything aligned at once—too much alcohol too quickly, too little sex too long ago, and too many feelings too close to the surface—and her control slipped. She might've stood a chance against one of her flaws, but in combination they were overpowering.

From behind, Rachel ran her fingers over Loane's close-cropped hair, massaging her scalp. It felt intimate and sensuous, and she wondered why it felt better with less hair. Rachel kissed her earlobe and tongued the sensitive rim of her ear, releasing a flood between her legs.

Loane wanted to grab hold of something tangible, not be tormented with one more thing she couldn't have. Erin rocked her pelvis forward, driving the seam of Loane's jeans into her tender clit. Driven by sheer animal need, she cupped Erin's ass and humped against her, grinding, straining for more contact. She buried her face between Erin's breasts and breathed the scent of arousal rising from her crotch. God, she needed to come. It had been so long and she physically ached. A few strokes would be enough. She held Erin against her, pumping faster. A few more—

"What the fuck? Get your damn hands off her."

Loane opened her eyes and saw the two bouncers she'd encountered before looming over her like a couple of tanks. She was so close to orgasm her legs trembled. For an instant she considered finishing. Erin didn't seem in a hurry to move.

"I told you not to cause any trouble," one bouncer said as he pulled Erin off her lap.

"You're the one causing trouble. I'm trying to have a good time."

"There's no touching the girls. You know the rules." The other guy nodded toward the front door. "Don't come back until you can follow them."

Loane didn't move. She couldn't. Every nerve in her body was firing toward her crotch. If she moved she'd have a screaming orgasm or rip something apart with her bare hands. Humping a stranger in a public place had nothing to do with intimacy or even sex. She needed a release…any release. Right now Mutt and Jeff looked like good targets for her aggression since they'd interrupted her method of choice. She balled her hands into gloved fists, rose from the chair, and started toward them.

"Hey, lover, why don't we finish this elsewhere? This place has become unfriendly all of a sudden." Rachel tugged on her arm, urging her in the opposite direction. "Come with me."

She looked from the two bouncers to Rachel—fight or fuck. Easy decision. "Yeah, sure." By the time they worked their way through the throngs of people and got outside, she'd sobered up a bit. "Maybe some other time?"

Rachel slid a hand down her chest toward the zipper of her jeans. "I could take care of this little problem pretty quick. I'm very handy."

"Those guys killed the mood. Rain check?"

Rachel backed away, obviously disappointed at the abrupt end of her sure-thing evening. "Okay, I'm here most nights. Come find me."

As Loane watched Rachel reenter the club, she doubted she ever would.

❖

"Yo, wait up," Vi called from across the street.

Loane kept walking. "I'm not in the mood."

"Know what you're in the mood for. Can't help with that." She caught up, looking like the same lost, bedraggled kid she always did. "Bad scene back there. You could get cooties from that one."

"Piss off, Vi."

"Look, dude, I know you're hurt, horny, and probably headed for a hangover, but don't take it out on me."

Her body quivered with the sexual energy she'd tamped down. Without thinking, she grabbed Vi's sweatshirt and shoved her against a building. *"Leave me the fuck alone."* She stared into Vi's startled green eyes, trying to decide if she wanted to hit her, kiss her, or beg her for a hug. As the adrenaline oozed from her body, leaving her weak and ashamed, she slumped to the pavement and buried her face in her hands. "I'm so sorry."

"Can't blame you. Everybody wants to touch me tonight."

Loane looked up at Vi's grinning face and laughed…and kept laughing.

"It wasn't *that* funny."

"How do you know when I need to lighten up?"

"Duh, you're always wound tighter than the inside of a baseball."

"Still, I had no right to do that. I'm not usually violent. I don't know what's going on with me lately. Everything pisses me off."

"Wanna talk about it?"

"No." If she talked, she'd have to admit that all her emotional issues were rooted in pain and sadness. And she'd have to acknowledge the growing possibility that Abby was gone forever. She didn't want to say those things out loud. It would hurt too much.

Vi slid down the building beside her and was quiet for several seconds. "You sure made a splash on your first night out. Should've waited for your wingman. I could've covered while you got your freak on with the brunette."

How the hell did Vi know about that? She hadn't seen her in the club. Her intelligence-gathering skills rivaled any organization, government or otherwise. "Are you following me again?"

"Nope. Whoever the brunette is, ditch her. I've found the perfect woman for you."

"Not interested."

"You don't even know who I'm talking about."

"And I don't care, Vi. I'm not interested in seeing anybody… special."

"Then you wouldn't like this woman. She's very special."

Loane rested her forehead against her knees and had the overpowering urge to cry. Abby had been a special woman. Why hadn't she told her? *History. Think about history.* Not one single fact sprang to mind, but words tumbled out of her mouth.

"One of the people who…died in the explosion was…my lover, Abby." Vi remained uncharacteristically quiet. "I should've been there, should've saved her. I tried, but it wasn't enough. Never quite good enough." She looked at her hands and then wiped her eyes as tears threatened.

"I'm sorry." Vi rested her hand lightly on Loane's shoulder. "I didn't know."

"How could you?" She took a couple of deep breaths and looked up at Vi. "I didn't mean to unload on you. I don't even know you."

"Yeah, but you know you can trust me. Freak." They both chuckled, now back on familiar ground. Vi went quiet again, as if changing the subject required serious concentration. "You interested in some case-related intel?"

Just because Vi knew the cop lingo didn't mean she knew good information from bad. But after her meltdown, Loane owed her the courtesy of listening. "What you got?"

"The new manager of the club drove a moving van in last night."

"News flash—that's not significant."

"I'm not done, brainiac. It was loaded with boxes marked 'furniture' that were never unloaded at the club."

"So…" Her patience was wearing thin again. She was exhausted, horny, and aching to slip into the condo and relax.

"So, the boxes weren't like any furniture boxes I've ever seen—long, rectangular."

Suddenly Vi had her complete attention. "Is the truck still at the club?"

"Nope. Ray, the tree-trunk goon, drove it to a storage place near State Street and off-loaded the boxes into one of the units."

"Playing detective?"

Vi shook her head.

"Then how do you know this?"

Vi shrugged.

"That's not going to get it. You need to be honest with me."

"I know things, that's all."

"No, that's not all. You could get seriously hurt or killed screwing around with these people, Vi." An image of the explosion ripped through her mind and she shivered. "I can't be responsible for that. Do you understand me?"

Vi seemed genuinely contrite. "Yeah, I do now. But I'm not doing anything dangerous. I watch stuff. I'm no hero."

"And promise you won't ever try to be."

"What's the matter, copper, starting to like me?" Vi nudged Loane with her elbow. "I knew I'd get you eventually. I'm like a bad cold."

She wasn't about to admit that she actually had a soft spot for Vi. Her ingenuity and independence reminded Loane of herself as a young officer, before the reality of procedures and politics blunted her enthusiasm. "Where is this storage place?"

"Gate City Storage on State Street."

"Did you actually see inside the unit?"

"Duh, yeah, number twenty, back side on the end. Looks like the place is full of boxes. Ray was pretty nervous while he was unloading. What do you think is in there?"

"Not sure yet." She pushed up from the sidewalk, pulling Vi with her. "You *have* to stay out of this. If you hear anything, let me know. Otherwise steer clear. I mean it."

"Okay. Don't blow a gasket. Wanna swap digits in case we need to get in touch?"

"Sure." After the exchange, Loane started toward her condo, then turned back. "By the way, how did the job interview go?"

"Got the job. Keep you posted." She slung her backpack over her shoulder and disappeared around the corner.

As Loane slipped into the back entrance of Center Pointe, she wondered again where Vi got her information. She obviously had resources. Did it matter? She couldn't afford to take anything for granted. She wanted to know who Vi was, what motivated her, and how she fit into the big picture, because Vi obviously had her own secrets.

Chapter Eleven

Abby clicked on the QuickBooks icon on the club's computer but nothing happened. She hated computers almost as much as numbers, so this was a double dose of hell—and all before lunchtime.

She'd come in early to search for the boxes of "furniture" that she was certain weren't here. Aside from the huge dance floor, lounge, and restrooms, the building had only three other rooms. She searched every space large enough to conceal even one of the mysterious boxes and found nothing. Frustrated and disappointed, she'd retreated to the office.

The paneled room resembled a walk-in closet, and every time she entered she was afraid someone would close the door and lock her inside. The air-conditioning system struggled to force cool air to this windowless part of the building. It was always stuffy and smelled of stale man scents—sweat, cheap cologne, cigarettes, and sex. She made a mental note to buy an air freshener and then scrolled down to the QuickBooks icon again.

She clicked the gold-and-green symbol, and this time the program opened. It might as well have been written in Egyptian hieroglyphics. Opening a few files, she scanned the endless pages of entries. They all looked the same, tedious and boring, with no obvious irregularities. She could be looking at thousands of dollars of embezzled funds or redirected monies and have no idea. A degree in fine arts didn't exactly prepare her for a foray into the world of cybercrime or money laundering.

"Damn freaking machine." She stabbed at the keys to exit the program.

"That doesn't usually help."

"Holy crap." Abby spun around in the desk chair and saw Kinsey Easton standing in the doorway. At least it wasn't Ray or Tiny, who'd be more inclined, though no more entitled, to ask questions. "You scared me."

"You're the boss. You're allowed to be in here. Me…not so much."

"I thought I was alone. What can I do for you, Kinsey?" The young woman was dressed more conservatively than she'd been last night. Khaki slacks and a subtly patterned blouse made her look even younger, if that was possible.

"You told me to come back at noon…about work?"

She pointed to a chair for Kinsey to join her. "It would be a godsend if you could figure out this accounting system. I have no clue."

Kinsey turned the computer screen toward her and took the wireless keyboard in her lap. Her fingers moved across the keys so fast Abby couldn't follow what she was doing. A few clicks later she sat back in the chair and smiled. "Yeah, I can do this."

"Did you major in computer science in college?"

Kinsey shook her head. "I picked it up. Like some people learn music, I'm basically self-taught."

"Impressive. Why didn't you tell me this yesterday when we talked about a job?"

"I didn't know what kind of system you had. That makes a difference. This sure beats waiting tables."

Abby's shoulders relaxed and she leaned back in her chair. Kinsey might be the answer to a prayer, and it would keep her out of harm's way in the club. "You're hired, but one thing." Now came the difficult part, explaining what she needed without it sounding like an unusual request. "I need a complete analysis of the books—account balances, income, expenses, a breakdown of operating costs, and anything that looks or even feels irregular."

"Sounds pretty routine for a new boss."

"I'd like you to back up the system every day and make an extra copy for me, just in case. If there's ever a question of tampering, I'll have daily tallies of everything. That should make finding any potential problem easier, shouldn't it?" She hoped she hadn't gone too far and looked to Kinsey for confirmation. Once she got her hands on the backups, she'd pass them along to Barrio or Bowman or whoever was now in the pecking order. She didn't need to worry about interpreting what was on them. ATF had experts for that sort of thing.

"Makes sense. I can do that, no problem. Who's my boss?"

"Me. If anybody else asks about the business, let me know. You can be trusted to do that, right?" For some reason she felt a little guilty for asking the question. Maybe it was the way Kinsey had handled herself with Ray that made her feel a kinship with her. Maybe it was her resilience. Either way, she was confident that she had a reliable ally.

"After last night, I'm not in the favoring mood with Ray or Tiny, the manhandlers." Her slight frame shook. "You can count on me, M. When do you want me to start?"

"How about right now?" Abby relinquished her seat at the desk and watched as Kinsey hunched over the keyboard, immediately lost in her task. With any luck she would find something that would either implicate or exonerate the Torre family. Abby hadn't considered life after this case in almost four months. Now she dared to hope that it wouldn't be long until she returned to some semblance of normalcy.

"Will you be all right here by yourself for a while? I need to run an errand." Kinsey waved her off like she were a pestering sibling. She scribbled her cell number on the pad beside the phone. "If you need me or anyone questions what you're doing, call."

Kinsey nodded.

Abby fast walked the few blocks to the historical museum, anticipation riding her like an impatient mistress. Something told her that her search for Loane would soon be over. The thought released equal parts joy and panic. She'd replayed their reunion in her mind thousands of times: a brief period of disbelief, the entire gamut of emotions, hours of explanation, ending with days of lovemaking and years of what—happily ever after? As she reached for the museum door, she wondered if she was fooling herself.

"I need to see Ms. Winters, please." Abby evaluated the woman manning the desk and decided that any disruption to routine daily operations would not be met with pleasantry. She had the look of a guard on death row: stocky build, black dyed hair, and thick glasses perched on the bridge of her nose.

"I'm sorry, ma'am, she's in meetings the rest of the day. If you'd like to leave your name and number, I'll have her call when she's free."

"It's important. I'd prefer to wait, if you don't mind."

The woman peered over the rim of her glasses as if Abby's refusal to leave violated royal protocol. "As you wish, but as I said—"

"She's in meetings the rest of the day. I'll wait." Abby settled into an uncomfortable straight-backed chair and pulled out her cell. Might as well be productive. She texted Carl: *Hope you got my message last night, arrived safely. Things going well. Hired office help. Nothing else to report.* That should keep him off her back for a while. Since she didn't know where the shipment she'd brought up was now, she assumed the guys had taken care of it. She put it on her list of things to ask about later.

After an hour of restless sitting, she did a slow circuit around the museum lobby, reading literature about the building and exhibits. She called Barrio and confirmed that he had indeed given Bowman her cell number and she was to channel information about the case to him. He didn't bother to elaborate on his motives for the change of procedure.

Two hours later she was still waiting to see Eve. The over-protective administrative assistant hadn't even offered her a glass of water. It was close to four thirty. She needed to get back to the office to see if Kinsey had had any luck or encountered any problems. "Excuse me, ma'am, can you contact Ms. Winters? It's important that I see her. It's a personal matter."

The woman looked at her like that was not even remotely possible. "I'm sure she'll be—" The phone rang, and she held a finger to her lips as she answered.

"Greensboro Historical Museum. Oh, yes, Ms. Winters. Things are going fine. No problems here." She looked at Abby as if deciding whether to mention her. "There is a lady who's been waiting for some time. She didn't have an appointment. I don't know what she wants. She said it was *personal*." The more questions she answered, the more flustered and embarrassed the woman became. "I don't know her name." She looked up at Abby.

"Abby Mancuso." She spoke loudly enough to be heard on the other end.

The assistant didn't need to repeat it. "Yes, ma'am, right away." She hung up and pointed to an office at the rear of the complex. "You can go on back."

"Thank you so much." Abby tried to keep the bite out of her voice but she'd wasted half a day. She knocked on the office door and Eve opened it immediately.

"I'm not sure if I'm shocked or on the verge of a heart attack. You look pretty good for a dead woman."

"The reports of my death are greatly exaggerated." Abby tried for a little Twain-ish humor as Eve evaluated her with penetrating blue eyes.

"I'm glad those looks come with brains…though I reserve the right to retract that statement." She motioned to a seating area in front of her desk and waited. She wasn't going to make this easy, but Abby didn't blame her. Apparently everyone in Greensboro thought she'd died in the explosion.

"Eve, is Loane okay? I had no idea that—"

"That she almost died trying to save you? That she doesn't know if you're dead or alive? That she's spent the last three months in hell looking for you? Or that she loves you so much that everything else is secondary? Which part didn't you know?"

Eve's words stung more than the burning cinders on the day of the explosion. She felt as if someone had squeezed the blood out of her heart. Her breath wouldn't come. "I…didn't know…any of it." Tears burned her cheeks. "So sorry."

"All you had to do was make *one* phone call."

Abby remembered how often she'd wanted to do that, the times she'd forced herself away from the phone, and the countless nights she'd cried herself to sleep because she hadn't. "I know."

"I'm not the one who needs to hear this."

"I don't know how to get in touch with Loane. If I can't find her, I can't explain this whole mess…and she could be at risk. I have to tell her."

"After everything she's been through, you show up bringing more trouble? I can't imagine why she would listen to anything you have to say." Eve stood up and walked toward the office door, her intent clear.

"Please, Eve, give me her number."

"Can't. If she wants to get in touch with you, she will. That's the best I can do."

"At least tell me if she's okay."

"She's still alive, if that's what you're asking, but she's far from okay."

Abby felt like her life was crumbling even as she tried to piece it together. If this crucial bit fell away, the rest wouldn't matter. "Thank you for seeing me, Eve. Please have Loane call me as soon as possible. I *have* to explain." She wrote her number on the back of one of Eve's business cards and handed it to her.

She had no idea if Eve responded to her request or if the assistant acknowledged her departure. She walked back to the club in a daze, Eve's words swirling over and over in her mind. *"She almost died trying to save you. She doesn't know if you're dead or alive. She's spent the last three months in hell looking for you. She loves you so much that everything else is secondary."*

She loves me.

Hope soared inside her like the ocean at high tide. She laughed aloud, skipped a few steps, and then stopped suddenly. Before she could fully embrace the euphoria, sickening guilt twisted her insides into a tight knot. She'd hurt Loane by leaving and not telling her the truth…about anything.

Loane had come after her that night, been injured, and spent months trying to find her. Abby had been through her own hell after the explosion, but she couldn't imagine what Loane had experienced thinking she was dead. So much had happened. Was it already too late for them?

Loane ducked between a building and landscaping timbers behind Gate City Storage, waiting for darkness. Fast-food wrappers littered the space, and the ground stank of urine and rotting garbage. Squatting for better concealment, she immediately regretted it, gagging on the unpleasant odors. She'd always disliked stakeouts for these very reasons. She turned her head sideways to take a shallow breath, and her cell phone vibrated against her hip. She ignored it. Time for action, not talk.

The storage manager had been very helpful earlier when she posed as a potential customer. Loane had located unit 20 exactly where Vi said it was and memorized the spot on the fence where she'd enter later to avoid the motion-sensor lights. Contrary to popular belief, the manager didn't retain keys to the units once they were rented. The customer kept all keys to his lock and distributed them as he saw fit. In practice it worked great. In police practice, it was a pain because it required a search warrant for entry. However, she wasn't acting in an official capacity. She didn't need a warrant because she was technically and legally breaking and entering.

It was the first time she'd ever intentionally broken the law, aside from the idiotic strictures still on the books that tried to regulate her sex life. She hated to admit it, but the repressed thrill-seeking side of her enjoyed lurking in the shadows and avoiding detection. The ordered, rule-bound side of her cringed at what she was doing. Part of her wanted to call her police buddies and do things the right way. But they'd failed her once, and when the system failed, somebody had to fill the void.

Nerves bunched in Loane's stomach and she searched for her customary balm. *1927 Charles Lindbergh piloted the* Spirit of St. Louis *to Greensboro and appeared at the War Memorial Stadium.* Her memory flashed back to family meals when she was a child. Her father entertained them with history facts disguised as thrilling stories. He was so proud of his city and the work he did as a cop. He'd wanted them to share his love of her past and gave them *Jeopardy* quizzes to test their knowledge. She'd taken to it immediately as a special bond she shared with him.

When she'd come out as a lesbian at fifteen, meal times were hijacked by her mother's rants against her lifestyle *choice*. Her father served as her champion over and over until the constant battles wore him down. Loane withdrew, reciting historical facts in her mind to avoid the conflict and pain. Three years of constant bickering and unrelenting homophobia later, her father filed for divorce and moved out. The separation had been her fault, and nothing she could do was enough to make him stay.

Her cell phone vibrated again, pulling her out of the unpleasant memory. She breathed through her nervous jitters, checked the area around the storage facility once more, scaled the fence, and dodged patches of light to the back row. Her heart pounded against her chest, and adrenaline filled her with daring. She'd heard arrestees talk about the high of committing a crime, like a cop's rush during a chase or a junkie's drug fix. She looked around again, fear dimpling her skin, and decided she preferred being on the legal side. Risking her life was bad enough, but the possibility of being punished for it wasn't appealing. Never again, she promised herself.

Removing the lock pick from her pocket, she held the tiny flashlight between her lips and jiggled the lock. On the third attempt, it sprang open. She took considerably longer to raise the squeaky door without alerting the entire neighborhood.

Once inside the unit, she stared at the stacks of boxes and shook her head. If even half of these contained weapons, the drug cartels along the East Coast would easily outgun the police. She opened the crate closest to the door—bingo. Every preferred weapon on the cartel's list to wage war against the police: FN 5.7 pistols, nicknamed cop killers because of their armor-piercing capacity; Barrett .50-caliber sniper rifles; Colt .38 Super automatic handguns; and AK-47 and AR-223 rifles. It couldn't be this easy. She checked several other boxes, and all contained weapons.

She reached for her cell to call the police but hesitated. She should report what she'd found so these weapons could be confiscated before they were distributed. How could she justify not doing that? Abby had probably died trying to find the source of this pipeline. If she turned the weapons over, they could be shoved into the same black hole with the rest of the investigation and she'd be no closer to finding the truth or Abby.

She tried to think like a gunrunner, but this didn't make sense. Why the huge supply in one place? The product demand had either dried up, the delivery pipeline had been compromised, or someone was stockpiling for a big payday. Why this place? If she was hiding millions of dollars' worth of illegal weapons, she'd use a more secure, more confined space with limited access. Maybe it was a brilliant move—detached from the rest of the Torre holdings and accessible by outsiders—plausible deniability. And how did Vi fit into the picture?

How had she found this place? Maybe she was involved in the case and pretending to help Loane as a distraction from some larger issue. What could be larger than a shitload of illegal guns on their way to a drug war? That idea was too convoluted. It was more likely Vi had a stake in bringing the Torres down. But what was her motivation and how far would she go to accomplish it? Those answers moved up her list of things to find out.

A dog barked in the lot next to the facility and the hairs on her arm prickled. She ducked into the shadows and pressed her back against the inside wall of the unit. All she needed was to get caught in a storage bin with a shipment of weapons—by the suspects or the police. She crouched on her hands and knees, peeked around the corner, and scoured the area, but didn't see anyone. She cocked her head to the side and listened for anything unusual. Breathing a bit easier, she dusted her palms on her jeans and stood.

Using her small flashlight and cell phone, she took pictures of the weapons. Not that she could show them to anyone without incriminating herself, but still she had proof. Maybe the storage manager would be helpful again and provide the renter's name. She'd bet money that it wouldn't be a Torre. She carefully replaced the container lids, slowly lowered the unit door, and slipped over the fence.

On her way back downtown, she looked at the missed calls on her cell phone. Eve had phoned a few times and Tyler once. She dialed her brother first. "Ty, what's up?"

"Hey, sis, a couple of things. Some woman called here looking for you. Wanted to know where to find you or how to get in touch. She didn't leave a name and I didn't offer any information. Sorry."

"Probably someone from the police department. I left you as my contact." She dismissed it as unimportant. "What else?"

"I've been snooping and got a look at the autopsy on Simon Torre."

"How did you manage *that*?" Her pulse quickened. She was so proud of her brother for going against the flow and trying to help her. Better late than never.

"Hey, I'm not without resources, and I'm kind of handsome, too."

"Yeah, you are. So, anything interesting?"

"As a matter of fact, yes. Simon Torre had more than a trace of phencyclidine in his system at the time of death."

"That shit causes hallucinations and paranoia. Why would a man his age take PCP?"

"Your guess is as good as mine. Thought I'd mention it since it was unusual."

"Thanks, Ty. Everything else okay?"

"Pretty much. The wife's still gorgeous, the kids are driving me nuts on my off days, the PD still sucks, and you're still gone."

"Sounds normal. See you later…and thanks again." Wealthy, elderly men weren't normal users of PCP. It usually appealed to a younger set that snorted it or laced their marijuana cigarettes with it. Another odd factoid of this case that she filed away.

She hung up and dialed Vi's number. She needed answers, and either Vi would give them to her or they'd part company. She'd had enough of unreliable people and their well-meaning secrets. When she got Vi's voice mail, she hung up and decided to find her downtown. She parked in the parking deck and strolled past the park, but saw no sign of the wisecracking kid.

After picking up a coffee, she walked Elm Street, checking the few places she and Vi had met in their short acquaintance. She didn't even know where Vi lived or worked, much less where she hung out.

And you told her about Abby. Not very smart. By the time she'd covered the eight-block central business district twice, she'd given up finding her.

As she passed the Sky Bar on her way home, she decided it couldn't hurt to put in another short appearance. After being thrown out the other night, she might not be welcomed like a high roller, but this place was connected to the case and she meant to find out how.

❖

When Abby got back to the club, Kinsey was walking out the door. Her mind was still at the museum with Eve Winters, but she shook off her preoccupation. "Hey, slipping out early?"

"Not really. Finished some of it and left an analysis program running." Kinsey's grin was childishly innocent, with a touch of pride thrown in.

"Finished?"

"It's easy if you know what you're doing—not that you don't, M."

"I don't. If you have a second, I'd love to see what you found."

Kinsey followed her back into the office and clicked a couple of keys on the computer. She pointed to a small icon at the top of the screen. "See that?" Abby nodded. "That means the program I installed is running in the background. When the little wheel stops spinning, it's finished and I'll be able to pull out the data."

"Okay…"

"Basically, I don't know anything yet." Kinsey's tone indicated that she had suspicions about something but wasn't ready to commit. "I'd rather wait."

"Wait for what?" Tiny stood in the office doorway glaring at them like they were trespassers.

Abby moved toward him to shield Kinsey and block the computer screen. The less he knew about what she was doing, the better. "I'm computer illiterate. I hired Kinsey to handle the club accounting."

"That's my job."

"Not anymore. Carl authorized me to hire any staff I needed. Besides, the way business is picking up, you'll be more valuable to me on the floor." She tried to massage his ego and downplay Kinsey's involvement so he wouldn't see her as a threat. "I want somebody to keep up with income and expenses, nothing too complicated." Tiny twisted his ponytail like a distracted first-grader. Maybe he was trying to wind up his brain.

"Yeah, I guess that'll be okay. If you need anything, kid, let me know. But don't change the password. I need to get in sometimes—payroll stuff."

We'll see about that, Abby thought. "Tiny, what happened to the furniture I drove in? I haven't seen anything new in the club. Did you unload it yet?"

"Nah, they sent the wrong stuff. Had to take it back."

"Too bad. We could use some new tables and chairs." Abby stalled until Kinsey signed off the computer. "See you tomorrow, Kinsey. Have a good night."

The young woman smiled at her and pushed past Tiny on her way out.

"I'll be here a while tonight, Tiny. How do I contact you or Ray if I have questions?" He scribbled two cell numbers on a Post-it and handed it to her. She walked out with him, locked the office door, and followed him into the club.

She watched in amazement as bartenders mixed drinks, waiters slung orders, and dancers enticed patrons of every description. If the very existence of places like this didn't insult her sensibilities, she'd be impressed with the simplicity of the operation—large open space, add booze and babes and open the doors. The bar seemed to operate at maximum efficiency with minimal problems. By midnight, she was emotionally exhausted from her talk with Eve, the run-in with Tiny, and hours on her feet. She wanted to go to the hotel, have a very hot soaking bath, and sleep.

As she headed toward the back door, she heard a yell from the front of the club and circled the floor behind a group of spectators egging on some sort of activity. The crowd broke into periodic cheers and she pushed in for a closer look. Two people stood against the wall, lost in the moment, undulating with a rhythm that broadcast their intent.

She recognized the woman facing her, an attractive, petite dancer with long brown hair and a curvaceous body. Abby couldn't see the other person's face. His hands were splayed against the wall on either side of the dancer's head, corded muscles bulging along his tattooed arms. His jeans-clad quads rippled with contained energy. The dancer knelt in front of him and teased her fingers up his calves, along his thighs, and toward his crotch, barely skirting the apex.

Abby shivered with excitement and immediately felt embarrassed.

Sex was a private matter. She wasn't used to intimate public displays, and this one was against club rules. She called Ray and worked her way through the crowd toward the couple.

The dancer straddled the man's thigh, her slender legs pressing against his like a rider on a horse. She bucked back and forth, rubbing their centers together. Then she cupped her breasts and offered them to him, withdrawing before his lips closed over an erect nipple. The dancer pressed her body tightly against the patron and ran her fingers through his close-cropped white hair—hair so similar to the color of Loane's.

Abby sighed as she remembered their last lovemaking session. Her mouth dried and her skin felt hot and sticky. She was tired, and fatigue made her susceptible to her real feelings and to mistakes that could blow her cover. It would only take a few minutes to help Ray break up the scene. Then she could leave. As she reached the couple, Ray grabbed hold of the man's shoulders and pulled him off the dancer. The guy turned around swinging, made contact with Ray's jaw, and sent him stumbling into the crowd. She moved toward the man, unsure how to stop someone almost twice her size. As she reached for him, someone grabbed her from behind.

"Not a good idea." *Loane.* Undeniably her lover's silky voice. Before she could respond, she was deposited like a sack of potatoes on top of the bar away from the ruckus.

The scene played out in slow motion. Loane stared at her for a split second, her crystal blue eyes haunted, hurt, and gouging into her soul. Then she turned and rejoined the fray. Abby squinted into the dim light desperate for another glimpse. It *was* Loane. She looked different, much thinner, with tight muscles close to bone. Her beautiful platinum hair color was the same but cut close and styled differently. The lovely shoulder-length locks that had feathered around her face were gone. And her face was marred by silver-studded piercings, hollow cheeks, and eyes dimmed by pain. But her lips were still full and kissable. She reached out, but Loane was already across the room.

She'd waited months for this moment, to see Loane again, to know she was all right, but now she couldn't move or formulate a single coherent thought beyond how much she wanted to hold her. Abby's heart raced as she struggled for an appropriate segue from this melee to love. The months of crying, waiting, and worrying flooded in and she ached—ached to go back in time and erase it all, back to that night and the decision she'd made that changed everything. Loane was here, safe, within arm's reach, and she was paralyzed with fear.

Across the room, Loane assumed a defensive stance and waited for the man to attack. When he advanced, Loane's arms and legs moved with the speed and grace of a master. She delivered one sharp kick to the side of his knee and he collapsed. Ray and Tiny gave Loane an appreciative nod, grabbed the man's arms, and dragged him to the exit.

Dancers and patrons immediately surrounded Loane, patting her on the back and standing way too close. Without even a glance in her direction, Loane backed up and made her way to the front door, followed closely by a busty brunette. Abby jumped off the bar and waded through the crowd after her. The music started again, dancers closed in around her, and she lost sight of Loane. By the time she got to the street, Loane and the brunette were nowhere in sight.

CHAPTER TWELVE

Hey, where's the fire, lover? Slow down."

Rachel's high heels clip-clopped behind Loane as she sprinted toward the condo. Tonight she didn't care who saw her, who knew where she lived, or who followed. The only thing on her mind was getting far away from Abby. She couldn't believe she was in the city and hadn't contacted her. But she hadn't bothered to call for months, so why was Loane surprised? Still, when she'd thought Abby was in danger at the club, she hadn't hesitated to act. What a sucker. She called back to Rachel. "Hurry."

It was the second time in as many nights that she'd left the club too fucked up, for one reason or another, to blow off some sexual steam. Well, not tonight. Rachel had offered her services and Loane wasn't too proud to say yes anymore. She needed to erase the image of a living, breathing Abby and to exorcise painful emotions that reignited with the slightest breeze.

Loane fluctuated between rushing to Abby and never seeing her again. How could she reappear as if nothing had happened? Didn't she know how much her leaving had hurt Loane, how much it still hurt? Perhaps she'd moved on with her life and for some perverse reason came back to put a period on their relationship. Maybe Abby had never truly cared about her.

She pulled Rachel into the elevator, pressed the button to the penthouse, and backed her against the wall. Rachel raised her skirt and lifted one leg onto the railing, revealing only a thong. Pulling Rachel's naked leg between hers, Loane rubbed against her from her knee to the apex of her thigh, then cupped her sex. She was already wet. Loane looked into her brown eyes and saw Abby's staring back at her. Desire vanished.

When the elevator door opened, she considered sending Rachel back to the lobby. *Don't be stupid. You need this.* She refused to let the past ruin her night. "Want a drink?"

"All I want is you. I've been waiting for this."

Soft illumination from outside flooded the condo, and Loane didn't bother to turn on a lamp. Too much light and she'd have too clear a picture of Rachel and what she was about to do. Besides, darkness suited her mood.

Rachel grabbed the waistband of Loane's jeans and pulled her to the white flokati rug in the center of the room. When she unzipped her jeans, unbuttoned her shirt, and shucked her clothes to the floor, Loane didn't object. Abby was alive and safe and *here*. Loane's heart raced. Abby was so close, but Loane hadn't deserved even a phone call. She looked out across the eastern skyline, willing her body to cooperate and her mind to disengage.

Streetlights twinkled in varying shades of white, yellow, and gray. Stoplights changed intermittently from red to yellow, then green, and back again. The muted sound of enthusiastic passersby and the steady thumping bass from the club wafted up from below. She struggled to connect as Rachel knelt in front of her. This *was* what she wanted. This was what she needed to feel alive and whole again, wasn't it?

Rachel grabbed Loane's ass and buried her face in Loane's crotch. Her breath was hot, her tongue searching. Loane closed her eyes. She saw Abby's face in the club, her brown eyes full of surprise and, what, love? Damn it. She pulled back. "I'm sorry." It wasn't working for her. *She* wasn't working for her.

"Please…" Rachel looked up at her.

"But I can't—"

"You don't have to do anything. Let me take care of you."

If only she could. Loane wasn't sure that was possible anymore. She didn't even seem to be able to take care of herself. Rachel lowered her head again as she slid a hand between her legs. Loane watched their vague reflection in the window like a black-and-white porn movie. Her legs were slightly spread, breasts exposed, facial expression nonexistent. Rachel knelt in front of her, her head bobbing up and down. She felt nothing.

The woman in the window was almost skeletal, bone poking out around muscle. The pallor of her skin was like that of a corpse. Sunken eyes stared out of a ghostly thin face. What had happened to her? *Abby*. She watched as the woman in the window grabbed hair in her gloved fists and pulled a lover tightly against her crotch. "Fuck me, harder," she begged. Rachel teased the tip of Loane's clit with her tongue, but Loane wasn't aroused. She concentrated on the warm tongue stroking the length of her shaft.

"So good," Rachel moaned. Loane flexed her knees to open wider, wanting to come but not wanting her. Rachel slid a finger inside her and she settled onto her hand. "That's right, hon."

Hon. "Oh, Abby, I need you. Make me come." Suddenly the hand was gone, and she pumped air. "What the—"

Rachel stared up at her. "I'm not Abby."

"I didn't say that…did I?"

Rachel's expression was the only answer she needed. Loane straightened and moved away. "Please leave. I've made a mistake."

"It's okay. I can be whoever you want for one night."

"No, you can't." Nobody else could be Abby. "Just go."

When Rachel collected her belongings and left, Loane went into the bathroom and closed the door. She couldn't look at the stereo images of the haunted woman in the windows any longer. The dim glow of a nightlight seemed perfect with the faint odor of disinfectant. This space was exactly what she needed—solitary, impersonal, cold, hard, and devoid of memories.

She stripped off her gloves and hugged the tile wall, pressing her body tight against the coolness. The throbbing between her legs spread to her limbs and into her chest. Why had she stopped? For months she'd silently suffered the pain and guilt of losing Abby, smothering any outward expression, refusing comfort. Now her insides felt like dynamite ready to detonate. Another wave of need spiraled from her center and she slid down the chilly tile wall to the floor, clutching herself as she collapsed.

Forking her clit between her fingers, she stroked and begged for relief. She pulled and jerked the tender flesh until it hurt. At least she felt something. Stretching out on the floor, she shoved a finger inside and flinched at the abrasive dry entry. But she kept thrusting, squeezing and milking her clit. She pawed and scratched like a deranged animal, desperate for release. Her body revolted, salty tears and fetid sweat the only moisture it would relinquish, mocking and confirming that she didn't deserve pleasure.

The pressure inside her was unbearable and she refused to give up. Continuing the painful penetration, she grabbed a breast and dug her nails in. She twisted and pinched her nipple until all she felt was pain at both ends. A twinge of desire sparked between her legs and she clutched her clit again, pulling and urging. *Please...please.* She pounded and plunged harder and faster. The spark disappeared. Exhausted, she surrendered to the burning ache of abused flesh and the sharp, coppery taste of blood.

She curled into a fetal position with a wail. The pain of losing Abby escaped like a torrential rain. It was so unfair. Three months had not been enough time. She realized now that she'd been falling in love with Abby—but hadn't had the courage to tell her. Was this her punishment?

Bottled-up emotions clawed their way out. She shook with staccato sobs and didn't try to stop. With each tear that fell, she remembered Abby—her head thrown back as she climaxed, her golden-brown eyes sparkling with morning light, her soft lips pressed against Loane's flesh, and her always-gentle words of support. Those times were the sweetest and now the most agonizing of her life. Abby was here again but still gone.

It felt like hours before she was aware of her body, stiff and exhausted on the cold tile floor. She rolled over on her back, every muscle objecting to the movement. She ached like she'd been beaten. She ran a soothing hand down her middle.

Tendrils of arousal trailed her touch. She closed her eyes and thought of Abby. Abby's hand caressed her now, gentle and encouraging. She relaxed, opened her legs, and gave in as delicate fingers soothed bruised flesh. Whispers of breath stirred and teased fine hairs across her clit. She bucked, desperate for a firmer hand.

"Relax, hon. Stay with me." She imagined Abby's soft voice, the tip of her tongue rimming her ear. The urgency disappeared. Abby was here. No need to rush.

Loane was wet, ready, and so willing to let her do whatever she wanted. Abby's finger slid inside her and her mouth claimed her swollen clit. "Yes." She wanted to look at Abby—to see her eyes staring up at her, her hand buried inside her—but knew she shouldn't. Instead she surrendered to the subtle rhythm, the goose bumps on the surface of her skin, and the gently building pleasure underneath.

"I want to make you come hard and fast."

"I'll come any way you want." She rocked back and forth as the pace increased. The pressure in her crotch built, filling her body with a fire demanding escape. Her heart was full of Abby—her delicate touch, her whispered words, and her desire to please and satisfy. "Oh God, yes…" With a long, deep thrust and one final tug on her clit, she came over and over and over.

All that had been confined and denied in her released in one continuous flood. The tightness in her chest evaporated. The tension that had bound her body disappeared. "I love you, Abby." She opened her eyes, searching for Abby's warmth, her smile. She found only cold tile, an empty room, and her own hands cleaving like a lover's between her legs. "Oh, Abby."

The tears came again, and again she didn't hold them back.

❖

Distantly, Loane heard a phone ringing and reached to answer it. Her hand brushed across the tile floor and stopped at the edge of the bathtub. She didn't want to open her eyes. She remembered where she was and how she'd ended up here. Abby. After she finally climaxed, she'd been too exhausted to move and had passed out on the bathroom floor. She'd slept soundly despite the hard surface. She pulled herself up slowly, stretching the kinks out of her back and hips. Then she made the mistake of looking in the mirror.

She flinched at the image staring back at her. Her short hair was plastered to her head like a ball cap, eyes red and swollen, and checkered tile indentions marked the side of her face. She followed the scored pattern from her cheek down her naked side, to her leg and onto her foot. Her left breast sported an obvious black-and-blue handprint, and her nipple showed traces of dried blood. She reached for her robe and pain shot from her breast to her crotch, almost bending her double. "Jeez."

Clinging to the sink, she tried to blot the previous night's events from her mind—running away from Abby in the bar, carelessly bringing a stranger to her home, almost having sex with her, the desperation of her own need, and finally making love with a ghost. For a brief moment last night she'd been with Abby again, at least in her mind. She shook her head at the reflection in the mirror. "You're pathetic."

Her cell phone rang again and she followed the sound to the pile of discarded clothes in the living room. "Yeah."

"Loane, where have you been? I've called half a dozen times since yesterday."

"Eve?"

"Of course it's Eve. You told me not to call unless it was urgent. This qualifies. We'll be right over."

"We?"

"Thom is coming with me. Be there in fifteen minutes."

If Eve needed her partner's emotional support, something had gone seriously wrong. "Can't you tell me over the phone?"

"No, and this can't wait." Eve's tone was all business, and she knew better than to question any further.

She showered, made coffee and, while waiting for her friends, tried Vi's cell again. This time when she got her voice mail, she left a message asking her to call as soon as possible. She checked her own voice mail next and got the six messages Eve had left, all the same: *call me, it's important*. No message from Abby. Surprise. With each second that passed, her anxiety grew. When the elevator bell finally announced their arrival, Loane had worked up quite an imaginative story in her mind.

"Is it Tyler? Has something happened to him? Are you and Thom okay? Is someone hurt…dead? Tell me!"

"Sit down." Eve guided her to the sofa facing the view of a city shrouded in fog as dense as the confusion in her mind.

Thom went straight into the kitchen, returned with a glass half-full of amber liquid, and handed it to her. "Drink this."

"You're scaring me now. Tell me what's wrong."

"Drink, for medicinal purposes," Thom said. She sat down beside her and waited. In times of emotional need, Thom was the person Loane wanted at her side. The fact that she was here both frightened and comforted her.

Loane took a big gulp of the Jameson whiskey and felt the warming sensation slide down her throat and into her limbs. She finished the drink and stared at Eve.

"This might be a shock, so prepare yourself. Interesting look, by the way."

Loane raked her hands through her short hair, wishing it were long again so she'd have something to hang on to. "I'm ready."

"Abby is alive."

For a second the world seemed surreal. She let the information sink in and confirm what she'd seen and momentarily questioned last night. How was it possible that Eve and Thom knew Abby was alive when she'd just found out? "I know."

"She came to see me yesterday and—what?"

"I saw her at the Sky Bar last night."

Eve flopped into a chair. "Well, give *me* a Jameson. So much for my big news. Did you talk to her?"

"No."

"Why not?" Eve said. "She wants to talk to you, pretty badly."

Her skin flushed and her insides quivered with a mixture of joy and irritation. One second she felt elated, the next she was totally pissed off. She should be ecstatic; it was what she'd prayed for, but it didn't seem real. Her heart was coming together again but the pieces were jagged and sharp.

"I…couldn't believe it. I've felt all along that she was alive, but seeing her standing in front of me was a jolt. And knowing that she's here and hasn't called…I couldn't handle it."

She thought about her erratic behavior last night and the despair she'd felt. She had actually seen Abby at the club. It wasn't an illusion, as she'd tried to convince herself later. She definitely hadn't made love to her, but Abby was undeniably back. It was inevitable that they'd have to talk sooner or later; too much remained unresolved. "Do you know where she is?"

Eve shook her head. "She left a number. It's different from the one we've been calling." Eve offered her a business card, but it hung in the air between them like something radioactive. She eventually placed it on the coffee table. "I didn't ask her any questions. I'm not the one who needs an explanation."

"Is she…" Loane wasn't sure what to ask. *Alive* pretty much covered her greatest concern. Anything else was a bonus. "How did she seem to you, Eve?"

"Perfectly fine and more gorgeous than I remember."

Thom glared at Eve and then rolled her eyes. "Miss Tact and Diplomacy."

"What? Well, she did." Eve didn't see the problem.

Loane entwined her fingers to stop them shaking. Emotion bubbled up, and she wanted to scream and release the pressure threatening to drive her mad. "Anything else?"

"She said you could be in danger and she needed to warn you."

"Danger?" Her life had been nothing but a series of potholes since

Abby left, and she'd handled them like an amateur. Facing danger with her would seem like child's play.

Thom placed her hand lightly on Loane's shoulder. "Do you want to see her again?"

"Of course she does," Eve said. "That's what she's been waiting for. That's why she changed her whole life and ended up looking like a street punk. She *has* to see her and put this thing to rest."

"Eve." It was the tone Thom used when Eve blundered across the line of acceptable behavior and trampled on someone's feelings. She turned back to Loane. "You absolutely do not have to see her if you're not ready. Take your time. Think about what's happened between yo and what you want."

Thom's words would've probably made perfect sense if she' been thinking logically, but the news about Abby had bypassed h brain and gone straight to her heart. The emotional void that had be her constant companion was now full but throbbing with uncertain and too much hope.

She needed to sort out her feelings before she tried to make a decisions about what to do. But she didn't want to think. She want to be with Abby, to forget everything else, and to pretend nothing h come between them. It just wasn't possible. She wasn't sure she co touch her again without feeling betrayed. Would she ever be enough keep Abby from leaving again? Had what they shared meant anyth at all to Abby? She blanked her mind, refusing to consider that opti and retreated to the familiar to mask her pain. *September 1862, Aut O. Henry, William Sydney Porter, was born in Greensboro. 18 Lunsford Richardson introduced Vicks VapoRub. 1944, servicem and later actor, Charlton Heston was married at Grace Un Methodist Church.*

"Did you hear me, Loane?" Thom asked.

"Sorry, what?"

"I asked how your palms are healing."

"Fine." She opened her gloved hands but kept her fin entwined.

"Mind if I look, to check on my nursing skills?"

Loane wasn't ready to take off her gloves, especially now. news about Abby made her feel too vulnerable. Her palms were stil and scarred, a constant reminder that nothing would ever be the s "Not right now, okay?"

Thom's brown eyes were full of the understanding Loane nee

"Of course. Do you want us to stay for a while? We can talk through this with you."

"No, thanks, Thom. I need time to think."

"It's probably not a good idea for you to be alone. Are you sure?" When Loane nodded, they headed toward the elevator. "Call us if you need anything. Seriously."

"Thank you for telling me this in person. I'll be okay." As she watched them leave, she wasn't sure she would ever be okay again.

She sat motionless on the sofa staring at the business card with Abby's number on it. The unresolved questions swirled in her mind but churned up no answers. Morning turned to midday before she acknowledged that the only way to get answers was to talk with Abby. Finally, with a shaky hand, she reached toward the small piece of paper that Abby had touched hours earlier.

Lifting the card to her nose, she inhaled—no scent of her. Turning it over, she looked at the number scrawled across the surface and her vision blurred. The bold strokes, curly ends of the characters, and the slash through the sevens were distinctively Abby. She dropped the card in her lap and wept for the losses of her past, for the fear of the present, and for the uncertainty of the future.

For two more hours she paced back and forth across the condo before summoning the courage to pick up the card again. She double-checked each digit before dialing and entered the number. After the first ring, she hung up. Opening the balcony door, she stepped out into the fresh air to clear her head, then tried again. Another misfire. Her courage waned in direct proportion to the number of rings.

What would she say when Abby answered? Would she be able to speak at all? Could she bear to see her or was it best to leave things as they were? Abby was alive, and that was all she needed to know. Maybe Abby had encountered serious problems, maybe even been injured herself when she exited her life. If she didn't ask, she'd never understand. Abby had chosen not to contact her and Loane had kept her feelings hidden. Any chance of a relationship between them was probably already gone. What harm could a conversation do? She made the call and this time waited for an answer.

"Hello? Hello? Is anyone there?"

Chapter Thirteen

"Good morning, M." Kinsey dropped her knapsack, pulled up a straight-backed chair, and turned the computer toward her.

"Kinsey."

"Mind if I check on the program I've been running?"

"Nope."

"You all right?"

"Yeah."

Kinsey peered around the side of the computer at Abby. "I don't know you very well and I don't want to get fired, but I'd bet that's not true."

"Why?"

"Hmm. Monosyllabic responses are usually a dead giveaway. No eye contact. You look like you haven't slept. Do I need to go on?"

Abby finally looked up. Kinsey practically bubbled with youth and vitality. Such optimism and hope was like an unwelcome splash of cold water, especially after she'd been up all night waiting to hear from Loane after the scene in the club. She'd left her number with Eve yesterday afternoon; surely she'd given it to Loane by now. Her anxiety level was maxed out.

"Sorry, Kinsey. I didn't get much sleep."

"A woman?"

"Is it that obvious?"

"Not usually. A friend of mine has that look a lot—like something has been ripped out of her by the roots."

She stared at Kinsey and marveled at the wisdom coming from her. "How do you know about such things at your age?"

"Loss and grief aren't age specific. Can I do anything to help?"

If only something could be done to erase the past, to set things right. "Thanks, but it's a waiting game at this point. I've done all I can." For the moment maybe, but what if she'd made another decision four months ago? How would things have turned out with Loane? Abby felt certain they would be together. Her feelings had been and still were true. *Then why did you leave?* The same question tormented her over and over, and her answer was always the same: *duty, responsibility, and an oath—it was the right thing to do—at the time.* Would Loane understand? She prayed that she'd have a chance to find out. Worrying wouldn't help. Work might at least distract her temporarily. "Any luck with the program?"

Kinsey tapped a few keys on the computer and studied the display. "It's still running. Maybe ten, fifteen more minutes." She was already reabsorbed in the information on the screen.

Abby flipped open a file folder marked SUPPLIERS and mindlessly stared at the list. The lines blurred into an image of Loane leaving the club with that brunette. She imagined a look of sexual hunger in Loane's eyes while every inch of her fair skin quivered and strained for release. She visualized a stranger teasing and tormenting her lover. Abby could satisfy her with one quick flick of her tongue. A sickening wave of jealousy bolted through her, and she clutched the folder until the sides buckled and the pages fell out. "Damn it."

She bent to retrieve the sheets but the image remained. Maybe Loane had gotten her message from Eve, and leaving with another woman was her response—screw you. But she wouldn't have known where to find Abby. The point was the same whether delivered directly or indirectly. So why had she bothered to rescue Abby from the combative patron? In spite of their differences, emotion still ignited between them. She'd felt it in Loane's touch and seen it in her eyes. Her tortured stare had initially conveyed disbelief, then fear, and finally something akin to rage. Her anguish had broken Abby's heart. Would she ever be able to soothe so much pain? Would Loane even let her try?

"M…did you hear me?" Kinsey asked.

"Sorry?"

"The program is finished, and we have a problem."

She moved her chair around beside Kinsey and stared at the computer screen. "What exactly am I looking at? You'll have to break it down for me."

"Well, the income and expense columns are pretty normal. The club makes a tidy profit and overhead is low. That's all good. But there's another account being run as a shell company. Someone's using the club as a front to launder money, depositing large amounts into this shadow account and then redistributing it to smaller outside accounts."

She tried to follow along as Kinsey explained, but the figures made no sense to her. "You're sure about this?"

"No question. I haven't nailed down the outside accounts that the surplus is coming and going from, but I'm certain of what I've found."

"Can you tell if it's illegal?"

"I'm not a forensic accountant, but I'd bet on it. Why else would anyone need to shuffle this much money through a back door?"

"Would you put a copy of your report on a flash drive for me? And let's keep this between us. I don't want to raise any red flags until I know exactly what I'm dealing with."

"Will do." Kinsey slid a drive into the side of the computer and a few seconds later handed it to her. "I've transferred my analysis program and the results to an external drive. If anyone else looks at the system, they won't see any trace."

"Perfect. You're turning out to be quite a star employee."

"Thanks, boss."

"Now go to lunch or something. I need to think." This could be a turning point in the case if she could show a connection between the large sums of cash and the guns—guns she had yet to prove even existed. There were too many loose ends. There had to be a link and she wanted to find it...soon.

She needed a break but wasn't likely to get one as long as her mind was on other things. It had been almost twenty-four hours since she gave her phone number to Eve, and she was tired of waiting for something to happen. As she grabbed her purse and headed for the door, her cell phone rang.

"Hello? Hello? Is anyone there?"

"Abby?"

"Loane?" Her pulse raced and she felt almost dizzy. "Hon, is that you?" She heard a small gasp on the other end, followed by a long pause, and her heart ached. "Talk to me. Please. I need to hear your voice."

"Yeah...it's me."

Abby collapsed into a chair and tried to steady her breathing. Those three words were the sweetest sound she'd heard in months. The timbre of Loane's satiny voice warmed her and sent a pleasant thrill up her spine. "Oh, I've missed you. Are you all right? Where are you?

Can we talk? When can I see you?" The line was quiet. "Hon? Are you there?"

"Yeah."

"Still as talkative as ever…and so am I. You know how I get when I'm nervous—blah, blah, blah. I'll do whatever you want, whenever you say, but we have to talk."

"I'm…not sure if…"

The momentary warmth that had filled her evaporated with the chill in Loane's voice. Of course, why would Loane want to talk to her? She'd chosen work instead of their relationship, and she'd let Loane believe she was dead for almost four months. Her pleas to be heard suddenly seemed selfish and insensitive. Maybe Loane had already made other choices and she no longer figured into her life.

"I understand if you don't want to see me." She almost choked on the words as she forced them out. "It's been a while and there are things I should've explained. I've missed you. If you could listen, please."

"Why were you at the club?"

Loane would get the wrong idea no matter what she said. The damage was already done, if the look in her eyes had been any indication. Either she was there officially and hadn't trusted Loane enough to tell her or she was there recreationally. It was a strip club. If Loane had been looking for companionship, why wouldn't she assume Abby was doing the same? "That's part of what I need to tell you."

"Not really. It seems pretty obvious."

The statement was like a jagged arrow, piercing initial pain followed by ripping and tearing with each subsequent breath. "But it's not obvious, Loane. Nothing is exactly what it seems."

"But given enough time, everything finds its own level. It's like a muddy river. It eventually settles and the water becomes clear again."

Abby didn't like the direction this was taking. Riddles weren't her idea of clearing anything up, especially the complicated events that affected her relationship with Loane. "Will you let me explain? Then I'll do whatever you want."

"I cared about you."

Past tense. Abby would've preferred a bullet, straight to the heart. Bullets were fast and the suffering ended relatively quickly. Did that mean she didn't care any longer? "I know you're hurting, and I am too. We owe it to ourselves to sort this out." It seemed like an eternity as she waited for Loane's answer.

Loane sank onto the sofa, her legs unable to support her as she listened to Abby's soft voice. She imagined that she could feel the warmth of her breath through the phone like a caress against her ear. Abby was alive and saying the things she wanted to hear, but could she take the chance? She hadn't taken it before and it had almost killed her.

"We can talk." She had to see her to make sure she was all right. If not, these past months would be meaningless. Whatever happened after that was a crapshoot. She knew what she wanted—still—but wasn't sure it could ever work. Damn Abby for making her care.

Abby exhaled a long breath. "Thank you. Where would you like to meet?"

Loane considered the possibilities. The home that she and Abby had loved in was no longer available. The condo was her hideaway and not a place she wanted to share with her yet. She had no idea where Abby was staying and didn't want to ask. "How about Lake Daniel Park at the picnic benches?"

After a pause Abby answered. "Sure."

"I'll be there in ten minutes." She imagined a hint of disappointment in Abby's voice. Did she expect a more private meeting place, a continuation of where they'd left off? A neutral public place where they'd have to contain their emotions and talk calmly was best. Considering Abby's avoidance over the past months, Loane wasn't sure even the constraints of public decorum could curb her reaction once she was near her again.

"See you then." Abby closed her phone and looked around the small office. Kinsey was at lunch. Tiny and Ray weren't due until late afternoon. None of that mattered. This place didn't matter. Loane had called and she was going to her. She'd hoped for a more intimate setting, but she'd take whatever she could get. She just had to be sure she wasn't followed and that Loane was protected.

She wanted to freshen up, change clothes, look her best but didn't have time. She felt like a teenager going out with the first girl she had a crush on. She was anxious, but this wasn't any woman; it was Loane. Their deep connection was still tangible, even through the phone line. What she wore wasn't important. What mattered was how to convince the love of her life that she was precisely that, when everything else she'd told her was a lie.

Five minutes later Abby sat at the picnic table and watched Loane walk across the wilting grass toward her. God, she loved to see her move. She made a slow walk look like a hooker's stroll down a high-dollar street. Loane wore tight, low-riding black jeans, an equally revealing black T-shirt, and fingerless black gloves. A red tattoo dripped down her right arm, and piercings dotted her usually unblemished ears and lip. Loane's short platinum-blond hair was like the whipped-cream topping on a hot fudge sundae. Her desire for Loane, though never truly dormant, flared. Moisture pooled low in her body, and her mouth dried as she recalled an image of Loane naked, prone, and sated on her bed.

"Abby?"

When she looked up, Loane was standing close enough to touch, but she didn't dare. The warmth of the day disappeared when Loane's cool blue eyes skimmed over her. She brushed a shaky hand through her hair and returned it to her lap. "Hi." How lame. She hadn't seen the woman she loved in months and that's the best she could do? "I mean, how are you?" Without asking she started toward Loane, needing to feel her, to hold her and know she was real.

"Fine…"

She wrapped her arms around Loane but cringed when she didn't hug back. She'd dreamed of this moment every night they'd been apart and refused to back away. This is where she belonged. She pressed her face into the crook of Loane's neck, inhaling the musky outdoor fragrance of her perfume. Quivers of excitement shot through her, and she stepped in until there was no space between them. Loane didn't stop her. She felt their bond immediately and closed her eyes to savor the moment. "I want to kiss you."

"No."

She'd gone too far, taken too much for granted. Loane edged out of her embrace and moved to the opposite side of the picnic table. Abby hated every inch that separated them.

"I'm glad you're all right," Loane said. Her attempt at a neutral expression couldn't hide the delicate worry lines that had cropped up between her eyes and across her forehead since Abby had seen her last. Her decision had cost Loane dearly, and Abby was beginning to realize how much. No job or oath was more important than the woman she loved. How had she rationalized that decision in her mind for even one second? And how could she explain something to Loane that she didn't understand?

"Like my new look?" Loane sat across from her and fingered the spike of hair over her forehead. Abby imagined that was her new nervous tell and found it charming.

"It's different. You've lost too much weight, but you're still the most amazingly attractive woman I've ever seen. Any reason for the makeover?" She regretted the question immediately. Loane's eyes darkened and her features clouded like a stormy afternoon. "Sorry, I'm prying."

"I'd rather talk about you, since I thought you were dead."

Though the delivery was cool, Loane's statement didn't carry the accusation or venom she thought it would. Her tone was that of a truly concerned individual weary from a long struggle and ready for answers. "I should start at the beginning."

"That's usually a good place."

She took a deep breath and sent up a silent prayer that she'd find the right words to help Loane understand what she'd done and why. "My name isn't Abby Mancuso."

CHAPTER FOURTEEN

Loane stared at the woman across from her as if she were a stranger… apparently she *was*. She was still the gorgeous brunette with brown bedroom eyes and an alluring body, so perhaps she'd misheard. Breeze rustled through the fallen leaves, creating a whirlpool of color and sound. Maybe she'd been transported somewhere else like Dorothy in *The Wizard of Oz*. Abby's statement seemed out of context and made no sense. "What do you mean your name isn't Abby Mancuso?"

"My real name is Abigail Marconi. Still Abby, just not…" When she looked at Loane, her attempt at humor died in the tension-charged air between them.

Loane's cheeks flushed with anger, her default response to all things not immediately understandable. She tried to speak but the words stuck in her throat, choked out by an overpowering wave of sadness. *Not Abby Mancuso*. Abby reached for her hands, but Loane withdrew.

"Loane, please listen. Let me explain."

"Is that even possible? If you lied about *who* you are, doesn't it follow that everything else you told me was a lie? Why don't I make that assumption and leave right now? You won't have to waste your breath and I won't have to be reminded what an idiot I've been." God, she didn't want to believe that. She'd changed her life on the slightest chance that Abby was alive. The thought that she'd been intentionally misled cast doubt on their entire relationship.

"There's more," Abby said.

"I'm riveted." Her sarcasm tasted bitter but she couldn't contain it. She wanted to be patient and understanding, to hear Abby out, but she'd been knocked off center.

"I'm an undercover ATF agent, not a confidential informant."

"And I'm the director of Homeland Security." She joked long enough to wrap her mind around what she was hearing. If Abby was an ATF agent, she would've gotten some indication, felt it somehow. Wouldn't she? Her handler would've known, but he wouldn't have told her. Bowman wouldn't give her air if she were in a jug. But the death of an ATF agent in an explosion would've made big news…unless there was a compelling reason to conceal it.

As if reading her thoughts, Abby continued. "Two people know who I work for and who I really am—Hector Barrio, Special Agent in Charge of the Miami Field Division, and now you."

"I don't know you at all." The shock of finding out she'd slept with a woman for three months and had no idea of her true identity or that she was lying to her every day rattled Loane's confidence. Her emotional intelligence had never been great, but she'd always been able to depend on her instincts—until now. Had she been kidding herself about Abby's feelings?

"Barrio shut the Greensboro investigation down after the explosion and put a gag order on any news coverage."

Some of the fragmented pieces in Loane's mind shifted and floated to the surface. "That's why I couldn't get any information, a gag order?" She'd painted everyone with the same brush of disloyalty, even her own brother. A sick feeling gathered in her stomach. It's not that they wouldn't help, they couldn't. She'd deal with that later. Right now Abby had more explaining to do. "How did you…ATF?"

"Barrio recruited me while I was in Moscow."

"Moscow? Are you some kind of Russian spy?" The more Abby talked, the less sense it made and the more Loane's head ached. She wanted a simple fix so she could move on, with or without Abby. Her life had been on hold for too long, and she was physically and emotionally exhausted. "Tell me the truth, all of it."

"I was on a three-month residency program at the Moscow Art Theater for a Master of Fine Arts degree from Harvard. At the time Barrio was in charge of international recruiting and we met at a job fair. I had no interest in ATF, but I went with a friend. Barrio made a compelling argument for utilizing my acting skills for something greater. He persuaded me to join the agency. I went from Moscow directly into training and undercover immediately afterward. Nobody knew about me, Loane. It was a condition of my employment."

"Acting, you studied *acting*?" Their three-month relationship flashed through her mind. She thought of how they met, their first kiss, and every time they'd made love, wondering if it had all been some elaborate performance—a way to distract her.

"I know what you're thinking and the answer is *no.* I wasn't acting with you. Everything that happened between us personally was honest and true. Everything I felt, and still feel for you, is real. Could you make love to me and not know that? I'm no good at hiding my feelings."

"Evidence to the contrary. You've fooled the Torres for almost two years and me for months." She wanted to believe their connection was real, but everything was starting to unravel. She didn't know this Abby Marconi, had no idea if she had a family, where she lived, or her background. Maybe their bond had only been about the job.

"That's work, Loane. People in jobs like ours compartmentalize or we'd go nuts from all the things we encounter."

It was the only way Loane had survived the horrendous acts of violence and suffering she'd seen. She wanted to trust Abby's feelings, but this news would have to marinate for a while. "Why did Barrio choose you?"

"He apparently saw potential in me. He had a personal interest in the gunrunning case because it was in Greensboro, and he'd set up that office before moving to Miami. He thought there was a leak and wanted me to find it. I started out working in one of the Torres' strip clubs in Miami and reported only to Barrio."

"What about Bowman?"

"He thought I was dead too. Now he thinks I'm an informant with clout."

At least Bowman was in the dark as well. She couldn't take it if his pompous ass knew things about Abby that she didn't. But none of this explained why Abby couldn't tell *her* the truth or where she'd been all this time.

"What happened…that night?" The memory of it struck Loane as if she were seeing it for the first time. She clasped her hands together to stop the shaking and the image of the explosion.

"Sylvia Torre called while I was at your place. Simon was paranoid, afraid someone was threatening his family. He was convinced they had to leave immediately. She begged me to talk to him. I was never certain Simon and Sylvia were involved in gunrunning. It didn't fit the picture of the people I'd lived with for a year and a half."

A young couple jogged by, and Abby stopped talking and checked their surroundings as if looking for someone. "Are you expecting company?"

"I'll get to that in a minute. When I got to Simon's house, he was out of control. His eyes were bloodshot, his pupils dilated, and he was talking nonsense. I couldn't reach him. Their grandson, Blake, was crying, and Sylvia was on the verge of hysteria. Their daughter-in-law, Alma, tried to calm Simon but nothing worked. So while they packed the SUV, I took Blake to the restroom and tried to think of another approach with Simon. I never got the chance."

"So, if you hadn't taken Blake to the toilet, you'd be dead?"

Abby nodded.

"Were you hurt? What about the child?"

"Fortunately for both of us, the bathroom was in the basement at the opposite end of the house from the garage. Blake was fine. Not sure how, but I shielded him. It was all a blur. My right leg was broken, but otherwise only scrapes and bruises."

Hearing Abby recount her ordeal was painful. It had to be agonizing for her. Loane reached for Abby's hands, unable to resist touching her a minute longer. She wanted to let her know that while everything between them wasn't perfect, she still cared.

"You saved a child and yourself, even with injuries. That's pretty amazing."

"I acted on instinct. I sure didn't have any training for that scenario."

"So the bodies in the SUV—Simon, Sylvia, and Alma?"

"Yes, but how did you know?"

"I followed you that night. I thought you were working the case and I wanted to back you up—whether you wanted me or not." Her skin chilled as she recalled the hopelessness of those moments before she passed out. "I thought you were in the garage and I tried to get to you. Hot metal and flesh don't mix." She glanced at the black leather covering her hands.

"Oh, my God, Loane. You could've been killed."

"Would say I was lucky, but it didn't feel that way. I was in and out of consciousness for a couple of days. Woke up in the hospital with minor burns, a concussion, and these mangled mitts." Would she ever feel comfortable enough to remove the gloves? She didn't want to see pity from anyone, especially not Abby.

"I'm so sorry, Loane."

"I wanted to die. Nothing mattered after that." She didn't want to admit that it still didn't, until today, but she had to know the rest. "You could've trusted me, Abby."

"I know, but I was new to the agency and undercover work, and I'd sworn not to tell anyone. My family doesn't even know what I'm doing. All my life I've been my parents' little girl and my brothers' baby sister—the one who needed protection. This job gave me a chance to stand on my own and do something that mattered."

Loane understood the need to be her own person, to be good enough. When her secret had ripped her family apart, she'd struggled to keep it together—and ultimately failed. The playful banter between her and Tyler had also been about finding her own niche. She got the whole independence thing. She hadn't accepted anyone's help the past four months either, but that didn't lessen the pain of Abby's exclusion.

"Why are you telling me this now?"

"I fell in love with you and that changed everything. I'd already made the decision to talk to you when I got back that night."

"But you never came back. You didn't call. Nothing." Loane heard the pain in her voice and hated her weakness. She wanted to be indignant, to hold Abby accountable, but it still hurt too much. The more she heard of Abby's ordeal, the more ashamed she felt for holding onto her resentment.

Abby raised Loane's gloved hands to her lips and kissed each one. "I was afraid for you. I was worried the bomber would go after anyone connected to the case. Since we don't know who the leak is in ATF, I couldn't take the chance of leading him to you, making you a target. I desperately wanted to call you when I got to the neighbors' house. Believe me."

"How did you make it with a broken leg, carrying a child?"

"I fashioned a crutch from a piece of pipe. It was a slow process."

Loane tried to reconcile the picture Abby's family had of her as a defenseless, dependent individual with the one she'd seen of a self-reliant, resourceful, and highly determined young woman. She'd had more courage than Loane to keep fighting against the odds instead of running away. Her heart swelled with pride at Abby's abilities and what she'd come through.

"After the shock of the explosion wore off, I was relieved because I thought the case was over and I was free to tell you the truth. But Barrio insisted that I return to Miami with Blake and reestablish myself with the Torre family. I couldn't walk for weeks, and when I finally got out of the house, Carl had guards around me all the time. He was afraid that whoever killed his family might return. I became even more determined to protect you. Tell me you understand."

Loane withdrew her hands from Abby's and rubbed her palms

together. She wouldn't lie to her. How could she explain how wrong life had gone? Their chance had been stripped away before she even acknowledged that she wanted it. Actually, she'd given up. She'd never felt worthy of that kind of love, and the universe had proved her right.

"I was out of it for a while, on pain medicine for the burns. When I'd healed enough to be coherent and asked questions, you were gone, presumed dead. I called your cell phone every day and left messages. I tried to find your family…that makes sense now. I wasn't looking for Marconi."

"That must've been hell for you. It was for me, and I didn't think you were dead."

They sat in silence for several minutes. Loane imagined neither of them knew what else to say. They'd shared so much, cleared up so many assumptions and misunderstandings, that it was hard to take it all in. How different their lives would've been if she'd had even a tiny sliver of hope that Abby was alive four months ago. Now that she knew the facts, the hard part began—figuring out how she felt about it.

"Carl said you got fired from your job." When she didn't answer immediately, Abby tried again. "I know that look. You quit, didn't you?"

Heat rose to Loane's face. "Not exactly."

"Let me guess. You went off on your own to find out what happened to me, the bosses didn't like it, and you quit. Am I close?"

Uncanny how accurate she was, but she'd always been able to read Loane like a transparency. "Pretty close. What else could I do? Nobody would tell me anything. I couldn't live not knowing. And I didn't quit. I took an extended leave of absence." She swung her legs under the picnic table like a kid, unable to look at Abby, waiting for her disapproval.

"Loane." When she met Abby's stare, the only thing she saw was understanding and acceptance. "I love you, Loane Landry. I waited too long to say those words for the first time, and I'll never hold back again. Can we get past this?"

This was everything she'd hoped for—Abby alive and well, declaring her love and wanting their relationship to move forward. Why was she hesitating? Because Abby had *chosen* not to tell her the truth about herself and her job. She hadn't trusted Loane and that stung. But they'd only been dating a short time. They hadn't made a commitment to each other, and Abby didn't owe her anything.

"I saw something in your eyes that night, Loane, and I so desperately wanted to hear you say whatever it was."

"Abby, I'm not sure if I can—"

"What?"

"Pretend all this never happened."

Abby straightened and pushed back on her seat away from Loane. The love and hope in her eyes changed to surprise, and the curve of her mouth tightened into a grimace. "I thought you'd understand the sacrifices I had to make starting out in this profession. I followed the rules to the letter to prove myself. It didn't feel like I had a choice, Loane. The commitment was made before I met you."

"One of the reasons I loved my job was because of that commitment, but there's something even more important. You have to depend on your partner in any situation. Knowing she'll be there, not having to wonder about it…ever. For that to happen, you have to totally trust each other. I thought we did." She shook her head, tears welling in her eyes. "I wasn't just your cover officer, Abby. I was your lover and you left me behind that night." She propped her elbows on the picnic table and slumped forward. All the emotions she'd bottled up for months gushed out at once, and she was exhausted.

Abby didn't respond. The only sounds were the rustling of trees in the afternoon breeze, an occasional robin, and infrequent street noises from the surrounding neighborhood. All of the possibilities from earlier had evaporated. Abby loved her, and she was pretty sure that she loved Abby, but it wasn't enough. "Love conquers all" obviously didn't apply to her life.

"So, what happens now?" Abby asked as she wiped tears from her eyes.

Loane's truth would hurt them both, but she had to be honest. "I don't know." Abby flinched and captured her bottom lip between her teeth. "I can't tell you what you want to hear."

"I won't walk away from you, Loane." Her gaze held Loane's and tears fell again. "You're my heart and soul, and if it takes the rest of my life to prove it, that's what I'll do."

"Abby…I—"

"You don't have to say anything, but don't shut me out, Loane. I need you."

She wasn't sure what lay ahead for them personally, but she couldn't let Abby pursue gunrunners alone. "We still have a case to solve. I can't set you loose on the world, a rookie ATF agent, with no guidance." Loane smiled, trying to lighten the mood.

"I have to see it through."

"Do you want some help?" Loane wasn't sure why she'd said that. Her feelings for Abby were all over the place. Though she wouldn't be much help without the GPD behind her, she wanted to maintain contact, even if it was professional, until she figured the rest out.

"I can't ask you to do that."

"You didn't. I offered." Abby looked around the park again like she was expecting someone, and Loane got an uncomfortable feeling. It was like watching Tyler when he was a kid trying to lie. He couldn't pull it off while looking her in the eyes. "What are you not telling me?"

"I don't want you involved in this anymore."

"It's too late for that." Abby's emotional struggle played out across her delicate features. Whatever she was holding back terrified her.

"Don't you get it? I've already lost three people I considered friends. If I lost you, I wouldn't survive."

"I can take care of myself, Abby. We're both in the protection business, so we better get used to trusting that we can take care of ourselves."

Abby's shoulders drooped. "Carl Torre thinks you had something to do with the explosion. That's one of the reasons he wanted me to come back here, to keep an eye on his business and you. He'll be snooping around too. I won't be able to hold him off forever. I'm afraid I might've led him right to you. So you have to really disappear. Let me handle this."

After everything that had happened between them, Abby was trying to take care of her. That had to mean something. Loane wished she knew, gut-level knew, what. "Thank you for telling me. I appreciate that you love and want to protect me, but I'm not going anywhere. We'll figure it out together. Is that why you were at the strip club, following a lead?"

"I'm the new manager. I drove a van up from Miami that I'm pretty sure was full of weapons, but I didn't get a look inside. Now my new office person has found some financial discrepancies in the books. If I could just connect the two, but I don't know where the guns are."

Had Vi met Abby, the new manager? She dismissed the thought. Vi would've said. She smiled across the picnic table at Abby. "I do."

CHAPTER FIFTEEN

"You know where the guns are?" Loane nodded and a spark flashed in her blue eyes. How had she managed to find a stash of weapons while dealing with everything that happened to her? Abby's admiration and affection for her grew even deeper. "Well, don't keep me in suspense."

Before Loane could answer, Abby's business cell rang. She looked at the caller ID and winced. "Sorry, I have to get this." Giving Loane's hand an apologetic squeeze, she answered. "Hello, Carl."

"How is everything?"

The tiny hairs on Abby's arms bristled. The warmth and familiarity that had been in his voice before she left Miami had disappeared. She hadn't been gone long but something had changed. "Things are fine, Carl. The club is running smoothly, capacity crowds every night."

"Where are you right now?"

Abby looked at her watch. She'd left the club before two and it was almost three. "I'm having a late lunch."

"How soon can you be back?"

"In Miami?" The conversation wasn't making sense and she had an apprehensive feeling.

"To the club. I'm in Greensboro."

She felt the color drain from her face and Loane gave her a questioning look. She mouthed, *He's here.* "Why? I mean, is something wrong?"

"We need to talk. I'm in the office and there's a young woman here I've never seen."

"That's Kinsey, the new office person I hired. I texted you about her."

"Still, I'd like to talk, and I have other meetings scheduled this afternoon."

"How soon can I be back?" She asked the question aloud so Loane would know what she was dealing with. Loane gave her a nod to indicate she understood. "Give me fifteen minutes."

"Good. See you then."

Carl hung up and she turned to Loane. "I'm so sorry, hon. He's not happy. I can hear it in his voice. Can we get together later?"

"Are you safe with him?"

"He can be prickly and a bit overbearing, but I've never known him to be violent."

"Do what you have to. I need some time to think."

"Promise me you won't make any decisions before we talk again." She was afraid that the grief and anger Loane had undoubtedly experienced the past months would resurface and drag her back under. "Promise."

"I promise. Besides, you still don't know where the guns are." The smile forming at the corners of her mouth gave Abby hope.

"You're absolutely right. But we better get some proof soon. What if Carl is here to make arrangements to have them moved?"

"I'll keep an eye on them." When they rose, Abby stumbled sideways and Loane circled her waist to support her as if it was the most natural thing in the world. "Are you all right?"

"A little stiff. Guess we both have scars from this ordeal."

"It's from the explosion, isn't it? Your broken leg?" She nodded, and Loane's lips tightened in an expression Abby recognized as an attempt to hide her emotions. She loved her for caring. "Let me know when you're free."

"I'll call you."

When Loane started to move away, Abby held her hand, took out a pen, and wrote her cell number on her arm above her glove. "In case you've already lost my new number. Now you have to do something with it soon. Number one speed dial would be good."

Loane smiled, and Abby watched the gentle sway of her ass as she walked back to her Jeep. Leaving Loane to ponder all this new information by herself didn't set well with Abby. She wanted to be there to answer questions before they became prickly needles in her mind. She wanted to be with Loane, not facing the unpleasant task that awaited her at the club.

When she opened the office door, Carl Torre stood over Kinsey staring down at the computer screen. She squeezed the doorknob until her composure settled. Was Carl computer savvy enough to figure out Kinsey had run an analysis program? Her best defense was a good offense.

"Carl, great to see you." She opened her arms, gritted her teeth, and gave him the most genuine hug she could muster. "What a pleasant surprise." She nodded toward Kinsey. "I gather you've introduced yourselves. Kinsey is fantastic. She's already done an income-and-expense report, and it looks great."

"Yes, we've met and she's shown me the program. Nice work, young lady. But do you mind if your boss and I speak privately?" The tone of his question made it clear that neither she nor Kinsey had an option.

"Of course not, Mr. Torre. Nice to meet you."

Kinsey grabbed her bag and gave Abby a wink on the way out. She prayed that meant Carl was clueless about her questionable discovery. When Kinsey closed the door, she turned back to Carl, the nerves in her stomach a knotted mass. "So what brings you all the way to North Carolina? You didn't mention anything about meetings here when I left Miami."

"Do I need a reason to check up on *my* business?"

"Of course not. I'm just concerned that something has happened." Carl wouldn't meet her gaze. "Or maybe someone isn't happy with my management style?" His head snapped up. One of his goons had whined to the big boss.

Carl motioned for her to take a seat. "Well, you can hardly blame the guys. They get a new boss, a woman, by the way. I forgot to tell them that part. And after only one day, you hire someone new. It had to grate."

"But you understand why I did it, right? I mean, it all seemed strange to me." Abby was taking a risk with her approach, but she had to stir the pot to make the dish she wanted. Carl's expression told her he had no idea where she was going with this but didn't want to look clueless. "The furniture?" she added.

He waited, obviously unable or unwilling to take the bait.

"The furniture you sent back with me disappeared. I thought Ray and Tiny were hiding something. The wrong-shipment story seemed plausible enough, but it didn't ring true. It made me wonder about other aspects of the business. As a new boss, I needed a financial baseline—

for my peace of mind and your protection. They've been running the club almost four months practically unsupervised."

The creases in Carl's forehead deepened. Had she gone too far? Ray and Tiny had worked for Simon, never directly for Carl. She was gambling on the possibility that their loyalty had never been tested.

"I see what you mean. That does make good financial and business sense."

"Thank you." She tried not to let her relief show. Acting was all about expressing emotions, but in this case doing the opposite was more challenging. Emboldened by his agreement, she pushed further. "Do you know for a fact that the furniture was returned? I haven't seen any new stuff come in."

"Let's not get sidetracked with furniture. I have something more important to discuss."

What could be more important than the stability of his business? The answer occurred to her before he spoke and she almost gasped.

"I've got a lead on that cop I told you about. Her name is Landry. Tiny said she's been in the club twice, apparently gone rogue and changed her appearance. Last night she helped the guys with a belligerent customer. I want to know whose side she's on."

Abby focused on Carl, forcing a blank expression when she wanted to scream, to direct his energy and attention away from Loane.

"I want you to get close to her, Abby."

"You want me to what?" She refused to involve Loane in this case any further. The risks were too great. Whatever his plan, she wanted nothing to do with it.

"She's like you—into women—so I figured you could make a move and find out if she had anything to do with the explosion. I wouldn't normally ask something so...personal, but it's for Simon, Sylvia, and Alma."

Get close to Loane? That was indeed her intention, but absolutely not for this man or any of his nefarious purposes. Even the appearance of complying with his request could cheapen her relationship with Loane. She needed to know his intentions. "For what purpose?"

"I don't know yet. I want to be sure she was involved. Maybe we just need enough leverage to get her on our side. Maybe..." He shrugged and Abby filled in the ending with an image of Loane injured or killed. "Consider it a test."

He wanted vengeance for his family, and he wanted to know that he could count on her completely. If she delivered Loane to him, she would have his trust. Never happen. She wouldn't relinquish one hair from Loane's head to this man. "I can't do that, Carl."

"I know I'm asking a lot."

"Why do we need her anyway? Is she still a cop?" She tried to reason with him without revealing things she already knew.

"She's on temporary leave. Sooner or later she'll be back in the fold. An inside source is always useful. Get close enough to exert a little influence. You don't have to sleep with her, unless you want to. I hear she's quite a looker."

The emotions that boiled inside Abby threatened to destroy her composure. A sickening taste crawled up the back of her throat and she swallowed hard. "I'm not comfortable with this, Carl. I'm not into violence or prostituting myself."

"Who said anything about violence? And the prostituting could be fun."

"If you find out she was involved in the explosion, what then?"

"Let me worry about that. In the meantime, think about it. You and I could have a long, prosperous business relationship. But first, I need to know that I can depend on you."

"I saved your nephew's life and might've saved you financially by double-checking the books. How much more proof do you need?"

"More, and you'll understand when we get to that point in our partnership."

What Carl didn't say concerned her as much as what he did. Why had she ever thought he had a kind streak? All that mattered to him was his business and money. "How long will you be in town?" She needed to get off the subject of Loane before she gave herself away. And she needed to know if Carl's offer had a timeline. While she didn't intend to accept it, maybe she could make him believe she had and gain his confidence.

"Until tomorrow. I'll be at the club tonight, to check things out. When I leave, I hope we'll have reached an understanding."

Abby forced her most charming smile. "I'm sure we'll come up with something." *We* certainly would. The sooner she told Loane about this development, the better.

He stood and started toward the door. "I'm off to my meetings. See you later."

Never would be good, Abby thought as he exited. She sat down and covered her face with her hands. This case had tested her endurance, integrity, loyalty, and now her discipline. Every choice she'd made chipped away at what she needed and wanted. If she didn't resolve it soon, she might lose herself completely.

"You okay, boss?"

She looked up into Kinsey's inquisitive green eyes. "I'll be fine if you tell me Carl doesn't know about the diagnostic you ran."

"M, you cut me deep." Kinsey turned her palms to the ceiling and shrugged. "Do I look like the kind of girl who'd leave a trace?"

Abby's sigh of relief bounced off the walls of the small office. "I guess you're wondering why I'm hiding things from my boss."

"I have a pretty good idea."

"You do?"

"You think something hinky's going on. And if I read you right, you don't want to get caught up in anything illegal. Based on what I found yesterday, I'd say you're right, and I'll help any way I can."

She appreciated Kinsey's discretion and offer of help, but still didn't understand her motivation. They'd only met a couple of days ago and didn't know anything about each other. In this instance, she had to follow her gut. Besides, she'd kept their secret from Carl, and that was good enough. "Thank you."

❖

Loane stepped out onto the penthouse balcony overlooking Center City Park and watched a thunderstorm move toward the city. Bursts of light like huge flashbulbs changed to jagged spears that stabbed the earth as the storm grew closer. She inhaled the fresh scent of rain and turned her face into the chilly wind. She'd stayed in the heated South partly because of the distinctive seasons and ever-changing weather. As fall approached, she appreciated it even more. It reminded her of life—never the same, never dull, always challenging.

Challenging, like her relationship with Abby. She'd spent the remainder of the afternoon and early evening thinking about their last encounter and anticipating their next. She'd imagined the warmth and intimacy of their reunion so many times, it was hard to accept the cool, disconnected reality. Abby's hug had stirred her, threatening to revitalize the closed-off corners of her heart and make her believe again. Her body hummed with anticipation while her mind resisted.

Abby had finally answered all her questions and she made sense, more or less. A law-enforcement officer often compromised personal goals for the sake of her career. Abby's reasoning was sound, and

Loane understood it from a professional standpoint, but the previously untouched part of Loane's heart still couldn't accept what had happened.

Fortunately, Abby hadn't pushed for immediate answers. She seemed willing to let Loane think about their situation and reach her own conclusions. So far she'd come to one: she still cared about Abby but wasn't sure they had a future. For the present, she had to solve one mystery at a time, and the gunrunner case seemed much easier than dealing with emotions. She dialed Vi's number.

"Hello?"

"Hey, Vi, it's Loane. You busy?"

"Not at the mo. 'Sup?"

"Can you meet me somewhere downtown? We need to talk."

"The park? There're some dark corners we can skulk around in. I got a rep to protect."

"Five minutes?"

"Yep."

Typical Vi, short, not so sweet, and to the point. Loane closed her cell and started downstairs. She had to envy Vi a little. Her life seemed so simple. Maybe it was her youth, the fact that she didn't have any real responsibilities or seem to care about much of anything. Loane couldn't remember a time when her life had been that uncomplicated.

She'd struggled as a gangly teenager when her hormones led her in the opposite direction from her peers. Fighting to come out in a family with a homophobic mother challenged her very nature. The test eventually destroyed their family, and she'd always blamed herself. She'd gone into law enforcement to prove she could overcome any challenges, but she'd already lost the most important ones. As she approached Vi in the park, she breathed a little easier. At least Abby was alive.

"Dude. Better not rain on my ass," Vi said as another strip of lightning zigzagged the sky.

"I need to know where you got the information about the storage unit."

"No hello, kiss my ass, go to hell, or nothing?"

"I don't have time to be nice." She sat beside Vi on a crescent-shaped wooden bench close to a small stand of trees that provided cover from most of the passersby. "I've given you a lot of leeway. Now I need answers, real answers. It's important."

Vi's green eyes lost some of their customary sparkle. The

persistently upturned corners of her mouth straightened and she suddenly looked years older. She rose and paced in front of the bench as she spoke softly. "The unit belonged to a friend of mine who went missing." Even her voice and the words she used struck Loane as more mature.

"Went missing?"

"She worked at the Sky Bar for six months. One night she didn't show up for her shift."

"What happened?"

"Nobody knows or wants to say."

The look she gave Loane almost broke her heart. She knew exactly what that was like and wouldn't wish that hopeless feeling on anyone. "What did the manager of the bar tell you about your friend?"

"That she quit and left town. End of story."

"Did you file a police report?"

"I tried. I'm not next of kin, and her family doesn't care what happens to her."

"But you should've been able to file eventually."

Vi shook her head in frustration. "After a month of badgering. By that time, she was long gone. You're a cop. You know how much attention a homeless person gets."

Loane wished she could erase the pained expression on Vi's face, but she couldn't dispute what she'd said. It was true, and that fact made her ashamed. She touched Vi's arm and urged her back to the bench. "I'm sorry. That's wrong."

"I just want to find her."

Loane now understood Vi's eagerness to help on the Torre case. She'd lost someone too and that was a powerful motivator. It could also be a reason for vengeance. "Is that all you want, to find her?"

"Well…if the Torres go down in the process, that's a bonus. Nothing crazy."

"We can't connect them to anything illegal yet, so it might not be so easy to find your friend. How does she…?"

"June, June Lennon."

"How does June figure into this storage unit?"

"She rented it when she got kicked out of her apartment, before we met. When she vanished, Torre's thugs somehow found out about it and moved in."

"That was pretty smart for a couple of thick heads like Ray and Tiny. No way to trace the unit back to the club or them."

"Yeah, but they didn't count on me." Vi's smile held a mixture of confidence and determination.

"You told me they took the boxes there. How do you know?"

Vi dipped her head and scuffed her Vans against the concrete walk. Voices from passersby fluctuated around them as Loane waited. Vi seemed to be struggling with how or whether to answer. After several more seconds, she found the courage and looked up at Loane. "I sort of wired it."

"You what?"

"Do I have to spell it out, dude? Electronic surveillance. I thought June might come back to the unit at some point."

"How do you know about that stuff?" Vi's look didn't exactly yell computer guru, so Loane was a bit confused about how a homeless street urchin became so tech-savvy.

"I was bored in school, so I rigged cameras in the teachers' lounge or principal's office for entertainment. It was sort of a hobby at first. Then I hacked the system and changed a few grades to help my peeps. I was good at it. And voilà, a star is born."

"Is the camera at the storage unit still active?"

"Well, duh, of course."

"You know that's illegal, right?"

"I kind of piggybacked on the CCTV system that the cops already had in the area for crime surveillance."

"Have you tapped into anything else I should know about?"

"Probably nothing you should know about, but I'm pretty wired. It's how I get most of the info I pass along."

Loane weighed her current situation against the possibility of finally putting an end to this life-sapping case. She wasn't technically a cop. Why not? If she could keep tabs on the guns without turning them over, she'd cover all her bases. "Can I access it?"

"No problem."

She stared at Vi, seeing her for the first time as not just a street kid but also as an adult who'd lived and lost and now wanted to make a difference. "You're full of surprises. You don't even sound like the same person. Who *are* you, your real name?"

"Why is that so important? Isn't it enough that I'm trying to help?"

"Call me suspicious, but I like to know who I'm dealing with. Don't you have any family?" Sadness enveloped Vi's face and Loane wished she'd found a more tactful approach.

"Not that you'd notice. Parents divorced. Dad skipped. Mother preoccupied with her career and no time for kid. End of family saga."

It was a story Loane had heard too many times, but this one made her want to get personally involved. Vi wouldn't accept her help, at least not directly. She was as proud as Loane and possibly as stubborn. In this instance maybe her identity wasn't necessarily as important as why she wanted to help. Vi had assisted her when she didn't have to, stuck her neck out when most wouldn't, and never asked for compensation. Maybe allowing Vi to be a part of this case would help. "Is this going to come back and bite me on the ass?"

Vi grinned. "Maybe, but you can handle it. Besides, you already know what's in those boxes, and you didn't exactly follow the rules to take a look, did you?"

"How do you know that?"

"I told you, surveillance. So, what's in the boxes?"

Loane thought about her interactions with Vi since they'd met and decided to trust her completely. She'd shared her motivation and proved that she could keep quiet and obtain useful information. Her technical skills had already come in handy and might save her and Abby hours of legwork. "Guns."

Vi's eyes grew wide as she stared at her. "Freaking guns? June's a goner."

CHAPTER SIXTEEN

Abby didn't like the idea of meeting Loane at the club for an update, but she couldn't sneak away with Carl lurking around. Since he already knew too much about Loane, it was best to keep her close. She stood near the lounge and watched patrons stream in like ants to a sugar cube. She didn't understand the attraction of looking at the near-naked bodies of strangers. It was too much like sale day at the produce market—things that were too cheap probably weren't very good.

The club walls vibrated with music so loud that normal conversation was impossible, but no one seemed to mind. The more the customers drank, the less they cared about what was being said and the more they focused on what their bodies wanted. Communication became a series of testing touches followed by responses leading to more intimate touching and finally a commitment between willing parties. Abby watched in amazement and tried to remember when she'd been so free with her body and affections.

She spotted Loane as soon as she entered the front door. Her platinum hair shone in the black light like a beacon. Several heads turned in her direction and Erin, one of the dancers, started toward her. Abby wanted to pounce and stake her claim like some wild animal. But if she appeared too familiar, she'd attract unwanted attention. To make this plan work, she had to take it slow, at least initially.

Erin followed Loane to the bar and rubbed seductively against her while she ordered her drink. Then Abby recognized her—this was the dancer Loane had rescued from the irate customer the first night she'd seen her in the club. A gnawing feeling settled in her gut, and she freely admitted it had everything to do with Erin's proximity to Loane.

"Bees to honey, I tell you." Carl had approached while Abby was preoccupied. "It amazes me that behaviors like this take place in such a conservative city. Guess it proves the old consumerist theory. Give people what they want and they'll gladly pay." His words dripped with sarcasm and a certain amount of perverted joy. "If you're going to distract our cop, you better move fast. Our girls have nice assets—no disrespect intended."

"Then why not have one of them seduce her?"

"Because I don't care about their loyalty."

"I'll take my chances. Besides, she might have more sophisticated taste."

"I hope for your sake she does."

As Carl walked away, she thought how easy it would be to end this charade. She could tell Hector Barrio she was finished and reclaim her life. No more acting, no more secrets, and no more putting up with scum. She and Loane could be together. But that wouldn't solve her problems, namely finding Simon, Sylvia, and Alma's killer, ending an illegal weapons ring, and proving herself.

She walked toward the bar where Erin had Loane pinned between the serving counter and wall. If Carl thought she should make a move, she'd be happy to peel Erin off Loane and get this show started. She would've preferred to give Loane some advance warning but didn't have time.

"Erin." She nodded to the dancer, then let her gaze slide up and down Loane's body in a languid display of interest. "Introduce me to your friend." She stepped closer and gave Loane a wink she hoped would be interpreted as *play along*. Loane inclined her head enough to confirm she understood.

Erin wasn't so easily deterred. "This is Loane. She's one of *my* return customers. Right?" She looked to Loane for confirmation and was obviously disappointed when Loane extended her hand to Abby.

"Loane Landry, nice to meet you…" She played the part beautifully, pretending they'd never met, looking back and forth between the two women for help.

"This," Erin nodded toward Abby, "is my boss, manager of the club. Guess I'll see you another time." She hesitated as if Loane might change her mind and, when she didn't, turned and headed for another mark.

"If she'd stood here one more minute, I might've clawed her eyes out," Abby said. "I don't like anyone's hands on you but mine."

Loane moved closer and whispered, "I love it when you talk dirty. And thanks for the heads up."

"Sorry, didn't have time to explain. Can you handle a little public foreplay for show or am I asking too much?" Loane tensed beside her and Abby feared she'd crossed a line. "You can say no." Using Loane wasn't her idea of a good plan, but she needed to prove herself to Carl while still being honest with her.

"I assume there's a good reason, which you'll tell me later?"

"Yes, but you don't have to go along with it. I don't want you to be uncomfortable."

Loane nodded and braced her elbows on the bar behind her, exposing a tempting swath of skin where her shirt collar gaped open. "I guess we better make it look good."

Now that she had Loane's consent, Abby wasn't sure what to do. She didn't know how to touch Loane and pretend it meant nothing. Public displays of affection weren't her idea of a good time, especially not with the woman she loved. Their moments of intimacy were private and not to be shared or exploited.

"Is something wrong?" Loane asked.

"I can't pretend you're a stranger. I'm afraid when I touch you everybody will know that." If Carl Torre was watching, he'd realize they'd been lovers and their lives would be in danger.

"I thought your degree was in acting, so act. We've just met. I think you're hot. Convince me I should go home with you."

Loane's suggestion of a role-play was exactly what Abby needed. "You're on, Landry. I'll make you yell uncle."

"Bring it."

The challenge in Loane's eyes heated Abby's blood like a siren call. She stepped closer until Loane's left leg tucked perfectly between hers. The chemistry between them grew like a living entity. She let her breath ooze out across Loane's neck and felt her twitch. "You look so good." Lightly, with the tip of her tongue, she traced the delicate ridges of her outer ear and slipped inside. "Taste good."

Loane still stood with her back against the bar, her legs firmly planted. She gazed into the distance as if trying to focus on anything except what Abby was doing to her. She wouldn't look at her and refused to touch her. Abby could almost hear her reciting those damn history facts in her head.

She lightly touched Loane's knee and smoothed her hand slowly up her thigh, redirecting at the last second to avoid contact with her crotch. Loane quivered slightly but made no sound. Abby had dreamed of stroking her again like this, but never under these circumstances. Her body couldn't tell the difference. She ached in places that hadn't been touched in months. She wanted to believe Loane wanted and needed her as much, but she seemed unmoved.

Placing her hand at the open collar of Loane's shirt, Abby slid her fingers between each button, touching skin all the way down to her waistband. Each time they connected, Loane sucked in a breath. Abby rolled her shoulders from side to side, working her breasts against Loane's arm until her nipples tightened. Loane licked her lips and Abby smiled. She was finally getting to her.

"Those jeans are so tight I can see the outline of what I want."

Loane's quad muscle tensed and trembled between Abby's legs, and she almost collapsed. She grabbed Loane's belt for support and yanked gently, twisting as she pulled up. "Are you wet?" This time she was rewarded with a groan.

Loane's excitement sent a bolt of heat down Abby's body and a release of moisture that felt like fire when it licked her flesh. She pressed her center against Loane's thigh and rubbed up and down, again and again. "I need you." She heard the urgency in her voice and hated that she couldn't contain it.

The loud drunken crowd around them faded into the background and all she felt was Loane—her scent, her eyes clouded with desire, her skin so close and hot, and her body straining for control. How was it possible to want someone so much that everything else disappeared?

"Abby…" Loane's hands were on her hips, but she continued to rub against her.

"Please, Loane. Touch me." She guided Loane's gloved hand to her center and squeezed, showing her what she needed. "Right there, just once." If Loane pushed her away, she'd combust. Abby rose on her toes and closed her eyes to kiss Loane, wanting their joining when she came.

"Abby!"

Loane's sharp tone startled her and she opened her eyes. Carl Torre was standing in front of them with a wicked grin. She chilled like she'd been freeze-dried. The thought that Carl had watched them in such an intimate moment sickened her. But she was even more upset that she'd allowed it to happen. She'd cheapened what she and Loane shared by putting it on display.

"Enjoying yourself, Officer?" Carl asked. When Loane didn't answer, he continued. "Do you like your gift?" Loane's confusion must've been as apparent to Carl as it was to her. He took great pleasure in clarifying. "Abby. I asked her to give you special treatment. I'm sure there's more where that little taste came from. Right, Abby?"

Loane looked at Abby, her eyes full of pain, but quickly concealed it before answering Carl. "Great, thanks. But I prefer someone I know." Her tone was as cold and biting as shark's teeth as she directed her next comment to Abby. "I'm not into stranger fucks. But thanks for the warm-up."

Loane turned away from her and walked toward the woman she'd left the bar with last night. Abby felt the life being pulled out of her with each step Loane took. She started after her but stopped when Carl spoke.

"Temperamental, isn't she?"

"What the hell was that about, Carl? I thought you wanted me to get close to her. How exactly did that help?"

"I was curious how far you'd take it. Get her back."

"Are you crazy? She's not a stray puppy."

"What's the matter? Don't think you can do it?"

Resentment rose in her as she allowed Carl to push her another inch past her boundaries. No one told her what to do in her personal life, but to him this was business. She had to go after Loane to maintain her cover but, more importantly, to explain what had happened. Loane seemed all right with the role-play earlier, but knowing Carl had orchestrated the seduction was probably more than she could handle right now.

"If you want me to do this, you have to let me do it my way." She glanced back and forth from the vile man standing in front of her to her lover across the room, being felt up by another woman. "Think fast, Carl, she's leaving."

"Do it. See if she knows anything."

"I won't be back tonight. I trust you can close up." She didn't wait for a reply as she pushed and squeezed across the crowded dance floor toward Loane. Her vision tunneled on the brunette pawing the woman she loved. She'd never experienced jealousy, but she'd also never felt so deeply for anyone. The feeling wasn't so much rage as a sickening dread that drained her.

When she was finally close enough, without saying a word, she simply held out her hand and prayed Loane would take it. Time stalled and the cacophony of sounds around her disappeared as she waited. And waited. Hurt reflected in Loane's eyes as she seemed to consider her options. The brunette rubbed her breasts against Loane's arm and moved in for a kiss. Abby watched the woman's lips getting closer to Loane's, and her stomach tightened with the gut-wrenching rejection.

As she turned to walk away, she felt the smooth glide of leather against her palm when Loane took her hand. "Thank you." Abby cleared a path to the front exit and, once outside, guided her away from the club.

"Where are we going?" Loane asked. Her tone echoed the emotional distance Abby felt between them.

"My hotel room. I'll explain when we get there."

"You've been doing a lot of that lately." Loane's voice held a slight edge of irritation, but she was glad it wasn't outright anger.

"I know, bear with me a little longer." She wrapped her arm around Loane's waist and sighed with gratitude when she didn't pull away. Their chemistry felt so perfect, but the emotional bond fluctuated as their precarious circumstances ebbed and flowed.

As Loane walked beside her in silence down Elm Street, she looked in the trendy art shops and clothing boutique windows as if seeing them for the first time. A casual observer would have thought they were just a loving couple out for an evening stroll. How Abby wished that were true. Could their lives be so normal, if they ever had a life together?

When she closed her hotel room door behind Loane, Abby pulled in a deep breath, preparing for the next round of explanations that seemed to do nothing but hurt Loane more. "Would you like something to drink? The minibar is pretty well stocked."

"No."

She hated it when Loane resorted to one-word responses. It usually meant she'd run out of readily available historical references and was nearing her patience threshold. The stare from her cobalt eyes confirmed it.

"You came on to me because Carl told you to?" Her tone was like ice.

"Absolutely not."

Loane cocked her head to one side and her left eyebrow arched in obvious disbelief.

"Well…not exactly."

"Jesus, Abby, I thought you loved me."

"If you'd listen for a second before you go off like a half-cocked brat." Abby couldn't believe she'd said that. The look on Loane's face said she couldn't either. She hurried to clarify. "I know this whole I'm-dead-I'm-not, coming-back-into-your-life thing is confusing, but for our sake, please don't do anything else stupid until you've heard me out."

Loane hadn't moved since she called her a brat. "You call self-preservation stupid?"

"No, I call taking a stranger home to your bed stupid." Abby regretted the comment immediately. "I'm sorry. That was a cheap shot. I can only imagine what a shock it was to see me last night after wondering for so long. You have a right to whatever comfort you can find."

Loane's shoulders dropped slightly as she moved away from the door. "Then tell me what the hell was going on tonight? I thought you wanted me to play along because we were in the club and it would give us a chance to talk, not because your boss wanted a free peep show."

Abby pulled Loane to the sofa across from the bed and held on to her hands as they sat down. She always felt better discussing difficult issues when physically connected. "Carl wants me to *get close to you* and find out if you had anything to do with the explosion. To him that means physical intimacy, sex, if necessary. I refused, of course, but then thought it might be a perfect way for us to keep in touch without drawing suspicion. It would also help me gauge how much danger you're in." She checked Loane's expression but it gave nothing away. "I didn't want to trivialize what we have by flaunting it in public, but when I got close to you, I got a bit carried away. Sorry." Her cheeks burned as she recalled her uncharacteristic behavior in the club.

Loane sat quietly for a few seconds staring at their joined hands before she looked up. The heat Abby saw in her eyes made her weak. "It was difficult, all the touching, when we aren't exactly…never mind. You did what you had to. It's part of the job."

She didn't want Loane to think her behavior was only about the job. "I enjoyed every minute of being close to you. So you're not upset?"

"That you enjoyed making out so much that you lost control in public? Not hardly."

"I…I…"

"I don't believe you're speechless." Loane sat back on the settee and pulled Abby against her shoulder. The gesture was intimate in its simplicity and Abby relaxed into the embrace.

She closed her eyes and let the steady thump of Loane's heart fill her with a sense of peace. She'd been alone so long that she'd almost forgotten how much she needed someone, and not just anyone—Loane. "This feels so right."

"Abby, I don't want to give you the wrong idea."

"I know. You still need time to think about us, but you have to admit, it does feel good to just sit quietly and hold each other. It's one of the things I missed most."

"It's best if we stay focused on the case right now. That doesn't mean I don't care."

"Sure." Though she agreed, she didn't have to like it.

Loane gave her a reassuring squeeze. "What's our next move, Super Special ATF Agent Abigail Marconi?"

"That just gave me serious chills. Say it again?"

"Super Spec—"

"Not that, the *our* part." Just hearing Loane say the word gave her hope. But she was right. They needed to keep an eye on the target. "First, tell me where the guns are."

"A storage facility. I've got it under electronic surveillance."

Abby raised her head from Loane's shoulder to check her expression. "You're not kidding. How did you manage that so quickly?"

"Wish I could take the credit, but I have an associate who was already watching the unit for another reason."

"Someone you can trust?"

Loane nodded. "Vi. She's actually a bit of a street urchin, but she's trustworthy."

"Have you seen the guns?"

Loane nodded.

"This surveillance isn't exactly legal, is it?"

"No, but we can use it in the short term until we come up with something that is."

"Pretty smug, aren't you, Landry?" Loane's voice was full of the old confidence and determination Abby loved to hear. "If we can tie the money trail to the guns, we're in business."

"Maybe you and I should meet with your office person to compare notes and make a plan."

"That sounds good. I'll check with Kinsey in the morning and give you a call." Almost as an afterthought, Abby added, "What about Bowman?"

She could tell by the silence that Loane wasn't happy about including Dan Bowman in anything. "What about him?"

"I probably need to brief him on what I'm doing. We might need him later."

"If he thinks you're making progress, he'll want to assign another cover officer. It's protocol. Too many people in the mix can be a problem. Why don't you send him the financial stuff and let him play with that? It'll keep him busy while we follow up other leads."

Abby nodded. "But everybody already thinks this case is over."

"Exactly, and it's to our advantage to keep it that way."

"I can't wait until it's done. I want to move on…hopefully with you."

Loane pulled her close and they huddled together for several minutes before she spoke. "And to clarify, I didn't 'take a stranger home to my bed.'" She fingered air parentheses for emphasis. "I freaked out when I saw you at the club. I wanted to have sex with her, to get you out of my head, but I couldn't. Jeez, I even called her Abby. How lame is that?"

"It's fantastic." Abby struggled to contain a laugh. "At least I won't have to take out half of Carl's staff and clientele because they've slept with you." She nuzzled against Loane's neck and whispered her next request, unsure how it would be received. "Would it be possible for us to sleep together tonight, just sleep? I'd like to be close to you again." She heard Loane's heart rate increase as she waited for her response, praying she wouldn't have to let her go yet.

"I'll spend the night, for appearance's sake, but I can't sleep with you, Abby."

Loane waited until Abby was ready for bed and tucked her in. Then she curled up on the sofa and snuggled under a blanket. Abby's heart was breaking. What if this was as close as they would ever be?

Chapter Seventeen

Loane snuggled into the softness against her cheek and inhaled a familiar flowery fragrance. She slowly opened her eyes and the hotel room came into fuzzy focus, light streaming in through the partially shaded window. Abby was sleeping upright on the floor beside the sofa, her head leaning against the cushion close to hers. Loane sniffed the spot in front of Abby's ear below the hairline that always held her unique scent. Her senses absorbed it like a drug. Abby's mop of wavy brown hair fanned out across her shoulders and Loane wanted to bury her face in it, then feel it cascade across her body as she writhed beneath her. Satisfied that Abby was real, she leisurely examined the dips and curves of her body, trying to memorize each one.

Several times during the night she'd woken and checked to make sure Abby wasn't a mirage. Though Abby slept on the opposite side of the room, Loane felt her presence. Even fully clothed, physically exhausted, and with no suggestion of sexual intimacy, it was the closest she had ever felt to anyone. Maybe she *was* ready to take the next step.

She listened to Abby's steady breathing and, with each affirmation of her existence, felt their bond deepen. This woman represented everything she'd hoped for in a partner—courage to chase her dreams, determination to stay the course, willingness to admit mistakes, and most importantly, vulnerability to show love. Abby had opened her heart, made her want things she'd never imagined, and shared all her secrets in hopes of making a life together. Had she been as honest?

She hadn't even told Abby she loved her yet. She'd almost given in last night. Feeling Abby's body against hers, she'd remained outwardly impassive while everything inside her screamed for their reunion. All she had to do was touch her, kiss her, or say those three words. But her most basic question remained: why hadn't she been enough to make Abby stay? Would she ever mean that much to her?

As her body awakened next to Abby, so did her desire. Heat rose like a sudden breeze of desert air. Her body tingled and a hard pulse pounded in her sex. She wanted to pull Abby closer, to explore the energy that vibrated between them. The hunger that clawed at her insides demanded attention, and she needed to satisfy or smother it. But she couldn't reach out until her emotional commitment was as strong as her passion. Abby deserved no less. Taking a final look at Abby's peaceful face, she forced herself to move, careful not to disturb her as she slid away. She quickly scribbled a note asking Abby to call and left.

Her stroll up Elm Street wasn't nearly as enjoyable as with Abby the night before. She missed Abby's arm around her waist, the gentle sway of her hips, and their slow pace as if nothing else mattered. The brisk morning air held a hint of autumn, making the empty space beside her more noticeable. Strange how a person she'd known only a few months could change her entire perspective. Abby had a way of making the ordinary extraordinary, and she wanted that in her life.

She stopped in the street and looked back toward the hotel. Abby was still there, warm and sexy. She could go back and give her a proper wake-up. Looking toward the small alley that led to her favorite sweet shop, she reviewed her options—fresh, flaky muffins and steaming coffee or soft, sexy buns and smoking-hot kisses. No contest. She started back.

"Good morning, Officer."

Carl Torre's voice, raspy like a pervert and full of self-importance, had become ingrained in her mind. He'd interfered with her plans for Abby twice now, and she wasn't likely to forget. She started to pretend she hadn't heard him, but he was persistent.

"Officer…I said good morning."

She turned and looked at him, forcing nonchalance. "Torre." He held a bag from Loaf in one hand and a cup of coffee in the other. It bugged her that he even knew about her favorite bakery.

"Did you have a nice evening?"

He had a smug look on his over-tanned face that she wanted to knock off. "Sorry?" She clenched her fists until her nails bit into her gloved palms enough to hurt.

"With my new manager, the gorgeous Abigail Mancuso."

When he used Abby's undercover name, she composed herself. He didn't know Abby at all if he thought she'd go along with his sick scheme to seduce her for his benefit. However, it was imperative that she maintain Abby's cover. "Absolutely, wonderful night. Thanks for that. How can I ever repay you?"

Carl waved his hands as if she'd offered him money. "Not necessary. Come by the club occasionally and check on her. Who knows? I might need your special skills one day."

"And what particular skills would those be?" She tried to smile but feared it came off as a smirk.

His gaze swept the area around and behind her, never resting on her. "You know cops, jack of all trades and master of none. I'm sure your talents extend beyond female seductions and fruitless surveillance."

So Ray and Tiny had reported their initial encounter on the street to him. Good. She wanted him to think she was curious, but not enough to pursue a police investigation without being paid. If he thought she was motivated by money, he'd drop his expectations and his guard. "You get what you pay for and police departments are notoriously cheap. I'm not easily bought."

"I'll remember that. Well, have a good day. I'm off to Miami. When you see Abby, tell her I'll expect a call later today."

"No problem." As Carl Torre walked away she visualized him covered in snakeskin, crawling on his belly. Maybe it was the fact that he might be an arms dealer or the questionable tactics he'd suggested Abby use to ensure her cooperation. Either way, she didn't want Abby around him any more than absolutely necessary. It was time to put a period on this case.

She turned down the alley off Elm Street that led to Loaf. After her encounter with Carl, she needed something to get the sour taste out of her mouth. Not exactly breakfast food, but she settled on a fresh lemon meringue cupcake and a nonfat latte. She sat at one of the small bistro tables outside, admiring the iron artwork and dazzling wall murals. The bright colors and creative arrangements immediately lifted her spirits as she enjoyed every morsel of the sweet treat and reviewed her plan for the day.

She needed to talk to Vi about the surveillance cameras, make sure she had access and everything backed up on computer. They needed the cameras in place long enough to figure out the dealer's next move. Then the pictures she had of the guns, though illegally obtained, combined with the outside shots from Vi's surveillance and the information from

Abby's new bookkeeper, should be enough for a search warrant. Even if the warrant was flimsy and the case was thrown out, at least the guns would be off the street.

As she scraped the crumbs of the cupcake from its paper wrapper and licked her fingers, Loane reflected on how convoluted and fragmented this case was. She'd gone about it backward, working from the inside out and trying to piece together evidence as she rebuilt a relationship. Procedures and rules worked better for her, gave her a roadmap. She'd even forgotten to ask Vi and Abby if they knew each other. Draining the dregs of her latte, she tried to convince herself she'd made the right choice between breakfast and Abby. A dozen cupcakes couldn't right that wrong. But it was too late to change her mind.

She reached for her cell and called Vi, got her voice mail, and left a message. As she walked back to the condo, Loane wondered what Vi did all day. She seemed to prefer the nighttime hours for prowling and annoying her. And what about her friend, June Lennon? What had happened to her, and what would happen to Vi once this case was over?

After a quick shower and change of clothes, she drove back to Gate City Storage to get the renter's name of the storage unit. A judge or magistrate would require that for a search warrant. Besides, June might have rented the unit in someone else's name. If possible she wanted to keep Vi out of the official investigation. She might be the president's bastard stepchild or a street urchin with no credibility. Either way, they'd both be protected if she verified all details herself.

When she pulled into the lot at the storage facility, she saw the owner's white Miata parked outside. They'd gotten along well last time, and she was hoping for a little more cooperation.

"Good morning, Ms. Hiatt." As Loane entered the office, the silver-haired woman rose to shake hands. Her clear blue gaze held Loane's in a look of total confidence. This was a woman she could be friends with under other circumstances. "Remember me?"

"Tori, please. Of course I remember, the renter who wasn't."

"Busted. I'm Loane Landry with the Greensboro Police Department. Sorry about last time. I didn't have enough information to ask the right questions."

"And now you do."

"Exactly."

"Am I allowed to ask what this is about? I have other customers to protect if this involves something dangerous or hazardous to lives or property."

She evaluated the woman before her, deciding how many details to disclose. Tori Hiatt's concern for the welfare of others indicated not only empathy but also integrity and character. "I believe someone is storing illegal guns in one of your units."

"On the back side."

Loane cocked her head in question. "How did—"

"That was the area you were most interested in last time, not the area where I actually had available units." Smart and observant too.

"Yes, unit twenty. I was wondering if I could get the name of the renter."

Without hesitation, Tori sat down at her desk and pulled out a handful of files. "I can't do that, privacy issues, you understand. It would be a violation of my customers' trust. Do you have a possible name?"

"June Lennon, though I don't believe she's involved. I think someone has taken over the space without her knowledge."

Tori flipped through several pages and pulled one out, placing it neatly on top of the stack. "As I said, I can't *tell* you who rented the space." As she spoke, she nodded in affirmation.

"I understand completely…and thank you. Please keep what I've told you in strictest confidence. This investigation has already cost three people their lives."

"You have my word." Loane had no doubt it was golden.

On her way downtown, Loane's cell rang and she looked at the caller ID: *Unknown*. "Hello."

"Have I ever told you how much I hate waking up in a cold bed? The only thing worse is waking up on a cold, hard floor." Abby's sexy voice was like fire coursing through her.

"Um…I don't believe so."

"Well, I absolutely hate it, especially after being away from you for so long. Can you come back?"

The temptation of Abby waiting in bed for her was almost too much. For the second time this morning, she thought about scrapping her entire day and spending it with Abby, in bed or out. "Wish I could, but I'm running down leads. Rain check?"

"Sorry, I'm pushing. I miss you."

"I know." She hated the disappointment in Abby's voice. "But the sooner we close this case, the sooner we'll have time for…other things. By the way, your *boss* is expecting a phone call."

"Which one? I feel like I'm buried under a tier of bosses, each requiring a more complicated layer of lies." Abby sounded tired and strained. She'd been pretending to be someone else for almost two years, skirting the edges of criminality, maintaining tenuous loyalties without the support of friends or family. Loane could only imagine what that sacrifice required of her. Loane had struggled to isolate herself for only a few months, missing the camaraderie of the department and her support group.

"Carl."

"When did you see him?"

"Ran into him on my way for coffee this morning. I sort of led him to believe we had sex last night…hope that's okay. It seemed to be what he wanted."

"That's exactly what he expected. I'll call him later. At least he's on his way back to Miami."

"Can we get together with your bookkeeper sometime today?"

"That's why I called. She's waiting for us at the office. It's best to do it early before Ray or Tiny shows up. Can you meet us?"

"On my way."

"See you soon…I love you, Loane."

Loane's breath caught in her throat. Abby's easy expression of her feelings always took her by surprise. She started to say something in return. What, she wasn't sure. Before she could decide, the moment passed and Abby hung up. Why was it so hard to say those three little words?

When she pulled in behind the Sky Bar and entered the back, she heard voices from a room to the left and pushed open the door. Abby sat beside a redhead with her arm around the back of her chair. A flash of jealousy streaked through her and took her by surprise. She'd never imagined Abby with anyone else, never even heard her speak of another woman with affection. The feelings she was having now convinced her that she never wanted to. She composed herself and cleared her throat. When the two women turned to face her, she felt her mouth drop open. *"You?"*

"Dude!"

Abby looked back and forth between the young woman and Loane. The small space was quiet for several seconds. "You two know each other?"

"Sort of, but not exactly." Her assistant rose, walked toward Loane, and extended her hand. "Allow me to introduce myself. I'm Kinsey Easton."

Loane struggled to find her voice as Kinsey's hand hung in the air between them. "*Kinsey Easton?* You're Abby's new financial wizard?"

Now it was Kinsey's turn to be surprised. "Abby?" She turned back toward her boss. "That's your real name?"

"What did you think it was, Vi?" Loane asked.

"I always called her M. This is *your* Abby? The dead chick?"

Abby's head swiveled like she was watching a tennis match. "Would someone mind telling me what the hell is going on? Who's Vi? How do you know each other?"

"Abby, this is Vi," Loane said.

"Your street urchin?"

Loane nodded. "And apparently your go-to person as well."

Kinsey smiled. "Yep, that's me. A woman for all reasons and all seasons." She waved her hands between Loane and Abby. "And I can't believe this. You two. Dude, this is the woman I wanted to introduce you to. Should've known you'd be way ahead of me on that one."

"Enough," Loane said.

"But the way you described Vi, I thought she was a…" Abby faltered.

"A destitute waif? Me too. She looks quite different as Vi. That hair of hers is more flame than subtle red, her ears and lips are covered with piercings, her clothes vintage homeless, and her language is just shy of indecipherable street jargon."

"No need to insult," Kinsey said. Her whole demeanor changed as if she'd flipped a switch in a dark room, and when she spoke her voice took on a refined air. "Perhaps you prefer an educated individual? Would you be more inclined to trust me if I sounded upper-class?" Her tone was confident, words distinctly pronounced with a hint of wealthy arrogance.

Loane couldn't suppress a grin of admiration. "Perfection. Where did you learn that?"

"Years of being shipped from one private school to another by a mother who didn't want me around." Kinsey's tone held equal parts bitterness and sadness.

"I assume Vi is responsible for the transformation of your appearance," Abby said.

Kinsey nodded. "Guilty. She had to fit in."

"Why do you call yourself Vi?" Abby asked.

"I'm a computer nerd. It's short for virus. Everybody either wants one or needs to get rid of one. It's how I make a very comfortable living."

"You mean you're not homeless or destitute?"

Kinsey shook her head as if Loane was totally clueless.

It was almost too much for her to fathom. The kid she'd encountered in the streets stood transformed as a young professional woman—smartly dressed, impressively intelligent and mature. She'd been working both sides of the case to find her friend. Vi skulked around in the dark unnoticed, scooping up tidbits of information that people dropped without a thought in front of a nonthreatening street child, while Kinsey Easton collected financial data and electronic surveillance from inside the organization. Even her altered looks served her two personas brilliantly.

"Well, this certainly is a surprise…and quite fortuitous. Everybody is obviously up to speed on everything," Abby said. "So, why don't we put our heads together and make a plan."

Loane pulled up a chair and listened as Kinsey explained what she'd found on the computer. The deposits into the shadow account coincided with dates on which there were transfers of personnel or equipment to the Torre clubs in upstate New York. Withdrawals overlapped with dates that shipments came from Miami. The pattern went back several years, with deposits toward the end of the month and withdrawals in the middle. Unfortunately, the records didn't indicate what goods or services were being exchanged for the money—nothing to tie in the guns.

"Numbers only go so far," Kinsey concluded as she closed the program.

"That leaves us one choice," Loane said.

"I won't like this, will I?" Abby asked as she scooted closer to her.

"Probably not, but I need to follow this shipment of guns, tomorrow or the next day, wherever it goes."

"No!" Abby's tone got Loane and Kinsey's full attention. "I won't have it."

"Oh, oh, a lover's spat." Kinsey bounced like a kid at the movies.

"Shut up, Kinsey, Vi," Abby and Loane said at once.

Abby patted Loane's hand where it rested on her lap. "I can't let you do that. This is my case and I have to see it through. You know the reasons why."

"And you can, but you've got to keep up appearances here without raising suspicion. I have more freedom if we go out of state."

"And less jurisdiction. Do I need to remind you that you aren't actively a police officer?"

"She's got you there, Dude," Kinsey interjected.

Loane gave her another sharp stare before returning her attention to Abby. "Just because you're ATF—"

"AT freaking F?" Kinsey practically vibrated in her chair. "How cool is that? Obviously we're *not* all up to speed. I had no idea." She looked at Loane and shrugged. "She's definitely got you now. ATF trumps local cops any day."

"*Please* be quiet," Loane said.

"Loane, what's the worst that can happen? They've already killed me once."

"Exactly. I wouldn't make it if anything else happened to you, Abby."

"I have an idea," Kinsey offered.

Loane wasn't sure she wanted to hear what Kinsey was about to suggest, but she and Abby seemed at an impasse. "Fine, go ahead."

"What if nobody goes all James Bond? I can attach a tracking device to the van and voilà. We'll know where they are at all times."

Abby shook her head. "We need a warrant for that."

"It'll be a backup," Loane said. "We're following them anyway."

"But we'll still need verification that there's an exchange of weapons for money. Without it, the case is no good," Abby said.

Loane skimmed her gloved hand over her close-cut hair. "Agreed."

"Then we do it together." Abby was staring directly at Loane. "No compromise on this."

Kinsey grinned at Loane, her green eyes sparkling with humor.

"What?"

"I'm loving the hell out of this," Kinsey said. "Waiting to see who wears the pants—big bad A-lone or sweet, sexy Abby."

"Shut up, Kinsey," Loane and Abby said again in unison.

Loane didn't want to attempt any further negotiations with Abby at the moment. Perhaps she'd have more luck in private. "Kinsey, how soon can you get the tracking device in place?"

"As soon as I know which vehicle they'll be using." She reached into her backpack and pulled out a contraption that rested in the palm of her hand. "Have gadgets, will travel."

"They'll probably take the same van I drove up from Miami," Abby said. "It's parked out back most of the time, unless Ray needs it for liquor runs."

"Then I'll do it tonight since there's only two more days in the month. Is that cool with everybody?"

Loane and Abby nodded agreement.

"One more thing," Loane said. "Take the cameras off the storage unit as soon as we confirm they've loaded the guns. Are you sure that little thing," she pointed to the device in Kinsey's hand, "will work?"

"Absolutely, top of the line." She ran her fingers around the touch pad on her laptop and turned the device on. "That little dot is what you'll follow. You can monitor it on your phone once I've downloaded the app, like the video feed from the camera." Loane handed her cell over and watched in amazement how quickly she updated and returned the phone. "Done." The dot on her screen flashed on a map of downtown.

"You're quite something, Kinsey Easton," Loane said with more than a touch of pride. She'd grown attached to the young woman and was pleased she wasn't a poor, homeless runaway. "Easton, Easton." She repeated the name, letting it settle in her mind, certain it should ring a bell. "Why does that sound so familiar?"

Kinsey squirmed and returned her attention to her laptop. "There was an oldies rocker named Easton, before my time. Maybe my mother had a soft spot for her music."

"Your mother. *Your mother.*" Loane rummaged through the articles and information she'd read about anyone local named Easton. The result was a stunner. "Councilwoman Brenda Easton Jeffries? You're Kinsey Easton *Jeffries*." The truth was all over Kinsey's blanched face. Loane felt the noose tighten around her neck. "And you didn't think that was worth mentioning?"

Kinsey straightened in her chair as if summoning all her courage and tenacity. "My mother has nothing to do with me or my life."

"It must be great to be so young and naïve. This will definitely come back to bite me on the ass. I'm the one conducting an unsanctioned investigation using questionable tactics involving an ATF agent and a councilwoman's daughter. And I didn't bother to check my sources."

"Sorry, Loane," Kinsey said.

"It's not your fault. I fell short again."

Loane pushed out of her chair and headed for the door without looking back. Vi had promised that she could be trusted, and Loane believed her. But she was a kid who'd grown up without the love and support of her parents. Instead of the customary annoyance Loane expected, she felt only disappointment and deep sadness. She'd grown very fond of Vi, but now their relationship seemed tainted. She'd have to question everything about Kinsey and each encounter they'd had. Once again, she'd failed to go the extra mile. The trust she'd so freely given might place Abby in greater jeopardy.

CHAPTER EIGHTEEN

"Wow, is she always that intense?" Kinsey asked as Loane exited and closed the door without a sound.

"In this case, don't you think she has reason?" Abby tried to keep the censure out of her voice. She wanted to understand Kinsey's motivation and determine the extent of damage to Loane's confidence and the investigation.

"What do you mean?"

She rolled her chair closer to Kinsey, forcing a neutral expression. "Think about what she's been through. She thought I was dead. The department abandoned her. She left her job and was so desperate she turned to a street kid for help. She trusted you without ever checking you out. Am I right?" Kinsey nodded. "Loane doesn't do that easily."

"Guess I fucked up."

"It's not about you. Loane blames herself. And for the record, why are you helping us?"

Kinsey scuffed her shoes across the worn carpet and looked down at the floor. She told Abby the story of June and how she'd gone missing while working for the Torres and her attempts to find her. When she finally looked up, her green eyes were rimmed with tears. "And my *mother* wouldn't lift one finger to help. Said she wasn't bartering her political clout for a teenage runaway. Can you believe the selfishness? That's the last time I spoke to her—nine months ago."

Abby put her arm around Kinsey's shoulder. "Honey, I'm so sorry. I had no idea. Did you tell Loane all this?"

"The part about June, not the stuff about my mother. Guess I should've, huh?"

"It might've helped avoid this misunderstanding."

"Will she forgive me?"

"I wish I knew. She's hurt right now. I wasn't totally honest with her, and I'm still waiting for the answer to your question."

"What do we do in the meantime?"

"The only thing we can. Wait, and give her space."

"You seem to know her pretty well."

"I'm in love with her, but I'm not sure how well I know her. She'll never believe or accept my love until she feels she deserves it. She's a complicated woman."

"Aren't they all?" Kinsey poked Abby's arm. "So…we're not just sitting here and feeling sorry for ourselves, are we? Don't we have work to do?"

"Indeed we do, my friend. You have a device to install, cameras to remove, and I have phone calls to make. Let's get to it."

When Kinsey left, Abby called Carl. She wanted to confirm what Loane had implied this morning and assure him that she was quickly falling under her influence.

If physical attraction and sex were enough to bind Loane, they wouldn't have any problems. But Abby wanted the whole package. During their little scene in the club, Loane had appeared totally unaffected by Abby's advances, her feelings now bruised and protected, unlike the woman she'd bedded before the explosion. But like she'd told Kinsey, all she could do now was wait and pray that things changed.

"Hello, Abby." Carl's gravelly voice returned her attention to her call.

"Carl, I trust your trip is going well."

"Fine. What news?"

"Loane Landry and I spent the night together. Congratulations, she likes me."

"Of course she does. Well done. When the time is right, ask her about the case the police were working on against my uncle. Someone has to answer for my family."

"I will, but these things take time. I have to build her trust first."

"Sure, sure…one more little favor?"

"Another test?" Abby was half-kidding, but the silence on the other end of the line told her she was exactly right. "Haven't I proved myself already?"

"This is the last thing. I promise."

"Why didn't you ask me before you left?"

"I wanted to make sure you could pull if off with the cop first."

"Fine. What do you want now? It can't be any worse than sleeping with a stranger."

"I need some merchandise taken up north tomorrow, and I'd like you to do it."

Abby wasn't sure if she'd heard right. It couldn't be a coincidence. Was this what they'd been waiting for—and what she and Loane had disagreed about—the gun shipment? She didn't want to appear too eager, so she downplayed the task. "Couldn't you have Ray or Tiny do it? I'm settling into the new job. They're more roadrunners and I'm the mind-the-home-front type."

"I need you to do this, Abby. Then you're in, all the way."

"It must be important merchandise."

"It is."

She was getting annoyed with his cat-and-mouse games. "Carl, I've been working for the Torres a while. I saved your nephew from an explosion, lived in the home with your family, and bedded a stranger to prove my loyalty. If you don't trust me enough to tell me what's going on, I'm walking, today." It sounded like a threat, and she hoped he took it that way. She held her breath as she waited for his answer, wondering if her bluff would work.

"Let's say we started providing a service to certain groups when the government dropped the ball in Operation Fast and Furious."

Carl had admitted he was selling weapons to drug dealers. Fast and Furious was the government operation designed to sell guns to the drug cartels in order to track their movements and make arrests of high-level members. She had to pretend this was all new information. "What is Fast and Furious?"

"You really are innocent, aren't you? We're basically selling street guns to drug cartels for a hell of a lot of money. And who cares? A bunch of dopers killing each other. The cops should pay us as a public service."

"So, Simon and Sylvia…"

"Had no idea."

"And your father, Stefan?"

"It's been my operation for years. The rest of the family thinks we make millions on titty bars." He seemed proud of his ability to carry on such an endeavor right under their noses. That pride would be one of the nails in his prosecutorial coffin. "I think Simon might've been suspicious near the end and I—"

"You what?" Abby's stomach twisted into a disgusted knot. Her instincts about Simon and Sylvia had been right. They'd simply been running what they thought was a legitimate business to support their family. And they'd been killed for no reason.

"I'm afraid that's what got him killed. If the people I supply had got wind that he was nosing around or was under investigation by the police, he would've been a marked man. But I have to be sure the cop wasn't in on it before I jeopardize such a lucrative endeavor."

It was absolutely ludicrous that Carl would suspect a police officer before his gunrunning, dope-dealing associates. That twisted way of thinking was one of the mysteries of the criminal mind that made law enforcement necessary. It also proved that Carl's number-one priority was money.

"Are you shocked, Abby?"

A sickening feeling rose in her throat as she recalled the months she'd spent in this man's home, questioning his involvement in illegal activity. She called on all her acting skills to present an air of nonchalance and callousness. "Maybe a little surprised, but any money is good money, right?"

"My sentiments exactly. I had a feeling you'd be on board, especially when I tell you your cut for making this little run tomorrow—a hundred thousand dollars, free and clear, no taxes. How does that sound?"

"Too good to be true. What's the catch?"

"No catch. Ray and Tiny will load the van and take it to the club about five. The GPS will be loaded with the destination information. All you have to do is drive and not get stopped by the cops."

"What happens when I get to the other end?"

"Someone will meet you, take the van, and give you another vehicle to drive back. Leave it where you got the van in the rear parking lot."

"When do we get paid for the merchandise?"

"That's the beauty of it. You don't have to touch the weapons or the money. The money's in the trunk of the car you'll bring back, in the spare-tire wheel well."

Carl's plan to include her made sense from a criminal perspective. As long as he involved his employees in the illegal operation with their knowledge, they were equally culpable under the law. Large profits, fear of prosecution, and threats of retaliation or death would keep them quiet. "Sounds like you've covered all the bases."

"So, you're in?"

"Absolutely…and thank you so much for trusting me with this." It took no effort at all for her to sound sincere. She meant every word. Carl's confession finally solidified his link to the weapons and brought her closer to shutting down the operation and getting back to a real life. The delivery run tomorrow would be the final piece of evidence she needed. But was it *too* easy? Maybe he'd begun to suspect her of disloyalty. She had no choice but to follow it through, setup or not.

Carl hung up and Abby made the other call she'd been dreading all morning. When the secretary at the Greensboro Field Office of ATF answered, she asked for Dan Bowman and waited. She wasn't exactly sure what or how much to tell him, but she was overdue to report in. Their contact had been sporadic since her return, and he'd even been good enough not to assign a new cover officer.

"Mancuso?" Dan Bowman's business voice cut through the line.

She launched into something tangible before he could start questioning her. "Dan, I have the business files I told you about the other day. They're on a flash drive. How do you want me to get it to you?"

"Oh…" He seemed surprised that she actually had something concrete to offer. "Can you send it in an e-mail, or is the file too large?"

"I think it'll transfer okay."

"Send it to this address, not the agency one." He gave her what sounded like a personal e-mail account.

"Have your financial gurus look it over. Carl Torre is running the gun operation through the Sky Bar accounts."

"And you found all this after a few days as manager?" He sounded skeptical.

"He trusts me." Bowman was silent for too long. "What's going on, Dan? You're never this quiet. I'm usually getting a policy-and-procedure speech by now." While their professional relationship hadn't been close, Abby never doubted Bowman's commitment to his job. His adherence to rules and regulations alone was the stuff supervisors wished they could sprinkle over new recruits like fairy dust.

"Hold on a second." She heard him put the phone down, and a few seconds later a door closed with a thud. "I probably shouldn't be telling you this. For all I know you're an internal plant gathering evidence against me, or a high-level CI with clearance beyond mine. Either way, I'm taking a chance."

She wanted to be honest with Bowman about her assignment, but she'd been forbidden to do so. There might be a leak in the ATF office, but she didn't believe it was Bowman, in spite of his shoddy treatment of Loane. She did the only thing she could. "Dan, all I can tell you is that you can trust me."

"You better be right about this." He paused momentarily, as if he wasn't sure how to continue. "I think we have a leak in the investigation. Well, not so much a leak as a plug."

"What do you mean?"

"I'm still trying to piece it together. After the explosion, somebody shut this case down completely. The coals were still hot when my supervisor, Gary Fowler, told me to wrap up the loose ends and put a lid on it. All my files were collected and the computer backups erased. The order came from above his head, and so did the order to put me back on the case. He has no idea. Everybody here thought you were dead, including me."

His last statement sent a chill through Abby's body. "And who knows I'm not?"

"I haven't told anyone that I'm in touch with you again. I don't think it's safe until I know who's running the show. From an organizational perspective this case is over, closed, no follow-up required."

"And that's why you haven't assigned a new cover officer and why you want me to send the financial info to a personal e-mail?" She wanted to tell him that Barrio was running the case now and had ordered the crackdown on information, but he wasn't authorized to know.

"Yeah."

"Why are you questioning all this now?"

"At first I was taking orders, but I'd never seen anything wrapped up this tightly. When I asked Fowler about it, he threatened to send me to the North Carolina equivalent of Siberia if I didn't drop it. He said we'd made a dent in organized crime in Greensboro and that was good enough for him. He and Councilwoman Jeffries held a huge press conference and crowed about our success. It didn't feel like a victory to me.

"And I got a call the night of the explosion from an anonymous source. She said I should go to the Torre home because something was going to happen, something bad. Then the line went dead. I was on my way there when I heard the explosion."

Abby made a split-second decision she was certain Loane, and probably Hector Barrio, wouldn't like. "Dan, you need to know more." In the next few minutes she filled him in on the delivery she was scheduled to make the next day without revealing Kinsey's part in locating the guns. The real struggle was whether to reveal Loane's involvement.

"Abby, I don't know how to advise you. You'll need backup and I'm not sure who to trust. I should've listened to Landry months ago when she suggested there was a cover-up."

"Since you mentioned Loane, she's been working with me. I assume you don't have a problem with her *now*?"

"Didn't she quit the department?"

"She's on voluntary leave of absence."

The line was silent for a few seconds. "Well, technically she's still covered under the year-long mutual-aid agreement between GPD and ATF. I don't have a problem with her, but she might very well have one with me. I was pretty hard on her during our questioning, but I had my marching orders."

"Let me worry about Loane."

"If she's willing, so am I. The two of us can probably handle the surveillance and cover you at the same time."

"Sounds good. I'll fill her in and get back with you about the details."

"Abby..."

"Yeah?"

"Thanks for telling me about this. You didn't have to."

"This needs to be a legitimate ATF investigation, and you're the only connection I have to make that happen. If all goes well, you could be in for a promotion when this is over."

"If I'm not out of a job for disobeying a direct order and listening to an *informant*." His emphasis on the word made her wonder if he already knew about her.

She hung up and for the first time felt guilty about not telling Bowman she was an ATF agent, but her instructions from Barrio were explicit. No one was to know until the case was closed for the very reasons Bowman had begun to suspect.

Abby spent the rest of the day and evening going through the motions of being a club manager. She helped inventory liquor supplies, dealt with personnel issues, and wrote employee paychecks like a normal boss.

Ray and Tiny had apparently been briefed about her pending trip because they suddenly treated her like a real member of their crime family. They brought her drinks while she worked in the office and talked openly about how they'd spent the profits from their side job. It took all of her practiced skills to feign enough enthusiasm to avoid raising suspicion.

She'd called Loane earlier and left a voice-mail message. Kinsey's news about her mother had surprised Loane, but she'd consider Kinsey's motives and adjust. Abby needed to talk to her, reassure her about Kinsey and about Dan Bowman. She wasn't sure which would be the harder sell, a woman she'd been misled by or a colleague who'd completely turned on her. If the situation between her and Loane was any indication, it would definitely be the former.

Chapter Nineteen

Loane sat in Eve's office the next morning staring into her coffee cup as though she'd find answers in the bottom. "What am I doing wrong, Eve? Do I have a sign around my neck that says sucker?"

Eve stared with one of her Pretty-Kitty-is-smarter-than-you looks. "When you're finished having a pity party, ask the real question."

"And what is that?"

"Are you upset with Abby, Kinsey slash Vi, Tyler, and everybody else in your life, or are you upset with yourself?"

"What do you mean?"

"Loane, I loved your mother like a sister, but she had issues. She never let anyone close enough to risk being hurt, not even your father. She drove him away. Did you hear that? *She* made him leave and made you feel like a second-class citizen for being a lesbian. I could've killed her for that one myself. Unfortunately, she passed all that insecurity along to you. It's time for you to make a decision about the rest of your life. Do you want to live or go through the motions?"

"I think I have a right to expect people I care about to be honest with me."

"You can expect anything you want, but that doesn't mean you'll get it. We make mistakes even with the best intentions. Abby thought she was doing the right thing. That's all any of us can do. Kinsey helped you when she didn't have to. Maybe she had other reasons for not telling you about her mother. And as for Tyler, that man loves you. Not a day has passed since you started this fiasco that he hasn't called asking if I've heard from you."

"Really?" Loane listened to Eve, letting what she said sink into the aching places in her heart. "He did get the autopsy results on Simon

Torre for me. That couldn't have been easy in a case under federal lockdown."

"Exactly. You listened to your instincts and trusted these people initially. Could you be so wrong so often? You wouldn't have survived two seconds in police work at that rate. And do you believe these highly intelligent people, myself included, would give a fat rat's ass about you if you weren't a decent, honest, caring person?"

"Maybe that's why I'm so confused. My heart is telling me one thing and my head another."

Eve placed her hand on Loane's shoulder. "If I could make a suggestion? I know this will sound strange coming from me. And if you tell Thom I said this, I'll deny it. Go with your heart. The head is great for facts, figures, and puzzles, but not so much for feelings. Settle whatever's unsettled, end this charade, and get back to your life."

"So you think I should give Abby and Kinsey another chance?"

"I think you should give yourself another chance."

"Huh?"

"Have you ever been in a relationship without an exit strategy?"

Her throat tightened with the certainty of her answer as she shook her head.

"Ever asked yourself why?"

"I guess I felt I didn't deserve real love."

Eve nodded. "Get over that old garbage and move on. Every woman is not like your mother or your father. They don't all leave."

Had she been looking at the situation all wrong? Maybe it wasn't Abby or Kinsey or even Tyler who'd let her down. Maybe she'd let herself down by not living up to her full emotional potential, even when her heart was urging her to do so. She'd fashioned an elaborate cocoon around herself with trust as the gatekeeper. Perhaps her self-concept caused her to doubt the actions of those she cared about. "Thanks for listening…and for the advice, I guess." She rose and hugged Eve good-bye.

"You're welcome, smart-ass."

When she stepped into the October morning, the cool damp air settled around her as tangibly as the decisions she had to make. Eve was right. She'd believed in Abby and Kinsey instinctively and opened part of herself to them. Her love for Abby had slowly seeped into her heart, but she'd been too afraid to admit it. The idea that she could love at arm's length had brought only pain and regret. She'd ignored Kinsey's calls since yesterday and hadn't responded to Abby's message either. It was time to talk—and not about the case—about relationships and what she wanted.

As she walked through Center City Park toward the club, her cell phone rang. She answered without looking at the caller ID, hoping it was Abby. "Hello."

"Officer Landry?"

Carl Torre's scratchy voice seeped through the line like a bad dream. "How did you get this number?"

"Cops aren't the only ones with sources. I have a proposition for you."

"In case you hadn't noticed, I'm into women." She didn't intend to make it easy for this guy to make an offer of any kind.

"I definitely noticed and this is strictly business. Are you interested?"

"Don't know until I hear the offer."

"Abby is making a delivery for me and I'd like you to accompany her—in case she runs into trouble."

Loane stopped beside the fountain, unsure if she'd heard correctly. This could be the answer to their investigative prayers—if the job involved guns. "A delivery? Of what, and what kind of trouble are you expecting?"

"I don't expect any problems, but I'm a cautious man. As for the cargo, Abby can fill you in if you accept the job. I'll pay you fifty thousand dollars."

He expected her to be financially motivated, and with figures like those, it wasn't particularly hard to play along. "Say no more. I'm all yours. That's nearly an entire year's salary with the GPD. But out of curiosity, why me?"

"The guys said you handled yourself pretty well at the club the other night. That's a good enough reference for me. Get the details from Abby. And carry a weapon. I want my interests protected at all costs. Understood?"

"Absolutely." Carl hung up and she shook her head in disbelief. Was he handing the entire case gift-wrapped over to an ATF agent and a police officer? Either Carl Torre trusted Abby completely or he was setting them up. Maybe he just wanted a cop solidly in his pocket. Either way this scenario was playing right into their hands. She practically ran to the Sky Bar, anxious to tell Abby the good news.

A few minutes later, she pushed open the door of the office and couldn't believe her eyes. Abby was sitting at her desk drinking coffee and talking with Ray and Tiny like they were old friends. She caught the end of an off-color joke before they broke into laughter. Abby saw her and straightened in her chair.

"Okay, boys, guess you better get back to work. I'll expect the van between four thirty and five this afternoon."

"Will do, boss." Ray said. As he passed Loane, he added, "Thanks for the assist the other night." Both men gave her a nose salute and exited.

"Did I walk into an episode of the *Twilight Zone*? Those guys hate you."

Abby came around the desk, reaching for a hug before she apparently thought better of it and dropped her arms to her sides. "We're like this." She raised three fingers pressed tightly together. Loane caught the hint of sarcasm in her voice. "Now that I'm on the inside, everything's peachy. I've been trying to reach you." Abby sounded concerned.

"Hold that thought." Loane went to the office door and looked out to make sure Ray and Tiny weren't still within earshot. She'd hoped she and Abby could talk about their relationship, but something more urgent was obviously bothering her. "What's wrong?"

"Have you seen or talked to Kinsey since yesterday?"

"No."

"She didn't come to work this morning and that's not like her, especially with everything we've got going on right now."

"Have you tried her cell? That thing's like an appendage."

"No answer."

"That is unusual." Abby was giving her a strange look. "What?"

"Are you upset about what she told you yesterday?"

"She's a kid, doing the best she can. I get that."

"She's not spying for her mother, if you were worried about that. They haven't been in touch since she refused to help Kinsey find her friend June."

"Her mother is a piece of work." Kinsey had been honest about her motives, if not all the circumstances, and she'd been justified in trusting her. Relief swept over her because, like it or not, she'd come to care about Kinsey.

"She was afraid you wouldn't let her help if you knew who her mother was."

"Yeah, maybe I was wrong…about a lot of things, but it doesn't seem like now is the right time to talk about them. You're worried about her, aren't you?"

Abby nodded and her bottom lip quivered. "We got her into this mess, Loane. If something happens to her…"

She hugged Abby reassuringly. "We'll find her. Do you know where she lives?"

Abby pulled away reluctantly and opened a file cabinet full of folders. "The only thing I have is her employment application."

Loane took the paper and scanned the contents. Kinsey's address and the owner's name leapt off the page like they were highlighted in a brilliant glowing color. She stared up at Abby. Her world became unexpectedly smaller. People who shouldn't know each other did. Things that shouldn't be linked suddenly were. "Did you know about this?"

"What?"

"That Kinsey was living in *my* house? That my brother was her landlord?"

Abby's eyes widened and the creases across her forehead deepened. "I never read the application. I liked her and went with my gut. How did that happen?"

"Guess it's a question we have to ask my brother or Kinsey, when we find her. I'll go see if she's home. By the way, Carl has employed me to accompany you and the shipment to New York. Either this is the best luck we've had so far, or he's on to us and it's an ambush."

"At least we'll be together." The upturned corners of Abby's mouth mirrored the pleased twinkle in her eyes before they suddenly drooped. "You should probably know…" The hesitancy in her voice warned Loane she wouldn't like it. "I told Dan Bowman about the delivery and he wants to help."

How could Abby involve a man who'd tried to railroad her? He'd gone after her in the inquiry like a man obsessed. As disbelief and indignation spun inside, she let them fill her, entice her, and finally drain away. She didn't lash out or withdraw like usual. Forcing her pulse to calm, she met Abby's gaze. "Why did you tell him?"

Abby maintained eye contact. "He's convinced there's a leak in the local ATF office. That's what Hector Barrio is worried about too. I believe he's sincere and I trust him. He's even sorry he didn't listen to you sooner."

"He said that?"

"Yep. He says you're still deputized under the original mutual-aid agreement."

She let this new information register as she stared into Abby's beautiful brown eyes. "You truly are amazing. Do you know that?" She drew her hand down the side of Abby's face and gently cupped her chin, the urge to kiss her almost overwhelming.

"I'm glad you think so. Does that mean you'll work with him?"

"If you trust him, that's good enough for me."

Abby straightened her shoulders and lifted her head a bit higher, as if suddenly infused with confidence. "You have no idea how much that means to me."

"I'll work with Bowman if he agrees to bring Tyler along. We'll need another person since I'll be with you in the van, and I can't think of anyone else I'd trust right now. If something goes wrong, I want at least two people covering us. Agreed?"

Abby stood on her tiptoes and kissed Loane lightly on the lips. "That sounds like an excellent idea. I called him, you know, when I was looking for you."

"You called my brother?"

"I was desperate. He couldn't or wouldn't talk to me, but I didn't identify myself either. I had to be the one to let you know I was back."

Loane allowed herself a moment of indulgence before the next round of chaos began in their lives. She hugged Abby tight and claimed her with her mouth, surrendering all the feelings she'd held back, praying that Abby received the message. It would have to do for now.

When she pulled away, she wobbled unsteadily. Her body was drawn to Abby's, desperate to be rejoined. "Save my place right here… to be continued." Before Abby recovered enough to respond, Loane ran out the back door of the club. She had to find Kinsey and talk to her brother before the trip.

The short drive to Tyler's wasn't long enough to cool the burn Abby's kiss unleashed or to dull the excitement of a pending reunion. She hadn't felt this optimistic about their relationship since their early days of lusty sex. Knowing Abby felt the same made waiting possible, at least another day or two.

With her raised fist cocked outside Tyler's door, she couldn't muster the courage to knock. *1910 Greensboro is the destination of the first piece of airmail sent in the U.S.* She felt like she was about to face a stranger, not a man she'd known all her life. *Fordham's Drug Store opens on Elm Street in 1898.* Would she actually be able to break the family cycle, admit she needed help, and ask for it? If she could, they might be able to establish a closer connection, and she wanted that. She started to rehearse what she'd say when the door suddenly swung open.

"Are you going to stand out here all day reciting history facts or come inside?" Tyler didn't give her a chance to answer as he drew her into a bear hug.

"I can't breathe," she managed to say.

"I've missed you, at least I think it's you. My sister had longer hair, no tattoos, and definitely no metal in her face."

"Cute. It's all fake, so don't freak out."

"Good, then you're still my sister." He ushered her into the family den filled with slices of domestic life. The boys' toy trucks and Legos littered the floor, and he playfully kicked them aside as he made a path to two leather recliners. Pictures of his wife and children lined the walls, and Loane felt a momentary pang of guilt that she didn't visit more often. The boys were growing up and she was missing it.

She sat down and fidgeted with the stitching on the back of her glove. "Ty, I'm sorry about the whole shutting-you-out thing."

"You're not getting all girly and mushy on me, are you?" When she didn't respond immediately, his tone changed. "Sis, you don't have to explain. You needed to get away for a while. That's what you do when you're hurt. You've always been that way, but you kept in touch this time. And as for the mushy part, I sort of figured you knew I love you."

When she looked at him, she saw only affection reflected in the blue eyes that mirrored hers. Some of her emotional awkwardness fell away. "I love you, Ty. It's good to say it occasionally. We never did that a lot. I was too busy trying to prove I was as good as you."

"Always were, sis. Everybody knew that but you." He winked.

"I should've trusted you…about Abby and the investigation. You didn't do anything wrong." Her vision blurred as tears formed. Though she was older, she'd always known Tyler would be there for her, and she'd denied him that opportunity. She hoped he could forgive her. "I'm sorry."

"It's all right." He shifted uncomfortably in the huge brown leather chair that molded around him like memory foam. He wasn't used to such honesty and raw emotion from her. Rubbing his hands along the arms of the chair, he said, "You did what you had to. So, what happens now?" As the wronged person, Tyler reverted to his familial training and shifted the topic, indicating he was ready to move on. They were back in familiar territory.

Their first heart-to-heart hadn't been long or probing, but it was a start. It was up to her to take it a step further. "I need your help." She never realized how good it would feel to ask and know without a doubt that it would be given.

He clasped his hands together, like a kid receiving a new toy. "I can't wait. What is it? Surveillance? Takedown? Kicking some serious bad-guy ass? Name it."

"It could be all the above. Abby…" He gave her a strange look. "Oh, yeah, she's alive and she's also the woman who called looking for me. *And* she's an ATF agent to boot. Who knew?"

"That's great news…right?"

"Absolutely, on all fronts, but that's a story for another time."

"Good. I love you but I do *not* want to hear about your sex life."

"Ditto. Abby and I are scheduled to drive a shipment of guns from here to New York this afternoon. We've nailed down the key players and have a money trail, but we need the exchange to finalize the case. Dan Bowman will—"

"That prick? The one who raked you over the coals? What the—"

She held up her hands to stay the string of expletives he was getting ready to unleash. "It's cool, Ty. He's apparently one of the good guys. Maybe a little misguided at first, but he's come through. Abby believes him and I have to go with her instincts. Can you work with that?"

"If you're sure." When she nodded, he added, "What do you want me to do?"

"Abby and I will drive the delivery van. You and Bowman will be our cover and surveillance. There's a tracking device on the van so you won't lose us. After the exchange, we'll make the arrests. Abby will coordinate with ATF in Miami for the arrests there. We'll have to inform local authorities as a courtesy, but we're covered under mutual aid and Abby has the real federal juice. What do you think?"

While she waited for Tyler's answer, she took in the comfortable surroundings. Would she ever share a life so full of love that it seeped from the walls of their home like a fragrance? She envied his love for his family and vowed to become more involved in their lives. They were all she had left of a bloodline. Was she being fair involving him in this case? What if it all went sideways and something happened to him?

"Ty, maybe this isn't such a good idea after all. You have responsibilities and I couldn't live with myself if something—"

"Whoa, I'm a big boy, and my family knows the risks that come with my job. Besides, what kind of brother would I be if I let you do this on your own? I want to help. And if I'm riding with Bowman, I can keep my eyes on him—in case."

"Okay. I'll call you with details of when and where to meet him. Now, about my house."

Tyler's smile reminded her of his victory grin when he beat her in a martial-arts bout. "Rented it and the money's going into your account like you asked."

"Rented it to Kinsey Easton?"

"Kinsey Easton Jeffries…the councilwoman's daughter. Quite a coup. She showed up one day, résumé in hand, and asked if I wanted to rent your house. I'm still not sure how she knew it was available. I hadn't even advertised it yet. She's a little strange but her cash is good and regular. How do you know her?"

"That's another long story. The short version is she works for Abby at the club and is the technological brains behind our whole operation. Have you seen her in the past couple of days?"

"Nope. She usually comes by on the next-to-last day of the month with the rent."

"She's a day late. Get your spare key and let's go to the house. She didn't show up for work today either."

Neither of them spoke on the drive to her Sunset Hills home. She imagined Tyler's cop sense was spiking, like hers. When they arrived, she knocked on the front door while he checked the back. The house was quiet and no one answered.

"Your busybody neighbor in the back said she hasn't been home since she left for work yesterday morning. I love nosy neighbors. Sure makes our job easier."

"Open the door. Let's make sure she's not inside injured or…"

Tyler turned the key and pushed the door wide. "Police, anybody home? Kinsey?"

The house was as quiet as the day her mother died. Loane's chest tightened as she moved into the room, fearing what she might find, praying it wasn't another body of someone she cared about. "Kin—" Her voice caught and she tried again. "Kinsey?"

She and Tyler both pulled their weapons and went into search mode, clearing the house room by room. The tension in her body grew as each area revealed no sign of disturbance and no trace of Kinsey. They worked their way back through the house looking for clues of where she might be and found nothing significant.

"We definitely have a problem," Loane said. "I'll drop you off. I need to keep looking." Leaving Abby in a lurch at the club, especially with the delivery coming up, was out of character for Kinsey. She pulled in front of Tyler's house and squeezed his forearm before he got out. "Thanks, bro. Call you later."

Loane checked at Loaf first. Kinsey stopped by occasionally for an afternoon latte, but the owner hadn't seen her. On her way up Elm Street, she spotted a redheaded kid a couple of blocks ahead and ran to catch up. The girl had a backpack exactly like Kinsey's. Loane tapped her on the shoulder, but when she turned, it wasn't Kinsey. Loane's next stop was Center City Park, where the city attendant was busy scooping leaves out of the fountain. He shook his head when asked about Kinsey. She checked every kid wearing a hoodie hunkered over a laptop in the park, with no luck. As Loane checked the last place on her list, the nerves in her gut bunched into a tight mass. Kinsey was in trouble.

CHAPTER TWENTY

Abby paced in the small office and stared at the wall clock as if she could make the hands move slower by sheer willpower. It was past four in the afternoon and she hadn't heard from Kinsey all day. If she'd gotten this young woman into trouble, she wouldn't be able to forgive herself, not after what had happened to the Torres. She wanted her work to be about making a positive difference. Glancing at the clock again, she dialed Loane's number and heard a ring outside her door.

"You called?" Loane walked into the room, her expression not reassuring.

"Did you find her? I can't make that delivery until I'm sure she's okay."

Loane shook her head. "I've looked everywhere." She took Abby in her arms and hugged her tight against her chest. "Don't worry. We'll figure this out."

"If something happens to her…"

"I know." Loane stepped out of Abby's embrace and looked around the office. "Let's backtrack. When she left yesterday, did she say where she was going?"

"To remove the cameras while I made some phone calls. You don't suppose she went to the storage unit and—"

"Let's not get ahead of ourselves." Loane pulled her cell phone from her belt and tapped the screen. "I hope she hasn't removed them yet. The video might give us a clue to her location. Plus it would be a bonus to watch the van being loaded with weapons from the unit."

"You can do that, on your phone?" She stepped closer and rested her hand on Loane's arm. The warmth of her skin and firmness of her muscles grounded her, and she breathed a bit easier.

"Kinsey put an app on it that gave me access to the cameras and the tracker. Let's see if either is still working."

She watched as Loane slid her fingers over the screen. In a few seconds a video of the storage unit appeared. The time stamp indicated the last update was about an hour ago. "That's Ray and Tiny loading the van. Perfect, and those look like the boxes I drove up from Miami." She exhaled when Kinsey's face blocked the screen as she removed the camera. "There she is."

As she watched the next shaky segment of the video, her heart pounded. The recording was like a roller-coaster ride, images bouncing up and down, in and out of view as Ray and Tiny dragged Kinsey across the parking lot toward the storage space. "Those bastards." Then the camera feed ended.

She tried to control her rising panic. "What have they done to her?"

"We'll find her." Loane's voice was tight with worry. "I promise, but I'm worried about you too. They know you hired Kinsey." Loane put her arm around her and kissed the top of her head. "Let me check one more thing. Then I have an idea." Loane tapped the phone screen again and a map appeared. "See that? It's the tracking device and it's heading in our direction. That means either Kinsey was able to place it on the van before they got her or she's in the van."

"How do we check without arousing further suspicion?"

"Tell them whatever you have to, just stall them. I have to check out the storage unit. Can you handle this end?"

She forced herself to breathe slowly and focus on what needed to be done. "This could be the performance of my life. I'll make it a good one. Go. They'll be here any minute." Loane turned toward the door but Abby stopped her. "And in case I don't get to tell you this again, I love you."

"I…" Loane feathered a gloved finger down the side of Abby's face. "To be continued."

Loane's touch left a track of chills, followed by searing heat. She pressed her body against Loane's and placed her ear to her chest, her steady heartbeat reassuring. At this moment she wanted nothing more than to wrap herself around Loane and never let go. But her personal desires would have to wait, again. "Hurry back," she whispered as she stepped away.

When Loane left, she dropped into her chair and gripped the sides of the desk. She pushed the images of Kinsey being dragged across the parking lot from her mind and replaced them with visions of Ray and Tiny behind bars. Maybe they had already called Carl about Kinsey and were on the way to kill her next. She buried that possibility, along with the memory of Simon, Alma, and Sylvia, under the very real probability that someone would soon answer for their deaths. Releasing her grip on the desk, she let the tension ooze from her body, and a sense of calm determination took over. She would not fail.

As the delivery time neared, she checked the hallway outside the office to ensure her privacy and called Bowman to update him on the delay. Had she been wrong to trust him? Maybe he was the leak and had blown her cover to Carl. Perhaps Carl's offer for Loane to accompany her on the delivery was a direct result of that information.

It was too late to second-guess her decision now. If the delivery was a trap, at least she and Loane would have backup they trusted. Bowman had already picked up Tyler and they were waiting nearby. Next, she made the call she'd anticipated for almost two years. "Director Barrio, it's Abby Marconi." She hadn't used her real name officially for almost as long, and it felt like freedom rolling off her tongue.

"Yes, Abby?"

"I'm making a delivery of weapons to New York tonight under orders directly from Carl Torre." She gave him the details and asked for further instructions.

"Once you've secured the weapons and money and made the arrests on your end, call me. And be sure to involve local ATF and law enforcement. I'll have a team standing by to move in on Torre at his estate. Any idea yet on the leak in the local ATF office?"

"Nothing concrete. Dan Bowman thinks there's a back door as well, but we haven't pinpointed it yet. Maybe some of the folks we bring in will be interested in a deal. At least we'll have some leverage."

"Maybe I was wrong to keep Bowman out of the loop. We'll see. Keep me posted." Before she had a chance to voice her own concerns, Hector Barrio hung up.

When a knock sounded at the door, she forced herself back into character. "Come in."

Ray and Tiny shuffled in with the same nonchalance they gave every task. If either of them suspected her of being involved in Kinsey's spying, they didn't show it. "You ready to go?" Tiny asked. "The van's in back."

"Where's your traveling companion?" Ray said.

"She had to run a quick errand, and I have to close out what I'm working on here. Why don't you guys get a drink while I finish up? Shouldn't take long." They nodded and headed toward the bar. "And I'll need to check the shipment before we leave."

Tiny stopped so quickly that Ray almost plowed over him. "Boss didn't say anything about that."

His objection made Abby think either they suspected her or Kinsey might be in the back of the van. It would be a stupid move on their part, but stranger things had happened in the criminal world. She wasn't going anywhere until she knew. "If you think I'm leaving here without making sure I have the cargo, you're very wrong. I don't trust you with my life. The guys at the other end of this deal aren't Boy Scouts. So either I check or you call Carl and tell him I'm not making the delivery. Your choice."

The air in the room seemed to thicken with tension. She counted the loud ticking of the clock as the seconds passed, wondering if she'd made a tactical error that Tiny had somehow pinpointed. "Fine. We'll check it when you're ready. I'm getting a drink. It's been a shitty day."

"Oh, by the way." She couldn't resist offering him one last chance at redemption. "Have you seen the new office person, Kinsey? She didn't come in today. Did she call or anything?"

Without turning to face her again, he said, "Nope." Abby added his name to the list of people she'd show no mercy once this case was over.

❖

Loane dashed out the back entrance of the club just before Ray and Tiny pulled in with the van. She dialed the storage facility while running to her Jeep parked a few blocks away. "Tori, it's Loane Landry. I need your help. Are you still on State Street?"

"Closing up for the day. What can I do for you, Officer?"

"I believe a girl has been abducted and left in unit twenty. I'm on my way there now, five minutes out."

"I'll get everything ready."

While she drove, Loane thought about Abby's good-bye. She'd wanted to tell Abby she loved her too, but not like that, not in a topless bar in the middle of an investigation. When she said those words for the first time, she wanted them commemorated in romantic style to show Abby how much she cared. Was she being overly sentimental or cowardly by not revealing her feelings? The answer didn't come.

When she pulled into the facility, Tori Hiatt was waiting by the storage unit holding a power drill and battery pack. "I appreciate this."

"I hope you're wrong." Tori's childlike face and blue eyes projected obvious disbelief. "What an awful thing to do to someone."

Loane pounded on the garage-type door at unit 20, praying for a reply. She had a sick feeling that Ray and Tiny had dragged Kinsey into the unit and killed her. They couldn't afford to have a witness. But she hadn't shared her suspicions with Abby, maybe because she couldn't bear to hear the words aloud, afraid they'd somehow become reality. She held her breath and pounded again. "Kinsey, are you in there? Can you hear me?" Nothing.

"Step aside, Officer." Tori raised the drill.

"Wouldn't a pass key or bolt cutters be quicker…maybe even a lock pick?"

Tori gave her a curious glance. "Don't have pass keys to customers' units, remember, and the locks are resistant to bolt cutters. Can't say about the pick. Fortunately, I've done this a few times. It won't take long."

Loane stood back and looked down at her hands, surprised to see them shaking. They were as unsteady as her insides. The image of charred bodies and the pain of loss flashed through her mind, settling around her heart. She wasn't ready to see someone she cared about hurt or injured again. The grinding of the drill pulled her back to the present, its insistent hum digging into her consciousness.

"Almost there," Tori said. A few seconds later, the lock fell away and she stepped aside. "This is where you take over." She reached into her back pocket and handed Loane a flashlight. "You might need this in there."

Loane rolled the unit door up and shined the light around the inside. As the beam swept the space, she saw nothing but small cardboard boxes piled almost to the ceiling and old furniture covered with dust. Hope drained from her like water down a falls, leaving her physically weak. She slid her hand along the back of a sofa for support and forced herself to move farther inside. *Please, please, let me find her…and let her be okay.*

"Anything?" Tori called from the front.

"Not yet." The steady sound of her own voice kept Loane moving forward. She swung the light to the opposite side of the small space behind a tower of boxes. The beam flashed across a familiar patch of red hair and a black backpack.

Kneeling beside Kinsey's body, she detected a pulse at her neck, slow and weak. "Call an ambulance," she yelled. "Can you hear me, Kinsey?" She kneaded along her arms, legs, and spine for obvious injuries, then took a deep breath and rolled Kinsey over onto her back.

As she repositioned Kinsey, she saw a large pool of blood underneath her body and a mass of dried blood and hair on the right side of her head. Her face was ashen, lips swollen, and one of her eyes and a cheek were already showing signs of bruising. Loane lowered her head and listened for breathing sounds, hearing no obstruction. "Kinsey, open your eyes. It's Loane." She felt helpless, and with no real medical training she hesitated to move her again for fear of doing further damage. In the distance the ambulance's siren wailed.

"Tori, can you make a path through some of this stuff so they can get to her?" Loane suspected Ray and Tiny had used the empty cardboard boxes to hide Kinsey's body after they removed the guns.

"I'm on it."

She looked over her shoulder and saw Tori plowing through furniture and boxes as if coming to assist her own family. A few seconds later, the paramedics arrived. Loane stood by as they checked Kinsey and carefully loaded her onto a stretcher and into the ambulance. "How is she?" she asked. "Can you tell how badly she's hurt?"

"Not sure yet. Do you know how long she's been unconscious?"

Remembering the time stamp on the video, she guessed. "Maybe an hour at most. I can't be sure. Is that bad?"

"We need to go. Is someone following us to the hospital?" The guy looked from Tori to her.

Abby was alone at the club with Ray and Tiny, and she didn't know if they were suspicious of her yet. Abby was waiting for her, but Kinsey was alone, with no friends or family, and she was injured. Loane was torn between her love for Abby and her need to protect her and the friendship and responsibility she felt for Kinsey. She couldn't let Abby make the delivery alone, and she couldn't leave Kinsey without anyone.

"I'll go," Tori offered. "You obviously have something equally important to do."

Loane glanced at Kinsey, then her Jeep, relieved yet afraid she was letting Kinsey down.

"Go, I've got this," Tori said.

"Are you sure?" When Tori nodded, she added, "Please tell her I didn't want to leave." She started toward her Jeep but turned back. "Let me know when you hear anything…and if you wouldn't mind, call her mother, Councilwoman Brenda Jeffries. Kinsey won't like it, but her mother should know. And thank you, Tori."

As she pulled away from the storage facility, Loane thought about how quickly she'd become attached to Kinsey in spite of her unconventional dress and behavior. Kinsey had filled a void, and Loane had opened up to her when she thought herself incapable of doing so again. Had that been a necessity or a desire to genuinely connect, and what, if anything, did it say about her relationship with Abby?

She glanced at the dashboard clock that read four fifty-five. Had Abby been able to stall the trip? By now Tyler and Bowman would be impatiently waiting and wondering what caused the delay. Speeding down Market Street, she dialed Abby's number with one hand. She couldn't make her wait another minute for news about Kinsey.

Abby's voice was strained with worry when she answered so Loane got to the point. "I found her." The sigh of relief from the other end made her smile. "Have you left yet?"

"Nope, finished checking the cargo. Will you be here soon?" Loane could tell she wanted to ask for details but couldn't because others were nearby.

"Turning in now." She hung up, skidded into the parking lot, and parked beside the van as Abby came out the back.

Her first instinct was to protect Abby, to get her as far away from this place as possible. That impulse was only slightly dulled when Ray and Tiny exited the van. She clenched her hands around the steering wheel until they throbbed, remembering what they'd done to Kinsey. They'd intended to kill her, she was sure of that, but botched the job. If she got out of her vehicle now, she'd lose any chance of bringing them to justice, clearing this case, or being with Abby ever again. She forced herself to stay in the Jeep long enough for her anger to pass.

She watched as Abby spoke briefly to Tiny, waved her good-byes, and walked toward the Jeep. When she saw Loane's face, she must've sensed her mood. "What's wrong, hon?"

"I want to kill those bastards with my bare hands."

Abby opened the door and pulled her toward the van. "Come with me. Now."

CHAPTER TWENTY-ONE

Abby drove through downtown and onto US 29 in silence. She could almost imagine the plethora of historical facts running through Loane's gorgeous head as she regained her composure. She had never understood how history could calm one's nerves, unless it was the boredom factor. It was Loane's quirk.

"When you're ready, I'd like to know about Kinsey."

The light in Loane's blue eyes turned dark and dangerous again, and she clenched her hands into tight fists. "They beat her"—her voice cracked—"and I think she was shot too. It was hard to tell with all the blood. She was unconscious. They tried to kill her."

"Oh, my God." Abby took one of Loane's hands and worked the fist loose enough to entwine their fingers.

"I didn't want to leave her, but you—"

"I'm sorry you had to make that decision. I know it couldn't have been easy."

"Tori Hiatt, the facility owner, went with her. She's a nice woman. I asked her to call Kinsey's mother and let me know when she had an update."

"Will she be all right?"

Loane shrugged like a guilty child unable to explain her behavior.

"You don't think this is your fault, do you?"

"Abby, I got her involved in this mess. She's a kid."

"And I hired her at the club where she met Ray and Tiny. If you want to compare guilt, let's start there."

"She kept them from assaulting me the night we met." Loane looked at her for the first time since getting in the van, a grin tugging at the corners of her mouth. "She was a redheaded fireball and a quick thinker. They never stood a chance. I thought she was a major pain in the ass, but she grew on me."

"I guess we both owe her, huh?" She squeezed Loane's hand and brought it to her lips for a light kiss. "Kinsey doesn't strike me as the type of person who'd do anything she didn't want to. She needed to find her friend and we needed her help. If she could hear us now, she'd tell us both to get over ourselves."

"You're probably right, but I'll still take great pleasure in slapping the handcuffs on Ray and Tiny when we get back," Loane said.

"I wish we could hear something." As if willing the phone to ring, Loane's cell chirped.

"Hello? Yeah. Right. Are you sure? Good. Did her mother show up? How was that? I can imagine. Was she upset because I wasn't there? Okay. Thanks so much. I owe you. Bye."

Abby punched Loane playfully. *"Tell me."*

"She has a concussion, broken ribs, bruised kidneys, a through-and-through gunshot to the side, and a few serious cuts. She'll be in the hospital a few days for observation. Her mother showed up, pissed because she doesn't know what happened. She thinks it's because Kinsey got mixed up with June. Tori said Kinsey came around long enough to say she'd get even with me for calling her mother. Oh, and she wished us luck."

"If she's coherent enough to threaten you, she should be fine." The air inside the van seemed to noticeably lighten with the good news, and Abby returned her attention to the case. She glanced in the rearview mirror. "I assume Bowman and Tyler are somewhere back there."

"Oh, crap, I was so focused on Kinsey I forgot to check with them before we left. Better make sure." She dialed her cell, and from her side of the conversation, things seemed to be in order. "They're a couple of cars back, and from the way Ty was laughing, it sounds like he and Bowman have made peace."

"Good…so…what would you like to do for the next nine hours?"

Loane looked at her like she'd suggested they pull over for sex along the roadside. "Uh, watch the beautiful nighttime landscapes rush by the window?" She oozed sarcasm and uncertainty.

They rode in silence for quite a while, Loane looking out the window and making occasional innocuous comments about the scenery or the weather, and Abby replying in kind. After the second bathroom break and a food stop, she decided that Loane might be content to squander a golden opportunity to reconnect, but she wasn't. If she didn't take this chance to clear the air between them, she might not get another one.

Abby lobbed an emotional grenade into her lap. "Want to talk about us?" The startled look on Loane's face prompted a gentler invitation. "We don't have to. I thought since we have several hours of uninterrupted time together and we're not sure what'll happen at the other end, we might talk. I dumped a lot on you at the park the other day. Do you have any questions now that you've had some time to think?"

"Not really."

"So, you understand everything?" It couldn't be this easy. She knew Loane too well to imagine one conversation would clarify all that had passed between them.

"Your job, the secrets, no communication, all makes sense in retrospect."

"Then why do I sense a great big *but* on the end of that sentence?"

"Because there is. Just because I understand doesn't mean everything will work out." She looked at Abby and the pain in her eyes was clear. "I trusted you completely. I've never done that before. And you left."

Loane's statement was heartfelt, but something about it didn't ring true. How could Abby say that delicately without discounting her sincerity? "When we had sex the first time, you wouldn't even let me hold you afterward. As we got closer, you let me cuddle and spend the night. You even shared some of your family stuff, and I know that wasn't easy. But what about the night I left? You wanted to say something. I saw it in your eyes, but you held back."

"I…Abby, it's complicated and it's not only about trust. When my mother rejected me for being gay and my dad left, I felt like it was my fault, like they'd abandoned me. Hell, I joined a profession where the clientele lies for survival and sport. I expect people to lie, so it's not that. I want to feel that somebody loves me enough to stay, for keeps, no matter what."

Abby wiped tears away with the back of her hand. She'd struck at the heart of Loane's insecurity—by leaving, she'd made her feel second best. Even so, Loane had continued to engage others, which spoke volumes about her capacity to care. "It will never happen again."

"How can you sound so certain?"

"Because I'm finally beginning to understand what you need from me. And in spite of your pain, you've been reaching out. That proves you *do* care, that you *do* have faith in the basic goodness of people because you haven't given up—not with your brother, not with Kinsey, not with the job you supposedly quit, or even Bowman, and certainly not with me. You believe even against the odds—that's faith, Loane. It's trust in the purest form and it's love. Give yourself some credit."

"I'd call it stupidity."

"Face it, Landry, you're an optimist at heart, like me. You couldn't do the job you do every day if you didn't believe people were worth saving." Loane's eyebrow arched toward her hairline, and she stared at Abby as if she'd said something profound. "One more thing and I'll be quiet. I think you love me, and I know I love you. I don't have any more secrets. The only thing left is to figure out how to move forward…if you want."

"I think I might, Agent Marconi." She kissed Abby's cheek before posing another question. "The night of the explosion, did you call Bowman on your way to Simon's?"

"No."

"He told me he got a call. I guess I assumed…" The pain in Loane's voice was obvious. She thought Abby had called him and not her.

"I didn't call him, but somebody did and told him to go to the Torre house."

"Do you believe him?" Loane asked.

"I want to. Otherwise we're in trouble. Trust is a two-way street. You have to start somewhere."

"I'm starting to get that…and maybe it's myself I don't trust, not everybody else." She swiped at her eyes and looked away. "I have more to say, Abby, but can we wait until this is over? A truck filled with guns isn't an ideal setting for an intimate conversation."

"I'll wait as long as you need."

Their talk had taken longer than Abby realized with their stops and starts and prolonged silences. In the end, she'd given it her best shot and their future was now in Loane's hands. Strangely enough, she felt comfortable with that, even after all her bravado about making her own way and being independent. Somehow letting Loane make this decision seemed right. Her parents had always said that love involved a lot of give and take. Maybe this was her next test.

Beside her, Loane pulled her phone off her belt and dialed. "We're almost at the meeting place. I'll let Ty know." When the call connected,

Loane said, "You guys find a place to stage nearby, but be careful. They might have lookouts. I'll dial your number when we get there and leave the line open so you can hear everything. When I say you've got enough weapons here to start a war, that's your cue. Let the locals know we're moving into position but to hold fast until they hear from you."

Abby pulled behind a warehouse in the industrial district as instructed, at almost four in the morning, and saw three men get out of a Ford Mustang. It was still dark, and the lack of streetlights in the area made her uncomfortable. She parked behind the men and left her headlights on. They were all dressed in black, bulky and rough in the street-worn sense. One held a weapon clearly visible, and another clutched an unseasonably heavy coat around a bulge. The man in the center stood with his hands clasped in front of him, his face almost completely covered by stringy hair and an unkempt beard.

Loane looked at the group then at her. "Don't take any chances. I mean it, Abby. We hand over the weapons, check the money, and call in the cavalry. Agreed?"

"Absolutely. Guess I'll do the talking since I'm the actor."

"Good plan." She gave Abby's hand a quick squeeze. Before they exited, Abby watched Loane tuck her small Walther .380 into the waistband of her pants. "Ready."

She and Loane got out of the van and walked toward the waiting men. As she approached, Abby sized them up and decided on the best tactic. They looked like street thugs, interested in money, guns, and sex. She decided to play the innocent. "Hi, I'm Abby. Carl sent me. I'm supposed to leave the van and take your car." She put on her best naïve expression. "Right?"

Beard man spoke. "Sounds right. Call me Grizz. You two got guns on you?"

"Of course we've got guns. We're not stupid. You've got guns." Abby nodded toward his two companions. "I didn't realize we were playing show-and-tell. I thought this was a business transaction."

For a second Abby thought she'd been too combative, but Grizz grinned. "I like a feisty woman." He stepped forward and his grin vanished. "I need to look at the cargo."

"Sure." She moved toward the rear of the van, certain Loane was covering her. Punching in the lock code, she stepped aside and swung the doors open. "Help yourself. It's all here."

Grizz motioned for the other two men to check while he stood beside her, taking visual liberties. Wanting to shiver in disgust, she looked across at Loane to calm her nerves. She was the picture of cool composure. Anyone else would think ice water ran in her veins, but Abby saw the barely contained anger mixed with love in her wild blue eyes. She wanted to put Grizz in his place for even looking at her.

"Everything all right?" Abby asked.

"All here, boss," one of the men said from inside the van.

"Now it's my turn to inspect the merchandise." Abby motioned back toward the Mustang.

Grizz lumbered to the car, popped the trunk, and lifted a duffel bag out of the spare-tire wheel well. "There you go."

Abby opened the bag and looked inside. Small bundles of neatly packaged bills almost looked like play money. She took one out and flipped through it like she'd seen on television to make sure it wasn't stuffed with newspaper. She handed the bag to Loane for a second look. When she nodded, Abby turned to Grizz. "Well, guess we're done here."

"You have enough guns to start your own war. We're out of here," Loane said.

Grizz held the car keys dangling between his fingers as if taunting Abby. "What's your hurry, pretty lady? We could go somewhere and party now the business is done."

"Not tonight. We have to get back." As she reached for the keys, Grizz grabbed her arm and twisted it behind her back, pulling her in front of him like a shield.

"I'm afraid not. Carl wants you two taken out," Grizz said.

The next instant, she felt the metal of Grizz's weapon pressed against her temple. Loane's shocked expression confirmed that the situation was as dire as it seemed. Abby heard the screeching of tires behind her as Tyler and Bowman arrived.

The muzzle of Loane's weapon looked like a cannon from Abby's perspective. She'd never been on the receiving end of a gun, much less two at once. "Don't do anything stupid, man," Loane said. "You're surrounded and your partners deserted you. It's four against one, not very good odds."

"Looks like three against two, and I've got the winning hand. I'll blow her pretty little face off if you come any closer."

Loane motioned for Tyler and Bowman to stay back. "Calm down. We can talk about this. Find a way out for everybody."

"The only way out for everybody is for me to leave here with the van and the money. Now move!" He shoved Abby toward the van. She struggled, but his grip around her waist was firm, almost cutting off her breath.

She knew Loane was only thinking about saving her and would risk her own life to do it. "Shoot him, Loane." She stared at her lover and sent the message she hoped would save them both. *Trust me.*

"I don't have a shot." Loane's eyes broadcast an uncertainty Abby had never seen as she planted her feet firmly, repositioned her weapon, and aimed.

"Don't give up, Loane. Shoot him, *now*!" As she spoke, Abby heard a gunshot, went limp in the man's arms, and dropped to the ground.

CHAPTER TWENTY-TWO

Loane watched the scene unfold in slow motion. Grizz held Abby around the waist, his gun pressed against her head, hiding behind her like a coward. When she looked into Abby's eyes, she expected to see fear but was surprised at how calm she seemed. Abby begged her to shoot, but could she hit Grizz without injuring the woman she loved? If she lost Abby again, and by her own hand, she'd never recover.

She planted her feet apart, rolled her shoulders to relieve some of the tension, and sighted down the barrel of her Walther. Her target was too small. The slightest deviation and she'd hit Abby. Could she take that chance?

"Shoot him, *now*!" Abby yelled.

Something in her voice and the intensity of her eyes convinced Loane to take the shot. She obtained her target. Took a deep breath. Held it and slowly squeezed the trigger. She saw the muzzle flash as her weapon discharged and Abby collapsed. Had her shot gone astray and hit Abby instead? *God, please, no!*

Grizz fell backward, his body bloody and still on the ground. From the corner of her eye, she saw Tyler and Bowman move in. She rushed to Abby's side, terrified to touch her, terrified not to. She felt as if her heart had been ripped out. A lump formed in her throat as she bent over Abby's still body. "Abby…" Tears ran down her face. She placed her hand tentatively on Abby's shoulder. "Please, don't leave me. I need you." She carefully rolled Abby over, visually checking for injuries.

When Abby landed on her back, she gasped a mouthful of air and coughed. "Told you I'd never leave you again. Jeez…that freaking pavement is hard."

"Abby! You're all right?" Loane scooped her up in her arms and hugged her against her chest. "Oh, my God, I was afraid I'd hit you."

"Got the wind knocked out of me."

"Are you sure you're okay? I'll call an ambulance and get you to the hospital."

Abby sat up, still leaning against Loane's chest. "I'm fine, hon. Did we get the bad guys?"

She hadn't even considered the suspect once Abby fell. She assumed Tyler and Bowman would do their jobs. Hers was to take care of Abby. She shrugged and they both looked around. Tyler stood over an unmoving Grizz, and Bowman was on the phone.

"How'd we do?" Abby asked.

"This one is out, but still breathing," Tyler said. "Ambulance is on the way. Bowman is updating local cops and ATF for the use of force. You two okay?"

She looked down at Abby, who smiled broadly and nodded. "We're fine, little brother. Thanks for being here."

"Always got your back." He returned his attention to Grizz as the ambulance pulled in behind the warehouse, followed closely by two city police vehicles.

"That makes two of us, you know," Abby said.

"Yeah, I'm beginning to believe that." Abby tried to get up. "Where do you think you're going?"

"Loane, I'm fine. I need to call Hector Barrio. He's waiting to execute search and arrest warrants. And I think *you* need to call the Greensboro Police and have them pick up Ray and Tiny and close down the club until we get back. I don't want them to find out about the arrests and leave town."

"But I—"

"I know. I wanted to personally take those two into custody, for Kinsey. But we'll be detained with this shooting and can't afford to wait that long." She brushed her hand up Loane's arm and cupped her jaw. "Agreed?"

"No fair using your feminine charms to seduce me into agreeing with you."

"Is that what I'm doing, seducing you?"

"I sure hope so." When Abby moved away, Loane's head cleared enough to process what she'd said. "Wait, why should *I* call Greensboro? As far as they know, I'm still on leave."

"Exactly. Who's to say you haven't been on special assignment with ATF since your supposed leave of absence? Surely your old friend Chief Hastings can arrange that, especially if it makes him look good.

We'll wrap this case up with a nice, neat bow that includes reinstating you with honors…if that's what you want."

When Abby turned to call Barrio, Loane said, "Have him bluff Carl about the PCP that was found in Simon's system. I have a feeling he might know how it got there."

"You think he could've been behind the death of his relatives?"

"It's possible."

While Abby finished her conversation with Hector Barrio, Loane thought about her conflicting feelings toward the people she worked with and how she'd left her job. In hindsight, perhaps she'd been too emotionally involved to see the situation clearly. Her only concern had been trying to get information about Abby and avenge her death. Maybe she'd judged others too harshly, like she'd done Tyler. If she wanted her job back, she'd have to eat a lot of crow. That would be much easier if she went back on a high note with her suspicions vindicated.

"Do you want to go back to the PD, hon?"

"That depends."

"On what?"

Something else she hadn't considered in a while floated to the surface. Abby could be assigned to work anywhere in the country. "Where will you be?"

"Good answer." Two black government vehicles pulled up and Abby nodded toward them. "We'll talk about this later. I better go play nice with the locals." She blew Loane a kiss and walked over to Bowman and the arriving agents.

❖

It was nearly eleven in the morning when Abby stared out the window of the ATF turbo-prop plane at the Piedmont Triad International Airport below. Hector Barrio had pulled a few strings for the ride, invoking urgent investigative necessity or some such government nonsense. He'd also arranged for Greensboro police to meet them at the airport and take them wherever they wanted to go. She'd gotten very little rest on the flight, but Loane was still sleeping.

As the plane's landing gear came down, she kissed the top of Loane's head where it rested against her shoulder. "Hon, we're about to land." She hated to wake her. The dark circles under her eyes had only deepened in the last twelve hours, partly due to lack of sleep but mainly to worry about Kinsey. Though Tori had called earlier with an update on her, they both wanted to see for themselves.

Loane raised her head and scrubbed her eyes with her fists like a kid. "We're going to the hospital first, right?"

"Absolutely. Officers have the club secured, and Ray and Tiny have been singing since five this morning. Suddenly they're not such loyal employees."

"What about Carl?"

"In custody," Abby said.

"Great. I love it when all the dominoes fall."

"What puzzles me is why Carl implicated you in the explosion when he put it all in motion."

Loane gave her hand an encouraging squeeze. "I think he was testing you…and it was a diversion plain and simple."

"Guess you're right. I can't wait to see Kinsey, fill in the missing pieces, and close the book on this one."

An hour after landing, they walked into Kinsey's hospital room. Abby wasn't prepared for the damage she saw. Purple bruising dotted Kinsey's normally pale complexion, and discoloration ringed her eyes. A bandage was secured to the right side of her head by several layers of gauze wrapping. Lying in bed, she looked childlike and helpless.

As they approached, Kinsey opened her eyes and smiled. "Pretty sick, huh?"

"You look like a raccoon," Loane said.

"Loane!" Abby bumped her with her hip and placed a hand on Kinsey's shoulder. "How are you feeling, honey?"

"Like I was flattened by a steamroller and inflated with a bicycle pump."

"In other words, not so great?" Loane asked.

"I hurt everywhere. Did you get those gunrunning bastards who shot me?"

Abby stroked Kinsey's arm, trying to keep her calm. "We sure did, and we couldn't have done it without you."

"Yeah, I might even recommend you for a departmental commendation or something," Loane added. "If I go back to the department."

Kinsey dropped her head and glanced toward the window. "You might want to hold off on that."

"Seriously, we wouldn't have caught these guys without your mad computer skills. You know that, right? Besides being the biggest pain in the ass I've ever met, you're also pretty amazing." Loane's kidding didn't seem to penetrate Kinsey's morose reverie. "What's wrong?"

"Whatever it is, Kinsey, we're here for you. After all you've done for us, we'll always have your back," Abby said.

"You might not say that when I tell you."

"Tell us what?" Loane asked.

She struggled to sit upright and Abby positioned a couple of pillows behind her. "I haven't exactly told you everything I know about this case."

Abby felt Loane bristle beside her and reached for her hand. When Loane's cool gloved fingers curled around hers, she knew they could handle anything together. "Tell us, honey. It'll be fine. Right, Loane?" She looked into Loane's blue eyes and saw the answer she knew Kinsey needed to hear.

"Whatever it is, we'll work it out. The three of us are a team now."

Kinsey took a deep breath and sank back into the pillows. "I think I know who set the explosion—"

At that moment, Abby's cell phone rang. "Damn. Hold on a second, honey." She punched the answer key. "Yes, hello."

"Abby, it's Hector Barrio. We've had some developments you need to know about."

"Can it possibly wait?"

"I'm afraid not."

She looked at Kinsey and mouthed *sorry*, then stepped into the hallway. "Okay, go."

"Carl Torre is trying to make a deal already. He says he'll name his ATF partner and another local player if he gets to walk. His offer is only good for the next hour. I don't want to give this bastard any consideration. Are you any closer to identifying the leak?"

Abby glanced toward Kinsey's room. "I'm not sure, maybe, but I'll need a little more time."

"The best I can do is thirty minutes. If I haven't heard from you, I'll have no choice but to authorize the deal. Understood?"

"Yes, sir." She hung up and checked her watch. Whatever Kinsey told her, she prayed it would answer their remaining questions and not implicate her in anything criminal. That would destroy Kinsey's life and jeopardize the trust she and Loane had placed in her. She took a deep breath and went back into the room where Loane was finishing the recap of the New York arrest.

"Jeez, you must be some awesome shot," Kinsey said.

"Have you told Loane yet?" Abby asked.

Kinsey shook her head. "I can only say this once."

Loane came around to Abby's side of the bed and put her arm around her waist. "You were saying that you might know something about the explosion."

Kinsey bobbed her head and looked down at her hands. When she finally spoke, her voice was barely audible. "The night it happened, I was tailing someone and sort of lost contact for a while. By the time I relocated them, the car was at the Torre house on Strawberry Road. A man came from the back of the house and got into a dark sedan. I followed on my bike, and when we reached 220, I heard the explosion." Kinsey wiped her tearstained face with an edge of the blanket.

As Kinsey told her story, Loane's grip around Abby's waist tightened. She looked at her face and saw a combination of comprehension and something akin to sympathy. "You were riding a motorcycle?"

Kinsey nodded.

Loane said, "I passed you on my way to the house…and the car."

"Do you know who this man is?" Abby asked.

"I do now. His picture was in the paper a few days later, making an announcement about getting rid of organized crime in the city. He's a bigwig with ATF, Fowler."

"Why didn't you tell someone right away, Kinsey? This case could've been cleared months ago and Loane wouldn't have…" Abby stopped. Stating the obvious would only make Kinsey feel worse and wouldn't help the current situation. "Why?"

"Because she wasn't following Fowler," Loane said.

Kinsey shook her head but didn't meet Loane's eyes.

"Then who?" Abby asked.

"Her mother."

Abby couldn't hide her shock as she looked from one to the other. "Your mother, Councilwoman Brenda Jeffries, was driving the car that night?" Then she remembered that Dan Bowman had told her about the press conference Fowler and Jeffries held after the investigation was shut down. "Of course. And did you happen to call Dan Bowman that night and tell him to go to the Torre house?"

Kinsey nodded again and finally looked up, her gaze fixed on Loane. "How did you know about my mom?"

"A hunch. Her press conference claiming credit for something that didn't happen was strange. Guess it was about throwing everybody off the track. They were pretty stupid to do the dirty work themselves, but I still think there's more to the story than the money."

"Probably didn't trust anyone else. I'm sorry, Loane," Kinsey said.

"Is that why you offered to help me that first night, because you felt guilty for not coming forward, for your mother's involvement?"

"Honest to God, I was trying to find June, but I did feel guilty for not telling you. My mother is a lot of things, most of them unpleasant, but she's still my mother. I couldn't turn her in. I thought if I helped you and Abby, we could find another way for this to come out. I can't be the one who implicates her."

"She'll do jail time for this, you know?" Abby asked.

"Yeah," Kinsey said. "Can you understand why I didn't tell you?"

Abby thought about her own relatives. Would she be able to turn one of them in if she knew they'd committed a crime? Her familial bonds were much stronger than Kinsey's. Maybe Kinsey's estrangement from her mother made her even more protective of their tenuous connection. It was hard to predict the intricacies of family ties.

"I understand," Abby said.

"Me too," Loane added.

Kinsey exhaled a deep, expectant breath and her face lit up. "Yeah?" When they both nodded, she asked, "So, what now?"

Abby pulled her cell off her belt. "I have to call Barrio. My thirty minutes is almost up."

"Wait a second," Loane said. "We have to keep Kinsey out of this if we can. Why don't you give him the facts without revealing your source? Then suggest that he offer Carl a deal *if* his statement provides any details we don't already have. Tell them to print out his statement in full and make Carl sign it along with an agreement to testify in court. That way we can use him as the source and not involve Kinsey."

"And we don't have to honor a deal with the bastard because he won't be providing any new information."

"Exactly."

"Thanks." She kissed Loane, dialed Barrio's number, and stepped out of the room. As the door closed behind her, she heard Loane say to Kinsey, "We have to talk about living arrangements."

When she'd finished briefing him, Hector Barrio said, "Those are excellent ideas, Abby. You'll make a great field agent."

"I wish I could take credit, sir, but they're Officer Landry's suggestions."

"Too bad the Greensboro police got her. You two are quite the team. Wonder if she'd consider joining ATF?"

"Not sure, but you can always ask. Your charms worked on me."

"You won't believe all the stuff we found at the Torre businesses. They were into a variety of crimes. We even found a stable of girls being held as prostitutes. These kids worked as dancers in his places along the I-95 corridor and drove guns and money back and forth. If they asked too many questions, they were sent down here until they outlived their usefulness."

"Do you have any of their names yet?"

"Hold on while I pull up the list on my iPad. Are you looking for anybody in particular?"

Abby sent up a silent prayer. "Is there a June somebody on the list?"

The line was silent as Barrio searched for what Abby hoped would be good news. "June Lennon, possibly? She's from the Greensboro area, pretty strung out, but she was able to tell us where she lived."

Finally, a bright spot in this horrifically convoluted case. Kinsey would be so happy that her friend was alive. "Make sure she gets back. She has friends here."

"Will do. And if it's all right with you, Abby, let Agent Bowman conduct the follow-up interviews with our suspects. They don't need to associate you with ATF until trial. I think we owe him that much."

"That's an excellent idea. Can I assume I'm officially no longer undercover?"

"There will be debriefings and such, but basically yes. You've earned a nice long vacation. When you're ready to go back to work, call me. You can pretty much choose your duty station after this, young lady. You've done yourself and this agency proud. Thank you."

Abby felt a wave of relief followed by an overwhelming sense of accomplishment. She'd lived in a whirlwind for almost two years, devoid of any significant personal connections. Not many officers could work undercover for such an extensive period. Now she understood why. It required selfless commitment, constant discipline to keep the facts straight, and a willingness to give up everything that mattered to accomplish the mission. She'd proved she was a capable agent who could handle anything the job threw her way. But more important, she'd learned there was more to life than work. She was ready to return to her family and, hopefully, to Loane.

When she reentered Kinsey's room, she and Loane had their heads together like a couple of co-conspirators. "You two are up to no good." She took Kinsey's hand and squeezed it gently. "Honey, I've got some excellent news. June is alive and will be on her way back here very soon."

Kinsey's green eyes filled with tears that spilled over onto the stark white sheet. "Really?"

"Agents found her and some others being held hostage in a club. They've been drugged, so she'll need some help readjusting."

"She can live with me," Kinsey said. "My new place is huge."

"And I'll do what I can," Loane added. "Speaking of which, I need to go."

Loane's sudden need to leave caught Abby by surprise. She'd envisioned a long night of getting reacquainted. Was Loane already distancing again? Why the sudden turnaround? "But I thought we'd go somewhere and…"

"Sorry. I've got to take care of a couple of things. Shouldn't take long. Can I call you later?" Abby nodded, and Loane kissed her and Kinsey on the forehead like siblings.

Kinsey looked at Abby with wide puppy-dog eyes. "I'd like some company, if you've got time. I hate hospitals."

Abby shook her head at Loane's hasty retreat and said, "It seems that I suddenly have nothing but time. I'd love to sit with you for a while."

Chapter Twenty-three

The remainder of the afternoon disappeared as Loane helped close out the case and made arrangements with a last-minute mover to put her personal plan into action. Hector Barrio faxed warrants on the additional suspects to the GPD, and she briefed Chief Hastings on the details. Barrio agreed to let the locals take Councilwoman Jeffries into custody while Abby and Bowman arrested Fowler.

Now she stood outside Brenda Jeffries's office with Tyler and Chief Hastings. "Can we wait a bit longer?"

"What's going on, sis?"

She couldn't admit to him, in the chief's presence, that she'd tipped off the news media about the pending arrest. Cops didn't leak information to the press unless it served their purposes, and in this instance it served hers perfectly. It was the most efficient way to release the facts about a case that had been riddled with propaganda and lies. She would be vindicated, but more important, the forgotten ones would be as well—Simon, Sylvia, Alma Torre, the girls who'd been held as sex slaves, the nameless victims injured or killed by illegal guns, and Abby.

"We have to move," Chief Hastings said. And as if on cue, the big red-and-white local news van rolled onto the lot.

"I'm ready," she said. The chief gave her a knowing glance and shook his head. "I'll have to promote you to keep you out of trouble on the street." She and Tyler entered the business while he fielded questions from the press.

Brenda Jeffries stood in front of the receptionist's desk, her perfectly arched eyebrows shooting toward her hairline. "What's the meaning of this?"

Loane waved the warrant in the air. "This means that you're under arrest for murder and conspiracy to commit murder. I'm sure we'll have more for you later—illegal weapons, malfeasance in office, things like that."

Jeffries squared her shoulders and assumed all her political prowess. "I'll have you fired. This is ridiculous."

"But you're such a *law-and-order candidate*. Surely you can appreciate officers doing their jobs, Madam Councilwoman." Tyler's tone was almost jovial in its mockery, and Loane had never loved him more.

"Yeah, what he said. Now put your hands behind your back."

"I want my lawyer," Jeffries said.

"Good idea. You'll need one. Actually, I'm shocked you weren't smart enough to leave town after your cohorts nearly killed your daughter. Or maybe you thought all that political clout made you bulletproof." Her comment wasn't exactly professional, but she couldn't resist a little dig on Kinsey's behalf as she locked the handcuffs and nudged her toward the front door and the waiting press.

"I know nothing about that." The woman's lack of concern made Loane wonder how someone with so much ice in her veins could even give birth.

The media pool had grown in the few minutes they'd been inside, and the cameras clicked like the rapid-fire banging of old typewriter keys. Loane smiled and maneuvered Jeffries in front of each one on the walk to Tyler's patrol car. She made sure Chief Hastings got a shot worthy of the front page before stuffing Jeffries into the backseat.

"Ty, could you handle the booking? I've got something to take care of."

"Would her name by any chance be Abby?"

"Smart-ass."

"Sure. The guys should be finished with the moving by now," Tyler said.

"How do you know about that?"

"It's my business to know…*and* the company you hired is mostly cops. So, Eve is okay with the swap?"

"Yeah, our friend Kinsey is quite well off, and Eve is happy to take her money. Besides, the penthouse suits her lifestyle much better than mine. We talked about it before I left the hospital. She can't wait." She hugged Tyler and whispered, "I love you. You know that, right?"

"Back at ya. Now go make an honest woman of my future sister-in-law."

As she walked past Chief Hastings, he asked, "Is your leave of absence over? It would be nice to have you back on the job… officially."

"Thanks, Chief. I'll let you know."

On her way home, she called Abby. "Where are you? Are you all right? Have you arrested Fowler yet? Are you free? When can I see you?"

"Hold on, hon, let me go somewhere more private." Loane heard a car door close and Abby's honeyed voice resumed. "Now…just leaving the jail. I'm fine. Fowler is in custody, spilling his criminal guts. I haven't been free since the day I met you. And you can see me anytime you want for as long as you want."

"Meet me at my house in Sunset Hills as soon as you can."

"I thought Kinsey was renting your place."

"I'll explain later. Will you meet me?"

"Of course. I'll be there after a quick stop at the hotel to change clothes."

Loane was grateful to have time for last-minute preparations as she waited for Abby to arrive. Now that she knew what she wanted and how to get it, the delay seemed interminable. Trusting herself, and anyone else, had always seemed like such a giant leap, but today Abby had made it seem easy. If she trusted Loane with her life, Loane could trust her with her heart. She could imagine traveling that two-way street with Abby and the other people who had stood by her. She'd have some bridge building to do, but it was a small price to pay.

She showered, scrubbed the damaged-heart tattoo from her right arm, and plucked the fake silver piercings from her face for the last time. Opening a bottle of chilled wine, she selected soft music on her iPod docking station and waited. Brisk autumnal air had replaced the warmth of day and promised a comfortable night as she staged the screened-in porch for Abby's arrival. All she needed now was the woman she'd waited for all her life. Time to show her hand, figuratively and literally.

Reclining on the lounger, she looked up at the cloudless sky and tried to count stars. She needed a distraction or she'd pop out of her skin. The last time she'd felt this unencumbered and ready to commit had been—never. She relished the idea of planning a future with Abby and returning to a job she loved. It wouldn't be as simple as imagining it and making it happen, but together they could do anything.

Abby's rental car pulled into the driveway a few minutes later, and Loane forced herself to stay put. The thrill of anticipation danced up and down her spine, and her hands sweated inside her leather gloves. She felt like a teenager waiting to be plucked from the stag line at prom.

The car door slammed and she heard the back gate squeak open, then closed. With each footfall of Abby's approach, Loane's heart beat faster. By the time she rounded the corner and stepped onto the porch, Loane was practically panting. Abby wore a pair of faded jeans that sported holes at the knees and a long-sleeved kelly-green sweater that hugged her breasts like Loane wanted to. Her body vibrated from the need to touch Abby, to hold her, and to solidify their connection.

"Is this a private party or can anybody join?" Without waiting for an answer, Abby sat down beside her and kissed her until she could barely breathe.

"Definitely…private." Abby's kisses started like a delicate ballet across her lips and deepened into a stomp dance of aching. "Abby."

Abby pulled back as far as Loane's hug would allow. "Am I going too fast? Do you still need time?"

"Your speed is perfect, and I don't need any more time." She poured two glasses of wine and offered one to Abby. "Business first. A toast to your case. Well done." They clinked glasses and Loane almost drained hers as nerves tangled in her stomach.

"Thank you for this, hon, and for all your help."

"Is everything wrapped up on your end?"

"Pretty much. Fowler is trying to make a deal. Those fancy cigars that Carl sent Simon every month were laced with PCP. That's why he was so paranoid the night he died. He'd found out about the weapons and threatened to close down the clubs. Carl left out that little detail in his confession. I guess I shouldn't be surprised that he would have three members of his family killed for money."

"And Fowler and Jeffries were protection?"

"Yep, distracting law enforcement while they collected giant payoffs. That's how the gunrunners successfully dodged arrest for so long. And Carl had been blackmailing Fowler and Jeffries to ensure their cooperation. Fowler has a proclivity for young girls, and Jeffries was desperate to keep her daughter's lesbianism under wraps. You were right that there was more to the story than money."

"So…our little street urchin is a lesbian. I didn't know."

"Me either, but with everybody flipping on everybody else, we'll have enough evidence and testimony to keep her out of it entirely."

"That's good. She needs a fresh start to go along with her new home. Thank you."

"And where is that exactly?"

"We traded places. She's in a condo downtown. You'll get to see it when we go check on her." She slid her hand up Abby's back and felt the heat through her glove. "I want you to know how very proud I am of you. This case would've fallen apart several times if you hadn't been so competent and determined."

Abby took their wineglasses and placed them on the table. "That means more to me than you know. It's taken a while, but I've become a pretty kick-ass agent. I'm sorry I had to keep so much from you in the beginning."

She leaned forward and sealed the sincerity of her words with a kiss. Loane never wanted to stop but there were things to say. "Abby, I want to talk to you before hormones take over. I need you to know that what I'm saying is sincere and not sex-induced."

Abby straightened on the side of the lounger and looked into her eyes. "I'm listening."

"I've been very unfair to you and—"

"Loane, it's all right."

"No, it's not. Please let me finish. Even if you don't need to hear this, I need to say it out loud for the first time in my life."

Abby stroked the side of her face and brushed her thumb across her bottom lip. The golden brown of her eyes deepened with such a look of love that Loane almost whimpered. "Go ahead, my darling."

"I'm in love with you, Abby. I've been afraid to admit it. But I've learned a few things. You kept your real identity from me and I kept my true self from you." Loane scrubbed her hands together in frustration. Her words sounded like a series of Harlequin romance one-liners, not eloquent, as she'd hoped. "We had the best intentions, but in hindsight I think my sin was greater. It's certainly more limiting. What I'm trying to say is I'm sorry. And I love you. And I'd like another chance if I haven't blown it."

In the past, this was the point at which she'd run for the hills, convinced that she'd never measure up to whatever expectation had been thrust upon her. Not this time. If Abby walked away, she would be devastated, but at least she'd know that she'd done her best and it *was* good enough. Loane held her breath and the seconds crawled. She could clearly hear the blood rushing in her ears. She'd bared her soul and this was what it felt like—naked and exposed, defenseless and afraid, vulnerable and hopeful.

Abby's gaze searched her face and settled again on her eyes as if divining the truth of her words. "I love you, Loane. You can have as many chances as you need."

She scooted behind Abby, wrapped her legs around her, and kissed the soft skin at the back of her neck. "I want you to know all of me. I promise, no holding back." Abby shivered in her arms. "Are you cold?"

"Needy."

"Let's take care of that right now." She stood and offered Abby her hand.

"Would you do something for me first?"

"Anything."

"Take off your gloves."

Loane hesitated only a second before sliding the leather coverings from her hands. She held them out for Abby to see. "Not pretty, are they?"

Abby kissed the crinkled, discolored flesh. "They're beautiful, and I can't wait to feel them all over my body."

The anxiety she'd felt about revealing herself to Abby vanished. Abby accepted her as she was—flawed, damaged, and scarred. "Well, let's get started." She pulled Abby from the lounger and wrapped her arm around her waist. Abby took a step forward and almost collapsed as her right leg buckled. Loane tightened her grip and helped Abby regain her balance. "I guess we both have our battle wounds."

"From now on, let's focus on the healing."

"Deal." Loane led her into the bedroom they'd left almost four months ago. "I hope being back here is okay."

"I wouldn't want to be anywhere else. This is perfect."

She kissed Abby but pulled back when she tried to bring their bodies together. "May I undress you?" A rich pink flush covered Abby's cheeks as she turned her palms up in surrender.

She hooked her thumbs in the hem of Abby's cashmere sweater and teased it up her body, bending to kiss each new expanse of flesh. She tickled the fabric across Abby's unfettered breasts and smiled as her nipples puckered. "So gorgeous." Heat sparked between her legs as if physically confirming her statement. She tensed her abs to stop the spread of desire and shucked Abby's sweater over her head. The tender, leisurely seduction she'd planned was slipping away.

"Touch me, Loane."

Abby's firm breasts called to her as clearly as her words, but she was determined to go slowly and commit every second of their reunion to memory. "Not yet." She skimmed her tongue over Abby's pleading lips, need coiling in her own body. Abby reached for her, but Loane knelt and grabbed the front of her jeans. She fumbled with the zipper, her fingers like clumsy mittens.

When the fabric finally fell away, Abby's creamy skin summoned her. She stripped the jeans down Abby's legs and inhaled the fragrance of her arousal. Her clit twitched, signaling the start of a process over which she had no control. "God, Abby."

"Will you touch me now? I'm dying here." Abby fell across the bed and kicked free of her jeans and shoes.

Loane peeled off her clothes, glad that nothing required unbuttoning, and eased herself down beside Abby. "I've missed you so much." She kissed Abby again, pouring all the feelings of the past months into it. "Never felt this way before." Tears of joy slid down her cheeks. She was about to come just looking at Abby, and she knew it.

Abby rolled over on top of Loane and wrapped her arms around her. "I love you, Loane." She felt Loane's tears on the side of her face. They'd broken through another barrier in their relationship. They were finally emotionally connected as deeply as they were physically. The hesitation she'd experienced in the past melted away. She wanted Loane more at that moment than she ever had. The force of it swelled inside her like a storm and she couldn't wait any longer.

"Are you okay?" Loane looked up at her.

"I need you, badly."

"Anything, name it."

"Our first night together. That's what I want."

Without breaking contact, Loane sat up against the headboard, and Abby straddled her. She guided Loane's hand between her legs. "Inside me." When Loane's finger slid inside, Abby rose to accommodate her and settled into a steady rhythm. "Yes. I love your hands on me."

Abby was in no hurry but knew she couldn't hold out. She'd waited too long to feel Loane's touch again. Rising and falling on Loane's skillful hand, she watched the muscles ripple along her arms and chest. She massaged Loane's breasts and tweaked her nipples, enjoying the increased pace her actions created.

"Play with yourself," Loane said.

Abby licked her fingers and circled her rigid clit. Loane timed her thrusts perfectly and Abby almost came at the first touch. "So good… you do remember."

"Everything about you. Look at me, Abby."

Abby opened her eyes and saw the love on Loane's face that she'd longed for. "I love you." She rubbed her clit faster and Loane kept pace. Stroke for stroke, Loane filled and emptied her until every nerve in her body was saturated with sensation. "More."

"Come all over me, Abby."

With a final frenzied pump, she slumped forward, rubbing herself against Loane's center. The orgasm oozed from her like warm honey on a summer day. Spasm after delicious spasm milked her until she couldn't move.

"All systems working properly, I see," Loane whispered in her ear.

"Finally." She rolled to her side and draped her leg over Loane's body. "We are so freaking perfect together, do you know that?"

"Of course."

"Pretty smug with yourself right now, aren't you, Landry?"

"Oh, yeah. I'm a love machine."

"Better be just for me." Abby hadn't been so happy or seen Loane so happy since their early days together. She hoped their future would hold as much promise as this moment.

"Only you," Loane assured her.

They lay entwined in each other's arms and legs until their bodies cooled and Loane reached for a blanket. "In case I haven't told you in the past five minutes, I love you, Abigail Marconi." Her voice sounded distant and serious. "So, what happens now, with your work, I mean… and us?"

"That depends on you. Bowman is taking over the Greensboro office and offered me a position. If you're staying with the GPD, I could be happy here. If not, we could start over somewhere else."

"You'd stay here, with me…and not leave?"

"I'm never leaving you again. Are you asking me to move in with you?" Abby asked.

"This is a good family home, so yes."

"That's good because I checked out of the hotel. Carl was paying for it."

Quiet for a long moment, Loane played with a curl of Abby's hair. "What about your family?"

"I want to be wherever you are. And my family can come visit. It's your decision."

"It's not just a decision, it's a commitment, and we make it together." Loane looked like she was earnestly weighing options. "But I'd like to make a go of it here, if you're willing. I could reconnect with my brother, mend some fences at the department, and rebuild my career. Would you be happy working here now that you've attained such celebrity?"

"Celebrity fades, what we have doesn't. Sounds like we've made a commitment." Abby rolled over on top of Loane, kissed her, and slid down between her legs.

Loane gasped when Abby strummed her nipples with the tips of her fingernails and ringed the base of her clit with light circles. "I need you, Abby." She wanted this more than anything she'd ever imagined. This wasn't sex. It was making love with the woman she adored.

Abby moaned and sent another shock of desire straight to Loane's crotch. She struggled to keep a slow rhythmic pace as Abby's mouth worked magic on her clit. Loane was mentally three steps ahead, with her fingers buried inside Abby, riding her thigh, and about to come.

The image was too much. She flipped Abby over, straddled her thigh, and eased her fingers through the slickness between Abby's legs. She parted the folds of delicate skin and flicked her rigid flesh. Abby twitched and thrust her pelvis.

"No fair." Her words were almost a whimper.

"I want you squirming under me when I come," Loane said.

"You've got the sexual patience of a rabbit."

"And you love it."

"Yes, I do."

Loane shifted her weight on her knees and brushed her pubic mound against Abby's. The light friction was like standing on a concrete slab while it was being jackhammered. Electricity reverberated through her body until she felt weak. Her arms shook and she almost collapsed. Abby's pelvis rose to meet hers and strong arms pulled her down.

"Now, hon. I'm ready now."

Loane lowered herself and the connection was complete. She covered Abby's mouth and claimed her with a kiss so deep she struggled to breathe. This was where she belonged. She poked and licked with her tongue, sucked and surrendered with her lips, and drank in all that Abby offered in return. She'd never thirsted for the taste of a woman like this and never been so sated by a kiss.

She looked into Abby's eyes, hazy with lust and need. "I love you, Abby."

"Show me."

She kissed Abby's ear, tongued her way down the side of her neck, and captured a breast. Her nipple was pebbled and rigid in contrast to the pliable flesh as she sucked and rocked in unison. She rubbed her center against Abby's, reveling in the mingling of their juices and the heightened smell of arousal. Heat surged in her veins. Abby's fingernails traced a path down her back and she stroked faster. "Oh, yes."

"Come for me, Loane, please."

She clamped her legs together. *I swear to uphold the laws of the State of North Carolina and the—* Her body stilled slightly.

Abby said, "Let go, hon. I plan to share a lifetime of climaxes with you, and I want you totally present for every one."

The only thing Loane needed to know about history at that moment was that it didn't have to repeat itself in her life again. She surrendered everything except the sensation of being connected to Abby. Feeling her skin. Sucking her breast. Tonguing her nipple. Riding her crotch. Her legs tingled and tensed as the orgasm built.

When Abby dug her nails into Loane's ass and forced her tighter against her, Loane lost it. "That's it, Abby, that's it." As her orgasm washed over her, she knew what was true. She pumped until her legs would no longer support her, until sensation drained her, and she collapsed on top of Abby. "Oh. My. God."

Her love for Abby was a gut-certain feeling, like the first time she'd kissed a girl or the initial taste of chocolate that left her craving forever. She trusted Abby and their love, and she'd never doubt it or herself again.

"I love you, Abigail Marconi."

About the Author

A thirty-year veteran of a midsized police department, VK was a police officer by necessity (it paid the bills) and a writer by desire (it didn't). Her career spanned numerous positions including beat officer, homicide detective, vice/narcotics lieutenant, and assistant chief of police. Now retired, she devotes her time to writing, traveling, home decorating, and volunteer work.

Books Available From Bold Strokes Books

Trusting Tomorrow by P.J. Trebelhorn. Funeral director Logan Swift thinks she's perfectly happy with her solitary life devoted to helping others cope with loss until Brooke Collier moves in next door to care for her elderly grandparents. 9978-1-60282-891-9)

Forsaking All Others by Kathleen Knowles. What if what you think you want is the opposite of what makes you happy? (978-1-60282-892-6)

Exit Wounds by VK Powell. When Officer Loane Landry falls in love with ATF informant Abigail Mancuso, she realizes that nothing is as it seems—not the case, not her lover, not even the dead. (978-1-60282-893-3)

Dirty Power by Ashley Bartlett. Cooper's been through hell and back, and she's still broke and on the run. But at least she found the twins. They'll keep her alive. Right? (978-1-60282-896-4)

The Rarest Rose by I. Beacham. After a decade of living in her beloved house, Ele disturbs its past and finds her life being haunted by the presence of a ghost who will show her that true love never dies. (978-1-60282-884-1)

Code of Honor by Radclyffe. The face of terror is hard to recognize—especially when it's homegrown. The next book in the Honor series. (978-1-60282-885-8)

Does She Love You by Rachel Spangler. When Annabelle and Davis find out they are in a relationship with the same woman, it leaves them facing life-altering questions about trust, redemption, and the possibility of finding love in the wake of betrayal. (978-1-60282-886-5)

The Road to Her by KE Payne. Sparks fly when actress Holly Croft, star of UK soap *Portobello Road*, meets her new on-screen love interest, the enigmatic and sexy Elise Manford. (978-1-60282-887-2)

Shadows of Something Real by Sophia Kell Hagin. Trying to escape flashbacks and nightmares, ex-POW Jamie Gwynmorgan stumbles into the heart of former Red Cross worker Adele Sabellius and uncovers a deadly conspiracy against everything and everyone she loves. (978-1-60282-889-6)

Date with Destiny by Mason Dixon. When sophisticated bank executive Rashida Ivey meets unemployed blue-collar worker Destiny Jackson, will her life ever be the same? (978-1-60282-878-0)

The Devil's Orchard by Ali Vali. Cain and Emma plan a wedding before the birth of their third child while Juan Luis is still lurking, and as Cain plans for his death, an unexpected visitor arrives and challenges her belief in her father, Dalton Casey. (978-1-60282-879-7)

Secrets and Shadows by L.T. Marie. A bodyguard and the woman she protects run from a madman and into each other's arms. (978-1-60282-880-3)

Change Horizon: Three Novellas by Gun Brooke. Three stories of courageous women who dare to love as they fight to claim a future in a hostile universe. (978-1-60282-881-0)

Scarlett Thirst by Crin Claxton. When hot, feisty Rani meets cool vampire Rob, one lifetime isn't enough, and the road from human to vampire is shorter than you think… (978-1-60282-856-8)

Battle Axe by Carsen Taite. How close is too close? Bounty hunter Luca Bennett will soon find out. (978-1-60282-871-1)

Improvisation by Karis Walsh. High school geometry teacher Jan Carroll thinks she's figured out the shape of her life and her future, until graphic artist and fiddle player Tina Nelson comes along and teaches her to improvise. (978-1-60282-872-8)

For Want of a Fiend by Barbara Ann Wright. Without her Fiendish power, can Princess Katya and her consort Starbride stop a magic-wielding madman from sparking an uprising in the kingdom of Farraday? (978-1-60282-873-5)

Swans & Clons by Nora Olsen. In a future world where there are no males, sixteen-year-old Rubric and her girlfriend Salmon Jo must fight to survive when everything they believed in turns out to be a lie. (978-1-60282-874-2)

Broken in Soft Places by Fiona Zedde. The instant Sara Chambers meets the seductive and sinful Merille Thompson, she falls hard, but knowing the difference between love and a dangerous, all-consuming desire is just one of the lessons Sara must learn before it's too late. (978-1-60282-876-6)

Healing Hearts by Donna K. Ford. Running from tragedy, the women of Willow Springs find that with friendship, there is hope, and with love, there is everything. (978-1-60282-877-3)

Desolation Point by Cari Hunter. When a storm strands Sarah Kent in the North Cascades, Alex Pascal is determined to find her. Neither imagines the dangers they will face when a ruthless criminal begins to hunt them down. (978-1-60282-865-0)

I Remember by Julie Cannon. What happens when you can never forget the first kiss, the first touch, the first taste of lips on skin? What happens when you know you will remember every single detail of a mysterious woman? (978-1-60282-866-7)

The Gemini Deception by Kim Baldwin and Xenia Alexiou. The truth, the whole truth, and nothing but lies. Book six in the Elite Operatives series. (978-1-60282-867-4)

Scarlet Revenge by Sheri Lewis Wohl. When faith alone isn't enough, will the love of one woman be strong enough to save a vampire from damnation? (978-1-60282-868-1)

Ghost Trio by Lillian Q. Irwin. When Lee Howe hears the voice of her dead lover singing to her, is it a hallucination, a ghost, or something more sinister? (978-1-60282-869-8)

The Princess Affair by Nell Stark. Rhodes Scholar Kerry Donovan arrives at Oxford ready to focus on her studies, but her life and her priorities are thrown into chaos when she catches the eye of Her Royal Highness Princess Sasha. (978-1-60282-858-2)

The Chase by Jesse J. Thoma. When Isabelle Rochat's life is threatened, she receives the unwelcome protection and attention of bounty hunter Holt Lasher who vows to keep Isabelle safe at all costs. (978-1-60282-859-9)

The Lone Hunt by L.L. Raand. In a world where humans and Praeterns conspire for the ultimate power, violence is a way of life…and death. A Midnight Hunters novel. (978-1-60282-860-5)

The Supernatural Detective by Crin Claxton. Tony Carson sees dead people. With a drag queen for a spirit guide and a devastatingly attractive herbalist for a client, she's about to discover the spirit world can be a very dangerous world indeed. (978-1-60282-861-2)

Beloved Gomorrah by Justine Saracen. Undersea artists creating their own City on the Plain uncover the truth about Sodom and Gomorrah, whose "one righteous man" is a murderer, rapist, and conspirator in genocide. (978-1-60282-862-9)

The Left Hand of Justice by Jess Faraday. A kidnapped heiress, a heretical cult, a corrupt police chief, and an accused witch. Paris is burning, and the only one who can put out the fire is Detective Inspector Elise Corbeau…whose boss wants her dead. (978-1-60282-863-6)

Cut to the Chase by Lisa Girolami. Careful and methodical author Paige Cornish falls for brash and wild Hollywood actress Avalon Randolph, but can these opposites find a happy middle ground in a town that never lives in the middle? (978-1-60282-783-7)

Every Second Counts by D. Jackson Leigh. Every second counts in Bridgette LeRoy's desperate mission to protect her heart and stop Marc Ryder's suicidal return to riding rodeo bulls. (978-1-60282-785-1)

More Than Friends by Erin Dutton. Evelyn Fisher thinks she has the perfect role model for a long-term relationship, until her best friends, Kendall and Melanie, split up and all three women must reevaluate their lives and their relationships. (978-1-60282-784-4)

Dirty Money by Ashley Bartlett. Vivian Cooper and Reese DiGiovanni just found out that falling in love is hard. It's even harder when you're running for your life. (978-1-60282-786-8)

Sea Glass Inn by Karis Walsh. When Melinda Andrews commissions a series of mosaics by Pamela Whitford for her new inn, she doesn't expect to be more captivated by the artist than by the paintings. (978-1-60282-771-4)

The Awakening: A Sisterhood of Spirits novel by Yvonne Heidt. Sunny Skye has interacted with spirits her entire life, but when she runs into Officer Jordan Lawson during a ghost investigation, she discovers more than just facts in a missing girl's cold case file. (978-1-60282-772-1)

Blacker Than Blue by Rebekah Weatherspoon. Threatened with losing her first love to a powerful demon, vampire Cleo Jones is willing to break the ultimate law of the undead to rebuild the family she has lost. (978-1-60282-774-5)

Murphy's Law by Yolanda Wallace. No matter how high you climb, you can't escape your past. (978-1-60282-773-8)

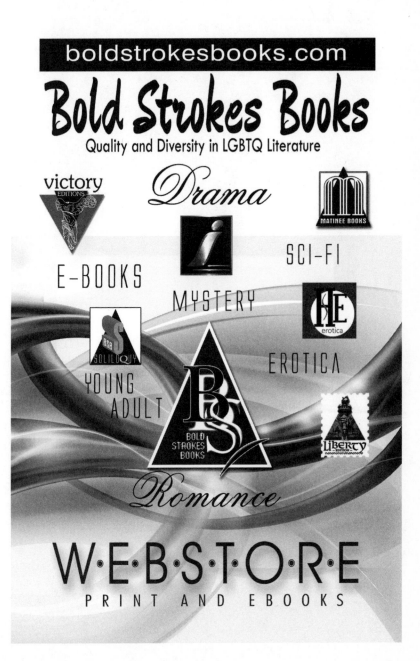